THE BASTARD PRINCESS

G. Lawrence

To Matthew,
for his love and support, and his patience.

PROLOGUE
FEBRUARY, 1603
RICHMOND PALACE

I am old.

I never wanted to admit that age had stolen up on me, but finally I can feel Death, a tangible presence, standing at my side waiting for me. I never took well to orders, and my reluctance to obey his call he seems to understand, but he will not wait for much longer.

He too has a nation he must maintain.

Soon he will beckon and I will have to obey this one, final command.

Most people do not think on Death until they are old. But my youth was such that Death was a constant companion, hovering at my side, waiting for me to slip, expecting me to fall.

If I have learnt anything during my long life that knowledge was formed in my youngest years, just as I was. There are three things that I learnt well, and learnt young.

The first is that this world belongs to men. If a woman is to survive, to hold any power of her own, then she must be clever, ruthless and above all...lucky.

The second is that power is a perilous, deceitful substance; its glowing surface conceals a wealth of darkness within. It should be approached and handled with the utmost of care, never forgetting its potential to corrupt and destroy. When the acquisition of power drives the soul of a person, they become blind and numb to all else. They will tread on the bodies of their friends and family to procure more of what they desire. They will pay for their purchase with their souls.

And the third... that the Heart is the most dangerous enemy any person may come to face in their lives. The Heart is treacherous. It is the best of spies, the most gifted of liars. It is the unseen influence over your choices and it is always with you, shaping your decisions, whispering to you in the dead of night. You may think that you choose your path in freedom and in liberty; you may think your head considers all its choices and forges ahead on the best course with intelligence and deliberation. But all the time you are deceived by the cunning Heart; the true master of your world.

Above all others, the Heart is the most dangerous enemy.

CHAPTER 1
LATE APRIL, 1536
SIXTY-SEVEN YEARS EARLIER...

The fish in the pool were little glints of gold twinkling in the afternoon light. I put out a hand to touch them and they flashed away like lightning. A small gurgle of laughter came from my mouth as I looked up with the wonder of a young child at the lovely woman who held me. I waved my hands and burbled my few words at her, trying to show her the amazing sights in the pond.

My mother looked down at me.

Even now, though I can barely recall her face, I remember her eyes; as dark and deep as the pond itself. I could see my own face staring back at me in them. And I could see the expression of gentle love in those beautiful eyes, for me.

Her only child.

I reached out a chubby little hand to her charming face. Much as I had sought to touch the fish in the pond, I sought to touch her fine eyes. But unlike the fish she moved towards me, nuzzling her cheek into the curve of my tiny hand and closing her eyes as she relished the feel of my skin against her own.

I laughed with delight. My little laugh bounced around the gardens. It was a fine afternoon in the late spring; there still was a chill in the air but that afternoon it was bright and sunny and I was with my mother playing in our gardens. I was happy, excited to be here with my hand against the cheek of the most beautiful woman in the world.

But when she opened her eyes they shone with tears.

I was worried then. The gorgeous creature who was my mother was all-powerful in my world. She could not be sad. There could be no reason to be sad. We were together and when we were together all was right with the world. She had spoken those words to me and they were true. I reached out both hands to her, frowning and she smiled gently to see the worry in my face.

Then, her eyes went from me and travelled across the lush gardens, up to the palace. There by a window stood the huge figure of the other most important person in the world. My father, the King.

He stood at the window, looking out at us in the gardens. He was a huge man, tall and powerful. His clothes and fingers sparkled with jewels and gold, flashing and twinkling as the sun caught them with her light fingers. But his face was as dark as the sky before a summer storm.

I saw him too and cooed with pleasure. Next to my mother, he was my favourite person. He often snatched me from my maids and bounced me around the room showing me off to many smiling faces, rewarded by my giggles of happiness. I sometimes felt a little afraid of him. He was a great giant! But I knew too that he loved me, so my fear of him was always mingled with pleasure.

My mother pulled me to her, lifting me, turning me, and pushed me in front of her, holding me out to my father. His dark face faltered at the window, he looked down at the floor and then up again at us. He frowned and then he turned away and walked off, disappearing into the darkness of the palace.

The window was empty. He had gone.

My mother held me for a while as though frozen, until I grumbled at being so long away from the loveliness of her face.

When she turned me to her I saw an expression she had never allowed me to see before. She looked into my eyes, and briefly in those dark waters I saw an expression of real fear.

She looked like an animal that was being hunted and knew not where to run.

She kissed my head and my lips, blessed me with a prayer and then gave me to my maids. Amid my noises of protest, she left the gardens abruptly.

My maids told me to be a good princess and to stay quiet. My mother was the Queen and she had many affairs to tend to. They took me back into the magnificent palace and as I walked away with them on my plump little legs, I looked back to see the shape of my mother, lithe and elegant, as she walked away.

Her gown was deep green and slashed with crimson velvet, bright gold thread twinkled at her long-hanging sleeves, catching the afternoon's light just like the fishes in the pond. Little seed pearls clung to her lovely dress as it swished from side to side as she walked. Her dark hair was covered by a hood of even darker silks that flowed down her slim back like water from a fall.

Her hands were by her side, clenching into fists and then unfolding again quickly into hands.

I knew she was scared and I wanted to help her. To reassure her that whatever it was, she would be able to conquer it. She was the most important person in the world, she could do anything,

But I never got to say those words, or any others to her.

A week later they took her away. My father's men took her head and he married another woman. A pale, flabby, insipid woman took my mother's place at his side.

They said that my mother had never married my father; she had never been the Queen. They said she had done *bad* things. And then… they stopped talking of her at all.

Her pictures and portraits disappeared from the walls. The badges that showed my father's *H* and her *A* entwined together in lover's knots were torn down and burned. The symbol of her crowned falcon became altered, painted over and re-cast into the phoenix symbol of the new Queen…

I was no longer to be called *My Lady Princess* or *Your Highness*. I was now just the Lady Elizabeth, the King's bastard daughter.

It was as though I had never had a mother.

But I remembered her. I was sure she must have been real. Although I was wise enough to never talk of her, I would go to bed and dream of her eyes. I was not quite three years old when she was taken from me.

My mother was dead, by the will, if not the hand, of my father.

My world would never be safe again.

CHAPTER 2
1537
HATFIELD HOUSE

It was October. The long, dusky nights of summer had turned into the heavy, swollen nights of autumn. Leaves were falling russet and gold from the trees. A crisp chill was in the air, bringing cool mornings promising frosts soon to come. The harvests had been brought in and the house was alive with the zingy scent of sweet vinegars cooking down apples and pears to make cider and sauce.

I sat at the window seat in a corner of Hatfield. My book lay open and ignored in my lap as I stared out of the window, thinking on what I do not remember. It cannot have been of much import, for I was a small child of only four at the time.

But I remember the sound of cannon fire from far away, cutting through the calm of the autumn air, then the sound of church bells as they started to ring out clear and true. I remember the smell of crackling bonfires lit in the towns and villages nearby.

And then the messenger came, riding fast with news.

Lady Bryan, both my friend and governess, came to me, ruddy faced and excited by the news, her cheeks flushed and her hands quivering. A son was born to England she said to me; I had a brother now.

At two-o-clock that morning, a prince had been born into the house of Tudor. He was named Edward and he was my new brother.

My father, the King, had waited for years to finally have what had come to him by the grace of God on that autumn morning; a son to rule England in his stead when he died.

My father, the King Henry VIII or the great *Bluff King Hal* as commoners called him, was overjoyed, as was England. London was afire with bonfires where people linked arms dancing for joy; wine flowed in place of water from the fountains. Churches sang out the *Te Deum* in thanks to God for assuring the King that he had made a lawful and righteous marriage. God had rewarded my father with the boy he had so longed for; there was no sign more sure or welcome of His approval.

After years trying to rid himself of his first wife, barren Queen Katherine, and many more striving to win the hand of my mother Queen Anne; after his anguish at my mother's betrayal and her subsequent execution, my father had at last, made a lawful marriage to plain little Jane Seymour, one of my mother's own ladies in waiting, and had been rewarded with the birth of a son. There could be no man in England as happy as its King on the day my brother Edward was brought screaming into this life.

When my mother was Queen, my own birth had come as a disappointment. If I had been the boy that she and my father craved, she would still be alive; a Queen honoured and respected as Jane was now. But a girl I was, a girl I always would be, and her position had become unsafe on the day that I was born.

Lady Bryan would have never allowed me to talk of myself or my mother in this way. Blood of the Boleyns herself, she had loved my mother and she was devoted to me.

But I could not help but hear the whispers of the servants, and I knew they were right. If I had been born a boy, that charming, beautiful mother whom I had scarcely known, and now barely remembered, would still be the Queen.

But now I had a brother. The future King of England was born and he was…younger than me.

It sounded strange to me, child that I was, that someone who was younger than me might come to rule the country. To my mind, nations were ruled by those who had grown up, not little babies who knew not one person from another.

Once, I had been placed in the line of succession. When my mother was the Queen my father had fought for my title to be recognised above all other claimants, above my older sister Mary; I too had been the heir to the throne when I was just a baby and knew nothing.

But with my mother's fall, with her arrest and execution, my father had announced that his marriage to her had been unlawful. Nights before she faced the sword she agreed to this, signed her name on a paper next to his and their marriage was made null. I fell from being the heir and legitimate daughter of the King, to being but a bastard daughter of Bluff King Hal…. the bastard princess of England.

Did that mean my father loved me not? I thought not.

My father was the most impressive man I had ever seen. A titan who stood shoulders above any other men I knew. To me, being so small, he was enormous and the jewels on his clothes, the rich fabrics and diamond buttons made him shine like the stars. When he laughed and threw his great arms around a man or woman he was fond of, the sound would resonate through the world, it would make the heart pound just to hear it. All his emotions could be *felt* by those around him like the heat that radiates from the flames of a fire. He was the largest person I had ever seen or sensed. He was captivating, enticing, fascinating. He was the King.

When his eyes rested on me, when his kiss fell on my head, I knew that he loved me. When he laughed and picked me up, I knew that I was special to him. But not quite special enough, it seemed, to warrant acknowledgment in the line of succession.

I longed to see him. So little time I ever had to see either of my parents. My mother was in Heaven and my father was often too busy with affairs of state to much visit his little bastard. As his daughter I wanted for nothing, but I was not wanted for anything. It was a stark realisation for a little girl to come to, and a lonely one.

Lady Bryan was holding the note in front of her like it was a holy volume. She bit her lip as she read, and then looked up at me.

"The King asks that his daughters come to court to celebrate with the family," she said to me in wonder. "You are to carry the robe of the Prince at his christening!"

I could see that she was pleased, but she looked at me with a little concern; I was after all very young to be placed in such a vastly important role at a state occasion. I smiled at her, touched to see her fears for me. Lady Bryan was easy to love. She was firm and meted out punishment when required, but she was warm to me; compassionate and close. She loved me I think a great deal. Her first devotion had been to my mother, and when she died, Lady Bryan had remained with me, to care for me as my mother would have wanted. She brought me a comforting link to the dead mother that I had hardly met.

I stood up and straightened my dress. Standing soberly in front of my governess I said; "Tell me what I must do, Lady Bryan, and I will do it as you say."

She looked at me with pride and surprise. She was always commenting that I was much more grown than my years.

She nodded to me.

"It will take work and diligence, my Lady." She smiled at me. "But we will begin as we should," she said, "at the beginning."

CHAPTER 3

AUTUMN, 1537
HAMPTON COURT

We came to Hampton Court, travelling along the river in a barge, the sides of the muddy, wet banks lined with people waving and cheering. Everyone was so happy to see a prince born.

I waved back to the crowds and was greeted by the common people cheering me, jumping around wildly on the bank to try and get my attention. One man was so keen that he tumbled, twisted, and fell backwards into the river, landing with a great splash in the cold water. I laughed a little.... until a face from Lady Bryan stopped me in my tracks.

The people of England liked to see me. It made me happy, made me feel less alone. They had hated, feared and despised my mother but it seemed that did not alter their affection for me.

"You are a *Tudor* to the core," said Lady Bryan, smiling down at me with pride. "Your red hair, your beautiful clear skin, the way you smile even… you remind them of your father and of all he has done to make this country great. That is why they cheer."

I pouted a little. "Do they not like *me* at all then?" I asked and she laughed.

"Of course, they love you," she said. "You are their *little* Elizabeth, your father's natural daughter. But your family and your house are what they show loyalty to; do not forget that you stand where you do because of the honour of the house of Tudor, because of their reverence of your great father. You are of royal blood; they honour you because of all that, but also yes, because you are yourself, quite charming"

I nodded. My family was great, and my father was the greatest of all the Tudors. My tutors were proud to impress this on me in each history lesson we had.

I waved again and the crowd screamed out to me with delight.

"They love you Elizabeth," said Lady Bryan. "Always remember that the love of the common people is something every good ruler and lord needs; either that or fear."

"Which do they have for my father?"

She looked sharply at me, her eyes wary, "love… of course. But for a king… it is also good that men should know to fear him. Kings must rule absolutely, like your father does. It is his God-given right and only God may decide who shall become King and wield that power."

"My brother will be King," I said.

"Not for a long time yet, God willing," said Lady Bryan crossing herself. "The Prince will need his father to teach him how to rule well, and King Henry is hale and hearty. He is married happily and they say he has a new lease on life. God willing, more children may come and the King will rule over us for many years yet."

I watched her look around a little as she said this. She was watching to see if any others had noted her words. I felt a little shiver run over me. Lady Bryan was afraid that her words would be carried to the King, and she wanted him to know that she spoke only good of him. She was afraid to speak openly.

"Yes." I said, perhaps a trifle too loudly, "my father will rule over this land for a long time, God willing, and we will all know the bounty of his good reign."

She looked at me and smiled. With a slight nod, she approved of my first foray into the world of diplomacy as we neared the palace.

My new brother, the little Edward, was a small, pink face that stared out at me with pale blue eyes. He looked tiny, surrounded by the magnificence of the great cradle he was in, covered in soft linens, cottons, silks and satins and topped with heavy cloth of gold that shimmered in the dapped sunlight of the enclosed chamber.

I curtseyed to my new brother and as I did, there was a little gurgle from him. His maids laughed and said he was already fond of his big sister. It took me a minute to realize they meant *me* and not the tall figure of my older sister who stood near me.

Mary used to live with me; when I had been the Princess, she had been made a part of my household, one of my servants and she had not been happy about it. My mother's marriage to our father had usurped her own mother's position and she had been made a bastard. She had been placed in my household perhaps as a punishment, but my sister Mary had shown affection to me all my life, never harbouring the grudge that some may have expected. She chose not to blame me for her fate, at least not when I was a babe.

When my own mother went to the block and I was made a bastard too, we shared something more in common than we ever had before. Two motherless bastards, girls of little importance, set aside by our father as he went on to try for a son… and to find a wife who was capable of giving him what he wanted. Our mothers had been found wanting, and they had been cast aside for it; we had been found wanting, and had been disregarded for it. We two sisters were united through this strange and painful bond.

Mary was auburn-haired, tall and willowy. Her face was pretty and flushed with the excitement of being brought back to court again. Our father had banished her when she had disobeyed his will. She had refused to admit her mother was no true Queen. Once she submitted to our father, agreed that her mother had never been Queen and she was not a princess, our father welcomed her back. Her new obedience pleased him and Mary was happy to have a family again. Years of fighting, of banishment, of being alone and unloved had brought disquiet to her soul early in life. She had known illness and infirmity, felt the wrath of our powerful father, lost a mother she loved passionately, and a title that she had once carried with pride.

Mary had lost a great deal too early in life, as I had.

But our father's presence was a powerful elixir, and Mary blossomed under the light that radiated from him like a field poppy in summer.

Whatever else the birth of our brother meant to us, at least we were brought back to our family, to our father, and together once again.

The Queen Jane lay in her bed when my sister and I were taken to see her. I had met her only once before, but even I could see that something was wrong now.

She was always pale, always plain, but her face now was darkened with shadows, her cheekbones pushed at the gossamer covering of her skin. Her pallid skin had a light sheen of sweat over it and her lips, that once were soft pink, were drained of colour. Her eyes did not focus on mine when she nodded to my greeting and blessing. She was dressed in a stunning bed-gown of black velvet with gold thread and her servants paid her all honours, but she tired quickly and our audience was brief.

I looked up with concern at Mary as we left and she reached out and squeezed my hand.

"You are so quick child that I forget how young you really are," she said shaking her head at me. "The Queen is very tired. The ordeal of childbirth is hard for women and in this case it was long and difficult. The Queen toiled for many days and nights to bring our beloved brother into the world and she faced the agony with courage and fortitude. She is weak and tired now, but she will be fine." Mary smiled and squeezed my hand again. "You must not be worried."

I nodded, but I was still unsure.

Our father greeted us with a shout and a great booming laugh as he strode towards us across the audience-chamber. Courtiers lined the room, all beaming and yet all looking as though their faces were stuck to their smiles. It was easy to see that they forced out more happiness than they actually felt to please our father in his effusive joy.

We fell to a curtsey before our King and father, and he reached out his hands to us. Kissing Mary heartily on the cheek and mouth, he greeted her with such warmth and friendship that I felt a little jealousy steal into my heart. Our father was well pleased that this daughter who had given him such worry had acquiesced to obey him, and when he was pleased with someone he would show it. He liked her submission to his authority; defiance was not something he took to kindly.

Then he turned to me and I found myself suddenly gathered up and brought up high into the air, right next to his big grin.

His face was large and round, with a red-gold beard and twinkling blue eyes. I laughed and screamed with surprise and pleasure as he lifted me up. I remembered how he used to parade me around, throwing me about in his huge arms. I giggled and hugged him, throwing my little arms about his shoulders. When I released my arms from my father I saw there were tears in his eyes. He was a deeply sentimental man at times.

He put me down and kissed me again.

"Many congratulations, your majesty," I said beaming, truly happy to have been shown such love in public. "On the birth of our beloved brother Prince Edward."

He looked at me, most merry and amused, but also surprised. There were touches of both pride and concern in his face as he thanked me, and a ghost of something else…something he sought to hide from me.

I understood what it was.

No one would have told me, but I remembered her eyes. When I looked in a mirror to see my heart-shaped face, pale skin and red hair... all *Tudor*...all my *father*... the eyes that I saw all this with were large and dark and glittering.

I had my mother's eyes.

My father had done all he could to forget. But here, in me, was a little uncomfortable reminder of *her*, staring back out at him through the eyes of his daughter.

I dropped my eyes to the floor and curtseyed again.

He was so happy on this day that he quickly blinked unhappy memories away and brought us both into the great hall to be paraded before the court; to share in the happiness of a nation who finally understood what it was to have a satisfied king.

CHAPTER 4
AUTUMN, 1537
HAMPTON COURT

The chrysom was heavy; weighed down and encrusted with jewels, thickly embroidered with gold and silver; it was a weighty christening robe for a four year old to try to carry. Before we entered the ceremony I held it nervously in my hands. They shook under its weight.

The thought that I might drop it was one of sheer terror to me. I flushed even to imagine the shame.

Luckily, my father had realized that I was perhaps rather young to be expected to carry it alone and had appointed Edward Seymour, now Viscount Beauchamp, the Queen's brother, to carry me in his wide, big arms as I bore the christening robe for my brother.

I breathed in a relief-ridden breath when I realized I was less likely to disgrace myself by dropping this most important cloth on this most important day.

We gathered in the chambers of the pallid Queen who received us from her bed where still she lay. Although there was great pride shining in her face as she watched the gathering of every notable and noble in the land around her, I saw a shadow of something else. It was as though she wore a mask of glowing satisfaction over her true, exhausted face. She would not show anything other than pride and joy to our father, but even I, a tiny child, could see that she was weakened and strained by the glorious day before it had even begun. I don't think our father was aware of anything amiss in his overwhelming pleasure.

Our convoy formed around the Queen's bed, and then we, the greatest of the nobles of England lined two by two, and processed to the chapel. Edward Seymour smiled at me as he lifted me into his arms. My hands wrapped as firmly as possible around the chrysom. I was determined not to disgrace myself on this most eminent of occasions.

The silver font was guarded by Sir John Russell, Sir Nicholas Carew, Sir Francis Bryan with his one eye glinting like the devil, and Sir Anthony Browne. All with ceremonial towels over their shoulders, ready to perform their parts. My sister too took her place at the altar.

To one side, holding a taper of virgin wax stood a tall man with dark eyes. I looked at him curiously and for a moment our eyes met. My mind started slightly as I saw the eyes of my mother's ghost in the face of a living man. A chill ran down my spine, for where the memory of my mother's eyes was warm and sweet, this man's eyes were hollow, haunted.

This man was my only living grandfather, the father of my mother, Thomas Boleyn.

He saw me looking at him, bowed his head gently to me and then looked back at the procession. At the time I did not think a great deal of this. I did not know who he was. But later, through the whispers of the servants at Hatfield House, I learned much. I heard of how he was despised for having betrayed his children, my mother, and her brother, leaving them to their bloody fates as he sought to save his own life. They said his wife was sick unto death after the executions of two of her three children, but he left her alone as he sought to regain his reputation at court. They said he had even been a part of the Council who had helped condemn my mother to her death; his own child. Whatever hushed and troubled tones were used when people described my mother and her fate, these were nothing to the grim manner people used to speak of Thomas Boleyn.

I did not speak to this man in my lifetime. I had no wish to know him, this strange man with empty, eerie eyes. My mother was dead but it was he who looked like a phantom. He died two years later. I do not think there were any who grieved for him.

A man is measured by the tears spilt for the end of his life, by the hearts and minds that miss his presence. I will wager that none cared to cry for my grandfather Boleyn, and that the world found itself a happier place without him in it.

The Marchioness of Exeter carried our little brother under a canopy borne by the Duke of Suffolk, the marquis of Exeter, the Earl of Arundel and Lord William Howard. It seemed our father had gone out of his way to ensure a part on this stage for every noble and person of note connected with the court. This was the first time a prince had been honoured into the Royal Household for more than a quarter of a century. Our father was not going to let it pass without every triumphant excess possible.

After I had carried the heavy robe, my own body in turn carried by the brother of the Queen, I stood beside Mary as we watched our little brother welcomed into the lands and law of Christ. Our brother screamed loudly as the priest dropped oil and water on his brow, his deep voice intoning prayers to God. Our father smiled with pleasure, looking around at all of those present with a huge grin on his face to hear the strong lungs of his son as their sound filled the air.

Edward was gifted with three godfathers; the Duke of Norfolk; Charles Brandon Duke of Suffolk; and the Archbishop Cranmer. Mary was made Edward's sole godmother, part-responsible for his religious learning in life, a role that I thought she was most suited for, as she took her faith most seriously.

It was a long ceremony and I was very young. Less than half the way through I could feel great pressure on my shoulders as though some huge unseen hand was pushing me down. The small of my back, the curve of my spine and my heavy head protested their tiredness to me, but I remained standing and watching. Towards the end of the ceremony I thought that I might whimper in pain as my bones screamed and my flesh quivered with fatigue; but I remained standing as I was, smiling a little to hide my grimaces of pain. I was not going to allow my body to let me down.

As the ceremony ended, long past midnight, tapers carried by the gentlemen of the court were ignited and suddenly my hazy, glassy eyes widened with tired shock as the world around me burst into dancing light. I stared with glazed amazement at the burning luminosity that surrounded us and Edward, blocking the darkness of the night. It was as though the light of God was upon us, protecting us, shielding us. I am sure my mouth hung open as I stared at the incandescence around me.

A loud voice made me jump startling me from my over-tired half-thoughts.

"God, in his Almighty and infinite grace, grant good life and long to the right excellent and noble Prince Edward, Duke of Cornwall and Earl of Chester, most dear and entirely beloved son of our dread and gracious Lord Henry VIII."

As I stared at the shining tapers and then at the tiny form of my brother I could not help but feel a wandering sadness enter my heart. I had been the focus, as Edward was now, of such a ceremony when I was this small. Had the same words been spoken over me? Had I once been the *most dear and entirely beloved* daughter of my father? Had I once been the centre of everyone's thoughts and dreams, the core of my father's world, as my brother was now?

I blinked away the thought and the lump that came to my throat. This was not a time to linger on the past. On what I had been or might have been. I was here, with my father and family, and a new time of peace and unity was upon us.

The night was deep as we went to leave the chapel; my sister took my hand in hers and looked down at me with a short smile. She was aware of the gravity of the ceremony but she was also willing to give me a little unspoken praise for my conduct. My eyes felt owlish as I looked up at her, blinking heavily in my tiredness. Our hands remained entwined as the Ladies Kingston and Herbert bore our trains and we walked from the chapel. My legs quivered and my hands felt cold although my cheeks were flushed. But I did not tremble as I walked out in honour. I did not falter, I did not fall.

I had made it through the ceremony.

As we were divested of our robes of state, Mary pulled me to her and embraced me. My tired feet and legs stumbled at the pull of her arms and I fell against her. She raised me to my feet, still within her arms and smiled at me.

"Well done child," she whispered to me, turning me back to my maids as their hands undressed me of my fine robes and put me into my nightclothes. I did little but stand yawning, my body and head lolling, as the women around me stripped me, changed me, and brought me to my bed.

In the court, the noise of celebration was still ringing through the very stones of the palace. The sound of music and celebration lingered and burst through the night's air.

My sheets were cool and soft, my chamber warmed by the cheery fire at its heart. My tired body sunk into my bed as my lovely Lady Bryan tucked the sheets and covers around me. My back and my legs clucked with approval at their soft resting place. I felt as though my bed was swallowing me; being eaten whole had never felt as welcome or as agreeable. My sleepy mind started to drift but I found enough sense in my thoughts to congratulate myself on maintaining both my own dignity and that of my family.

My maids shifted on their pallet beds on the floor, sighing for happiness at the end of their long day. The noise was one of familiarity and comfort. I was never really alone.

As I fell into the arms of sleep I heard Lady Bryan speak to Mary as they left the room.

"The Lady Elizabeth did well for one so small and young," she said, and Mary replied in a little warm whisper, "she did very well Lady Bryan, a credit to you, to herself and to the King."

I smiled as I drifted into sleep.

A credit to the King was what I genuinely desired to be.

CHAPTER 5

AUTUMN, 1537
ELTHAM PALACE

Queen Jane was dead.

After enjoying ten days of glory and adoration after the birth of my brother, the Queen of our realm lay white and cold, her body emptied of its soul, awaiting burial.

I had been taken to Eltham Palace after the ceremony, and Mary had stayed at court to help the Queen with her recovery. But soon the Queen had started to fever and sweat. She would not eat nor drink and the heat of her body became a raging fire. Delirium took hold of her mind until she knew not who was around her or where she was. She knew nothing of her son. She knew nothing of the world.

Our father, Mary had written to me, was frantic with worry over the Queen's illness and then, was crushed by her death. Finally he had found a woman who had given him his longed-for heir, he had thought he had found the perfection he had sought for so long… and then his perfection had sickened and died.

It seemed that love and marriage for our father was never going to have a happy ending.

Queen Jane was buried in state as a Queen; the first of my father's wives to be given that honour. Katherine of Aragon was buried as the Princess Dowager of Wales somewhere in Portsmouth, or so I was told, and my mother lay in the Chapel of Saint Peter Ad Vincula, in the Tower of London, her decapitated body bundled into an arrow chest, her last resting place on this earth unmarked.

Perhaps Jane, dying as she gave the King his greatest wish, deserved a place in the halls of kings… perhaps not. Despite my father's love for her, I could little forget that this woman had directly replaced my own glittering mother.

Our father was plunged into dark grief. He appeared for state occasions but I was told that apart from that, he preferred to keep to the company of only his greatest and closest friends. He did not seek to visit me.

Our little brother, Edward, joined the same household as Mary and I. It was special to me as suddenly all three of us, children of the King, all without a mother, were brought together to grow up together.

Mary was of course much older than Edward or I, and I felt much, *much* older than Edward who was just a baby. But still, in those early years at Hatfield and Eltham there was a sense of family, of kinship and closeness.

There was however a down-side to all of this, as there often is in life. My beloved Lady Bryan was in charge of the *Royal* Nursery and now that Edward was brought to Eltham *he* had to become her priority. Although she took time and care to explain this well to me, I could not help but seethe a little with jealousy that my brother should have taken the ministrations of my governess from me. I was not her sole care in the world anymore, and I admit that it rankled with me, no matter how fond I was of my fat little baby brother.

But with Lady Bryan leaving my intimate care, a new person entered my life, one who would become my greatest friend and confidant but also one who would perhaps place me in the greatest of dangers. But when one opens one's heart to love another, it is always placed in some danger. I would never trade all the perils I faced, perhaps partly because of her, for a quieter life without her.

I loved Katherine Champernon from the first moment she leaned close to my ear, whispering to me with a little sideways grin, and told me to call her *Kat*.

Kat was the daughter of Sir Phillip Champernon of Devon; Sir Phillip was a learned man, who saw the benefits, as some enlightened families had, of educating his daughters well along with his sons. My own mother had belonged to such a family herself, and my father the King believed that his daughters should be of much more use to him if they understood not only to read, write and sew, but also learned languages, philosophy and history so that our minds may be quick and useful.

Kat was an excellent tutor; she was learned in classical history and languages and had an enthusiasm for reading that was infectious and pleasing. Although I had never been indifferent to the pleasures of learning, under her tutelage I started to find it a joy. There were *so many* books to read in the world and I wanted to read all of them. She started me on a diet of French, Spanish and Latin (which I had already started) and then history, dancing and philosophy for my sweet. It was a rich dinner certainly, but I feasted on books every day. Any time I looked tired or bored with a lesson, she would find a new way to make it agreeable; we would take walks where we conversed and discussed both historical events and new ideas. She taught my mind from a very early age to hone the skills of conversation and argument, to find my own view and to be able to support it. She was a fine tutor… and a good friend to a lonely little girl.

She was also the most incorrigible gossip you would ever chance to meet and had not learnt to guard her tongue, as she would have to do one day.

As I grew older, she talked to me more and more as a friend, letting slip little nuggets of scandal or court politics, so that, as she said; "I should have an education in current affairs as well as historical matters." But of course this was really just an excuse to gossip.

Kat's fine tutoring of my mind was tested when Sir Thomas Wriothesley paid a call to our house, now moved once more to Hatfield, in 1539. He had business with Mary, but as a courtesy, stopped to pay a call on Edward and myself.

He came into the room after seeing my brother. I stood from my writing table and smoothed my dress. He bowed to me as the King's daughter and I curtseyed to him, and indicated that he may sit, if he wanted, on one of the floor cushions.

We started by discussing my health and that of the King and the Prince, and then he asked me if I was reading much that I found interesting as he had come to see me during a time when I was deep in study.

"Is it perhaps the fables of Aesop?" he said in a gentle, if slightly patronizing tone, I thought.

"It is *De Re Publica*," I said, stroking the volume with my long-fingered hand. "I find Cicero fascinating and his language is beautiful. Excellent writing can be as valuable to a nation as any wealth. Even Julius Cesar said; "It is more important to have greatly extended the frontiers of the Roman Spirit, than the frontiers of the Roman Empire."

Wriothesley stared at me for a moment in astonishment. He blinked.

"My lady," he said a little weakly. "I must have forgotten in my advancing years, but how old are you now?"

"I am six years old." I said smiling at him. I loved to surprise people with my age… they always thought I was older because of my gravity; I had a certain vanity about that I suppose.

"You are so like your father," he said with affection and a little wonder. "When he was a young man, and when he was in the nursery, he loved books more than anything in the world they say, and he still has a fine library now."

I beamed at him. There was nothing I liked more than being compared to my great father and hearing that I was like him.

"You are pleased to be likened to your father?" he said, noting my face and smiling at me.

"Indeed," I said. "For there is no greater king on this earth."

His smile broke out all along his face. "I agree most heartily my lady," he said. "And you, as his daughter, are a great credit to him. I shall be sure to tell him not only of your most advanced and educated mind, but of your graciousness and most excellent conduct."

I smiled wider at him; he was fast becoming one of my favourite people.

"Thank you my lord." I said. "And please do come again to converse and visit with us. Your company has been most agreeable."

He bowed to me and left, shaking his head and smiling still; perhaps marvelling at my old head, on little shoulders.

CHAPTER 6
HATFIELD HOUSE
1538 - 1540

As my brother grew up, he and I were more and more in companionship with each other. Our households were joined for much of Edward's infancy. My poor Lady Bryan spent the majority of his childhood in fear for her life, for Edward's well-being and health were of paramount importance to the King our father. He was both paranoid and obsessive about keeping his precious son safe from harm and infection.

Edward's walls and floors were washed daily, no one who had been near a site of plague, sickness or infection was allowed near the house. Only those with the express permission of the King were allowed to visit, and even I was quarantined away from my brother for the slightest sniffle, headache or cold.

Edward was the heir to the throne, the only legitimate boy that our father had, and since the death of our bastard brother Richmond in 1536, Edward was the only boy surviving of any of our father's marriages or affairs. I did not remember Richmond, that son born of my father's affair with Bessie Blount. He had died in the same year as my mother, and if I met him, I must have been too young to recall the face or voice of my half-brother. They said that our father had adored him; Richmond was the first proof that he could get living sons. But after his death, our father did not mention him. Our father was unwilling to speak of painful things in his past. Once he had left something or someone behind, they were to be forgotten.

Edward was a serious child, even as an infant. Much like myself; he loved books, stories and learning, but that did not mean that he did not love to joke and have fun. There was a natural type of rivalry between us to learn and out-do each other. I believe we learnt more together than even our excellent tutors would have been able to teach us, as we vied with each other to excel. I was secretly rather jealous that my little brother was the centre of everyone's world. It was a position I would have liked to have. That jealousy encouraged me to try to stand out more and more. Without Edward, and my envy of him, I would not be the person I grew to become.

When I started to outstrip the teaching methods of Kat, she arranged that Edward's tutors recommend a male tutor for me. William Grindal was taken on for my education and I grew most fond of him. Grindal had been the star pupil of Roger Ascham who in turn had been the star pupil of Edward's tutor John Cheke. They all were in contact with each other whenever possible, these men with lively minds and active tongues ready to leap into discussion at any time. Roger Ascham was a constant visitor to our houses, and he taught both Edward and me how to write in a beautiful italic hand. Grindal tutored me through ever more difficult stages of Latin and Greek, allowing me to work on translations from Greek to Latin, then into English or French, which broadened my mind and gave me both fluency and understanding of many languages.

We were also allowed to share tutors to a certain extent, and Jean Belmain, Edward's French tutor helped me to master the language of spoken French and the accent that would serve me well in the future.

Our house was a little hive of learning and activity, but our education was also taken outside where we learned to hunt, to hawk and often, to play against each other shooting at the archery butts.

I was better at it than my brother. My arm was strong and my aim was true. Kat told me that my mother had been an excellent archer, as she said I was.

Perhaps one of the reasons I loved Kat so, was that she was the only person who talked of my mother to me. Never in public, for my mother's name was not to be mentioned before others, but in private, she would tell me of my mother, of her passions for learning and for religion, of her private ways with her ladies and of the great love that once existed between her and my father.

I learned early on that my mother's fall from grace was not something that I should mention. Some things were too dangerous to ask of in our world. But I longed to know more about the mysterious woman I had barely known, and Kat was my only source for knowledge about her. She was the only one who would dare, out of love for me, to talk of my mother the Queen Anne.

"There was *no one* like your mother." she whispered to me when we were alone together in my room as I was going to bed. "No one was so enticing, or interesting. She was tall and willowy, like you, but her hair was dark and long. Her skin was clear and soft and when she sang, she sounded like an angel."

"They say that your mother kept a good house as the Queen," she continued nodding with approval. "And there was never such good order amongst the ladies of the royal house as when she ruled. She had a merry spirit and a pretty laugh. She loved to read and to talk, she loved to discuss ideas and ideals; she loved to ride and to hunt with the falcon. She was *fascinating* to all men and women who met her."

"Perhaps *too* fascinating," I said. I was not unaware of the accusations that had been levied at her before her execution.

"You should not believe everything that you hear," Kat warned softly. "There are many who think she was unjustly accused and that you are still the legitimate princess of the realm."

"You should be more careful in what you say Kat," I said fearfully. "What if someone overheard?"

"I am *whispering* to you my lady," she said. "And I trust *you* would not betray me?"

I shook my head. "Never," I said. "But why would my father have had my mother executed… if she did *not* do terrible things?"

Kat looked around her and dropped her voice further. "Your mother had enemies," she said. "She was of the reformed mind, she leaned to the *Protestant* faith, and there were others who did not like her passion for the new thinking. They did not like her influence over your father. They feared that she might sway him to leave the Catholic Church for good. For her, he had already broken with Rome, dissolved the monasteries, become the Head of the English Church in the place of the Pope. Her enemies feared that she would influence him further. They thought if they could remove her, then they could bring back the old religion and join the country once more with Rome."

"And they...made things up about her?"

Kat nodded. "And the King was so in love with her that hearing their stories of betrayal, of her giving her love to other men, made him wild with jealousy. It was not his fault; men who are in love with women as he loved her can do terrible things, things born from fear and pain. He believed her enemies, their tales wounded his pride and his love for her, and she was executed because of their lies."

I looked around again, as though a spy might be hiding behind a tapestry and overhear our whispers. "My father is very clever," I said softly. "He would not just believe anything without knowing it for sure."

Kat shook her head. "You are very young," she said. "And although you know many things, you are still a child when it comes to the matters of the heart. When a man loves a woman *so completely* as your father loved your mother, it is a fragile thing that can be destroyed so easily, it can be abused, turned into blinding hate and rage. Such it was with your mother and father. The lies of her enemies made him think that she had betrayed him. He was afraid that she loved him no longer, and so he sought to destroy her before *she* could destroy *his* heart. He has never faced the truth, for he cannot. It would be too painful for him to admit that she died innocent of the things she was accused of...too painful for him to admit that he killed the woman he loved... unjustly." She looked at me with serious eyes; "there are some things that every man and woman in this world can never face about their actions or their own selves. We seek to hide the parts of us we do not understand or like. This is so for your father, in the case of your mother."

I shuddered and felt on the verge of tears. I could hardly believe that my father would be so easily deceived, and yet neither did I want to believe my mother was capable of such wrongs as I had heard of her. Neither version of the past was easy, or enjoyable.

"The position of kings and queens may seem all-powerful," said Kat snuggling her body to mine in the warm bed and wrapping her arms about me. "But you know well from your study of history that this is not always the case. Emperors and kings, queens and generals have been destroyed by betrayal as often as others have triumphed and won. These things you should remember, for one day you will be grown, and perhaps you will help to rule a country should your father marry you to a king. Keep the memory of your mother in your heart, know that she loved you and was a good woman. What others say can never affect your love for her, but know too that it can be dangerous to speak the truth; the enemies that brought forth her death, may still be enemies to you…just for the kinship with her which flows in your blood."

They were hard words for a little girl, but I was shrewd enough to understand her well enough.

CHAPTER 7

1540 - 1542

My father married again in 1540. I did not meet the new Queen whilst she *was* Queen as it seemed there was a problem with the match. Our father quickly turned this wife, the Princess Anne of Cleves, into his *Most Beloved Sister*, and she settled into a life in England as a rich woman with a royal allowance and many goodly houses to her name. She became my aunt; a strange arrangement where a stepmother may become an aunt in the blink of an eye or with the scratch of a pen. But such was the will and power of my father; what he wanted, became the truth.

Kat told me that Anne of Cleves was betrothed to another prince before she had married my father, and this was a lawful impediment to the marriage between them, forcing its end. But servants whisper well, and I heard another rumour… that my father had not thought her *pretty* enough to be his wife. There were other stories travelling in murmurs across the breeze of the courtyard and the stable block too… that our father had already found the woman he wished to marry instead of the Princess of Cleves, and he rid himself of his ugly wife, for a new appealing one.

Her name was Catherine Howard, of the house of the Duke of Norfolk, and she was a young cousin of my mother's, making her something of a second cousin to me. She had been a lady in waiting during the short-lived reign of the Cleves princess. I could not help but remember that this was how our father had met Jane Seymour before he replaced my mother with her. It was also how he had met my own mother before he replaced Katherine of Aragon.

My father it seemed, never needed to look far to find a new bride.

I was taken to meet the new Queen, my stepmother, one afternoon. We met formally in her new apartments at Hampton Court and I was surprised that she seemed younger even than Kat, which Catherine was, being but seventeen. She was little, plump and pretty; she laughed a lot and had lovely eyes that sparkled when she saw me.

"We must be *good* friends," she said to me after I had curtseyed to her. "They tell me you are very clever and very well learned. I am not so. My tutors always despaired of me when I was your age." Her little face pouted a little with the memory and I was surprised to see how easily she showed her emotions; living on the outside of her features. This little woman could hide nothing it seemed.

My father was enraptured with her. Everywhere he went he took her and he was very fond of touching her, pulling her to him when they walked together, stroking her as they sat at the head of banquets and entertainments. He rode with her body crushed against his, never allowing her to ride her own horse. He could not bear to be apart from her. It seemed she was doing him good. He had taken to riding and hunting with vigour once more and the increasing girth of his waist seemed to stall and retreat at his new enthusiasm for exercise.

Kat said to me that he had never shown such affection to a wife, apart from my mother.

There was something in Catherine Howard that was so easy to like. She loved to laugh and to dance. She was flighty to be sure, and had no great intellect, but she was friendly and warm. There seemed to be no malice in her and she was very keen that she and I should see much of each other, which made me like her more. Possibly, this was due to our connection by blood, but I think it was also because she had not succeeded in getting my sister Mary to warm to her.

Mary was unlikely to approve of any lady as unbidden in her emotions as Catherine in any courtly position. But I think that the idea of the merry, flighty, slightly silly, Catherine taking the lofty place once held by her regal mother, Mary's paragon of all womanly goodness, was vastly repugnant to her. Mary was polite to Catherine, but she did not attempt to do more than was strictly necessary to honour her as queen.

Edward was young and serious, but Catherine managed to get even him to giggle and stare at her with adoration. The King loved her, all seemed happy and well at the palace after the great mourning of Queen Jane and the strangeness of our father's brief marriage to Anne of Cleves.... and I thought therefore that this would be my father's happy ending.

I was wrong.

They had hardly been married for any time at all before Catherine was arrested, sent to the Tower, accused of adultery and executed.

She did not have a trial as my mother had done. She was not allowed to defend herself. They said when my father heard what she was accused of, that he had screamed for his sword, wanting to strike her head from her neck himself.

The night before she died she asked that the headsman's block be placed in her rooms at the Tower of London, so that she could practise dying with dignity as her cousin, my mother, had done. They say she walked to it over and over, practising her steps, rehearsing how to place her head carefully upon it. When she had done so a dozen times, she rested her head there and wept quietly, her tears rolling down the sides of the block, where later her blood too would flow.

I shivered when I thought of her pretty, sparkling eyes weeping through the night against the block on which she was to lay her head and die. On the morrow of 13th February 1542 they came for her, and Catherine Howard passed from this life with the stroke of an axe. She was not quite nineteen years old.

Catherine was the second Queen in all of English history to be executed by the King. My mother had been the first.

Kat was sorrowful. She had liked the Queen's spirit and her merry ways.

"They say that she took a lover, the same Master Culpepper who was in service in the king's own house and was executed with her," she whispered to me when we were in bed at night. "And even before that," Kat leaned towards me, her voice catching with both excitement and horror at her own tale. "When she was a young girl in her grandmother's house... there were other men she took to her bed."

I shivered again. "That is what they said of my mother too," I said.

Kat nodded. "But in this case, unlike your mother's, it seemed that all the men admitted it," she said. "Apart from Culpepper."

I sighed, feeling sorrowful. "Does it seem to you, Kat, that marriage and love are… dangerous things for women?"

Kat tusked and shook her head. "Not for all women," she said.

"But for royal women, or those who become royal?" I shivered still, even though the covers were warm about me. "I think that I should not want to marry when I am older."

Kat laughed. "You will change your mind on that, my lady," she said. "Marriage is the most natural and most glorious state for a woman, and besides," she grinned at me, "would you not wish to have a child? You will find that hard without a husband."

I smiled at her. But my thoughts were uneasy. Pretty little Catherine Howard and my beautiful mother both ended their days at the executioner's block. Jane Seymour had died after giving birth and Mary's mother, Katherine of Aragon had died abandoned; shut up and forsaken in a castle… Which of them had had a glorious state? Would any of them have chosen differently, perhaps not married, if they had thought their ends might be as awful as they had been?

I had started to think that marriage seemed like it only led to one thing for a woman: death.

CHAPTER 8
SUMMER, 1542

Since she and my father had ceased to be married, my new *aunt*, Anne once of Cleves, now of England, had become an attentive member of my family. Interested in becoming closer with her adopted nieces and nephew, she wrote to each of us, sending books and little presents such as pretty ribbons, fine cloths and gems to us. It is easy to win the affections of children in such a manner.

Our time at Eltham and Hatfield in our youth was spent largely in seclusion from the court; fears about the corruption of the court on the young, both from diseases that spawned in the city and from the activities that adults seemed to censure, and yet engage enthusiastically in, were impressed on us as reasons for our absence from the court *proper*. We came to visit at times, on state occasions in particular, and our father visited us when he could, mostly to see Edward of course, but also to spend time with Mary and me. He would take us walking in the gardens; ask about our lessons and what we had learnt since last we saw him. Since the end of his marriage to Catherine Howard he had remained unmarried and seemed to have lost some of the resolute and awesome spirit which I had always previously felt resonating from him. He was sad I suppose, sorrowed by the failure of another marriage, lowered by the betrayal of someone he had loved. When I slipped my little hand into his as we walked, I felt him squeeze my fingers slightly, as though in thanks for my little offering of love to him.

When I was not with my father, I would think of Catherine Howard with sadness, but when I saw him, brought lower than I had seen before after her execution, I felt more sorry for *him*. It changed from day to day I think. I could never entirely reconcile the feelings of both love and fear I had for my father. Perhaps it was because, as my Lady Bryan once said, subjects must both love and fear their King... that is the source of his control.

As much as I was his daughter, I was also his subject. It was the same for his wives I suppose, they had two roles and both ordered them to obey his will. But my father had a habit, it seemed, of picking women who did not wish to obey him as a husband or as a king. I wonder sometimes if his overwhelming disappointment in marriage was because he saw his wives as having betrayed him as a man, or as a king?

It was rare enough, but sometimes our father would allow other visitors to come to us when he could not. Courtiers vying for his favour would seek to impress us with their gifts, or fools they brought to the house, in the hopes that we would offer a kind word to our father about them. It was easy enough to tell which were in truth interested in us and which were only interested in advancement.

One of those he allowed to visit was our aunt, Anne, his new sister.

My aunt of Cleves was a good woman. Although the impediment to her marriage with my father had deprived me of her as a stepmother, my father's careful arrangement to make her his beloved sister had given me a loving and considerate aunt.

Anne was a plain looking woman with a rather over-large nose that she sought to hide by adopting a shy, down-cast expression that made her seem most humble. She had pretty eyes though, and a sense of acceptance about her which was easy to like. She had been pleased to marry my father, she told me, but no less pleased to become his sister and to remain in England which was "a great country". It seemed that she held the country she came from in little regard.

I could get very little from her as to the type of land that she hailed from, but when she did speak about her country and especially her brother the ruler, she had a wild, frightened look about her eyes that made me think she would have been scared to return to it. She loved England, that was sure enough, and she had been made a rich woman by submitting to the will of our father. She gambled and played at cards a great deal with her servants, and her English, although accented and heavy, was getting better daily. She was not discontented with her life at all.

No other queen had fallen so gratefully or so gracefully from her place at the side of our father. Every other queen he had sought to depose or replace, to annul, divorce or kill... And every one of them had fought to stay where they were. All but Anne; and now every one of the others lay in a grave, every one of them. The only memory honoured was that of Jane. The names of my father's other wives were never mentioned at court. My father's anger at them had removed their existence from life, and from history.

Anne was not a queen anymore, but she was alive, she was prosperous, she was independent in her means.

Is it better that one should strike through life like a flash of lightening that once it strikes the earth vanishes without a trace…. or is it better that one should be like the changing brightness of the sun? Able and ready to bend and to fade when required, but always present somewhere, and always alive?

If my mother could have guessed at her fate, would she have changed her actions? Would she have taken a lesser place, if it meant that she would not die…. that she might still be with me? I knew not. Something within me told me that my mother was not made of the same mettle as my living aunt of Cleves.

Anne of Cleves was indeed a rich woman. She had a royal pension on which to live which was vastly generous in its terms, servants, a fine stable of good horse and my father had bestowed upon her several palaces when he made her his sister. One of these had been the family home of my own mother, Hever castle in Kent. On occasion when I was young, I was taken there to see Anne.

Having found out, from Kat of course, that Hever was the castle my mother had grown up in, I was eager to see it. The first time I rode over the little hill and spied the white-washed walls shining in the failing light, surrounded by the dappled waters of the gentle moat, I felt as though I had found a part of my mother. As though I had stumbled into a memory of her which I could not place; it was like waking from a dream where the pictures and events of the dream have gone, and yet the emotions raised by it still echo in the fibre of your heart.

I stopped my horse and those around me did the same as I gazed on the little castle. Hardly bigger than a manor house really. A small village stood not far from it in the distance, where blue smoke rose to mingle with the dusk from many chimneys. My mother had been related to the Howards, to the Dukes of Norfolk, but my grandparents had been Boleyns; a family who had impressed my father with their skills in courtier ship and diplomacy. I wished I had had a chance to know something of them, although I think my father might not have approved. I think at this time my aunt Mary Boleyn was still living, but her reputation was as wild as could be, so I would never have been allowed to meet with her.

I leaned forward on my horse, patting his sweating sides and looking at the childhood home of my mother. This was where she had played as a child; this was where she had learned her lessons and danced. This was where she would have laughed and sung. This was where she and my father had met and courted in secret when they first found love together. My heart swelled and tears came to my eyes as I tried to place that distant faded memory I had of her within the gracious gardens of Hever, as I tried to reconcile the half-thoughts and strange emotions that came from finding another part of my mother, in my own life.

My aunt Anne came out to meet us in the little courtyard followed by her many attendants and saw me looking around with interest at the castle. Her gown was glorious in black velvet with ermine at her cuffs and collar. She was allowed to wear all the trapping of royalty with the permission of our father, and she was keen to take advantage of this generous allowance.

"Yes," she said in her heavy English, nodding at me and following the long gaze from my eyes around me. "I knew you would want to see Hever. For your own blood, it speaks to you... calls to you, does it not?"

I smiled but did not answer her question. I did not speak of my mother often, and certainly not in public. I curtseyed to her and embraced her, telling her of my pleasure in receiving the gifts she had sent to me. Anne smiled; that habit of pointing her large nose downwards gave her, in the shadow of the castle, a strangely sly appearance.

We ate together in the great hall; a weighty, grand room with a roaring fire at its heart. All around us, encrusted on the ceiling and around the fire were emblems and badges of the Boleyns. My grandfather had obviously wanted to ensure his family were remembered. What a shame, I thought, that he could not do that by ensuring the survival of his children, rather than the survival of his insignia.

When we had finished the sweet at the end of our meal, and my belly was filled with slice after slice of thick marmalade and wafer, I was taken to my bed.

The next morning, Anne took me on a little tour of the castle and of the grounds.

"This room was your mother's... when she was a child," she said, swinging open the heavy oaken door to a dark little room, and then she shrugged, "or so they tell me."

We stood in the little room. Once my mother had been here as a child, perhaps at the same age as I was now. Feelings fought to well up inside me and I pushed them away. I could not be seen to show emotion, to show anything at the mention of my mother. Servants could see and report many things.

"It is a good room," I said pressing my hand on hers. "But it is *you* whom I have come to see."

She smiled at me; her plain face was gentle with affection. "I was so pleased when I became your aunt," she said, still stumbling over some of the words. "For it meant that I could see you and your brother and sister. I did not have a lot of family in Cleves, and none that are… as clever, or as friendly, as the one that your father gave me here in England." She grinned at me. "He gave me many things," she said, "but I think his great gift was my new family."

I reached out my hands to her, "I too was glad to take you as my own blood," I said. "My father was wise to keep you in our family as a sister."

She looked almost crafty as she turned a little away. "They say that your father looks for a new queen," she said. "Perhaps one day, he and I might once again become husband and wife, rather than brother and sister. Then you would be my daughter. Would you like that?"

I looked at her with surprise and alarm and then looked around me. Her servants were some way away from us, as were mine, and she had not spoken loudly, but still…she was unguarded in her speech. It was not clever, or careful.

"Perhaps those things are better left to my father," I said quietly, wondering slightly at her words. She had all she could ever want for here. I could not understand why she would want to return to a position fraught with so much uncertainty when she had all that she had as the sister of the King. She was the only one to have ever escaped with her life, and yet she might be willing to give that up, just to be the Queen again.

Power, it seemed, was worth risking all present happiness for, for just a chance to be the highest of the land.

"Perhaps…" she said and smiled again. "Come," she said, "I would show you the rose gardens. They say that your grandmother was gifted with flowers and the gardens are most beautiful."

I took her hand and let her walk me through the roses. Even if she had no guile and no idea that what she was saying might be dangerous, I did. Roses were a much safer topic of conversation than the next marriage of my illustrious father.

CHAPTER 9
HATFIELD HOUSE, 1543

"I have news," Kat said, throwing herself onto my bed one evening. Her face was alive with expectation, as it always was when she had discovered a new titbit of tasty talk.

"You always do," I said smiling at her, and playfully slapped at her shoulder.

Kat was turning into an incorrigible gossip. Always ready to fill me with some dainty morsel of court life. I learnt almost all that was going on in the world through the ready lips of my governess.

"They say that your father will take a new wife soon," she said. "Shortly enough, you are to have a new stepmother and England will have a new Queen."

"*They* are always ready to talk aren't they?" I said frowning at her. I did not like this news. I had heard it end too often with disgrace and sorrow and death.

"Are you not interested?" Kat said looking at me with feigned shock. "Then I shall go away and say no more!"

I caught her by the sleeve and yanked her back onto the bed; we both fell laughing in a jumble together.

"Fine," I said, my curiosity giving in to paths my heart feared to tread. "Tell me what *they* say this time."

Her face puckered a little. Whilst she was excited to tell me her news, she was also bringing further enjoyment to herself as she held back from the brink of telling me. It was in her nature to tease and to flirt with those she was friends with. It was not that her character or reputation was ever in doubt, but she enjoyed playing with people, enticing their expectations to increase her own enjoyment of each and every moment of life. Some people are like that; able to squeeze every last pleasure from each hour of their life. It is a good trait to have.

"*They* say," she said laughing, teasing, "that your father is spending much time with the household of your sister Mary...They say that there is a certain woman amongst her ladies whom he is spending a lot of time with...*They* say that he has sent away a certain Thomas Seymour, brother to the late Queen Jane, who might have been a-courting this *certain lady*."

"Who?" I said, slapping at her again in frustration; my hands hit her arm with greater strength this time. Although I loved her, I found her infuriating sometimes. I think that was what fuelled her to tease me, because to tease is no fun whatsoever, unless the person being teased is not riled by it.

She rubbed her arm. "My lady is too free with her hands against her loyal servants," she said ruefully, pouting at me. "The lady is named Katherine Parr, widow to the late Lord Latimer. A good English woman."

"A widow?" I said in some surprise. "Is she old?"

Kat laughed. "No my lady, she is young and comely. Just because a woman has the misfortune, or fortune, to lose a husband does not mean she has to been old and ugly to do so. The Lady Katherine has buried several husbands who were much older than her. She is a gentle and beautiful woman and it is said the King admires her greatly."

I shivered a little. "He admired Catherine Howard too," I said softly.

Kat crossed herself. "May her soul rest peacefully," she said. "But this is different my lady. Catherine Howard deceived the King. She said she was a virgin come to his bed when she had in fact invited all and sundry to it before him. In this case, the lady is well-bred and raised, and the Lady Parr is a widow, so we know that she will not be pretending virginity to his majesty. At least he will have no surprises there."

I shook myself, I felt cold. "Does he love her?" I asked.

Kat smiled, pressing her hands to mine. "It would seem that he does, and soon they will be married and you will have a new mother," she said.

"Do I need another?" I said waspishly. "I just hope that this time my father finds happiness. He does not seem to have the best of luck with wives."

Kat nodded at me. I could see that she was excited to think of a new queen. When there was a queen at court there were always more entertainments that we might be invited to. There was always more to talk of, to think about and to gossip about. But I was not so sure.

When Kat fell asleep at my side, I lay awake looking at the hangings over my bed in the darkness, wondering about the Lady Parr; another woman, another wife for my father. What was *this* lady thinking as she lay in bed this night? Was she feeling excitement and pride to marry a king and become a queen, to be raised up from her place as a noble woman of little importance, to be the most powerful woman in England? Or was she afraid? Did she feel the cut of the axe in the night breeze chilling her throat, or feel the cold walls of a prison at her back? Did she want to marry my father... or was she compelled to marry him because he was the King? Did she love him, or was she afraid of him?

I wondered on what kind of woman would want to marry our father. But it was likely that she would have little say in it; women did not have a say in who they married much, and if the King beckoned, she could hardly say no.

I loved my father. He was a great man and a great king. But it seemed to me that even though he was all these great things... it was a dangerous thing for a woman to become his wife.

CHAPTER 10
HAMPTON COURT
JULY, 1543

I looked up from my curtsey into gentle, almond shaped grey eyes that shone with merriment and happiness.

My new stepmother, the Queen of England, was a beautiful woman. Her clear skin smelt of fresh milk and sweet herbs, her breath was like crushed mint leaves and her long fingers reached out to me with all the best appearance of friendship.

Her crimson gown set off beautiful auburn hair adorned with a stylish hood, her mouth was pink and pretty and there was all together an air about her of enjoyment of life. I was overcome with admiration for the woman who had captured my father's heart.

She was lovely.

"Come," she said, extending her hands to me and bidding me to rise. "You are my daughter now and the best of friends we should be. It will please your father, our dear King, and also me. I hope that you and I shall converse often and I shall hear everything about your life that I do not have the power to share in, when you write to me."

"I would be honoured to, your majesty," I said and went to bow again, but her tinkling laugh stopped me as I saw she was trying to hold me upright rather than bowing to her as I should.

My father stood behind us, looking at our interaction with pleasure. His eyes shone with delight as he looked at Katherine and me as we conversed. But I could not help remembering that same look had adorned his face when another Catherine stood in the same place as this one.

"Tell me of your studies," she said. "I hear that you are a most gifted scholar and I am most pleased to hear of it."

She paused and sighed. "My own education was not one benefiting the station that your father has raised me to, I fear," she said. "But I have tried hard in my adult life to learn what I should have done when I was a child. Your father..." she paused and looked at him affectionately, "has the great wisdom to educate his daughters as well as his son, for he knows that they will come to benefit the country and to aid the Prince Edward as he grows."

My father laughed and reached out to kiss her.

"You heap praise on me, as ever Kate," he said with warm affection in his voice.

My father had grown larger, so much larger than I had seen anyone grow. Although his body was covered in jewels and cloths of gold and purple that made his girth stunningly royal, there was also a paleness to his skin, and an air of illness about him that I had never seen before. It made me uneasy. I was so used to my father being all-powerful that I was unprepared for him to seem in any way fragile... or human.

But he looked happy at least. For some time now there had been a dark cloud cast over the country that spoke of the unhappiness of its King. My father could affect the feeling of the very land. He and it were linked so entirely that when he was unhappy, the very fibre and feeling of the grass and the trees, of the skies and the clouds felt sorrow too. That was what it meant to be the King, I thought to myself; to be connected as one with the land over which you rule.

That was why he was a great king. He was England, and England was he.

Katherine was kind, sweet and merry. She was beautiful and charmed Edward immediately. She was fastidious in her toilet, always smelling of musk and jasmine, and even concocted her own sweet lozenges to sweeten her breath. She loved books, and loved to read which endeared Edward and me to her from the start. There is nothing like sharing an obsession to bond people together.

More than anything, I hoped that this marriage would make my father happy. My feelings about the various awful fates of his frequent wives were complicated to say the least. I did not want to believe ill of my father; I admired him a great deal. But I could not help but think that either he was terribly unlucky when it came to choosing wives, or perhaps there was something at fault with him, as well as his wives.

I did not speak these words to anyone. To do so would have been foolish and reckless. But I could not stop thinking them.

I liked Katherine a great deal… and it made me afraid. Growing close to people was dangerous, I had learned. For in time you were sure to lose them. I liked Katherine. It made me afraid to lose her.

CHAPTER 11
HATFIELD HOUSE, 1543

Mary and I had fallen out...again. It was becoming a common occurrence.

Our tutors were educating Edward and me in the new religion and the new thought. Our father was the Head of the English Church and so it was fitting that we, as his children, followed his lead in matters religious. Mary, remaining true to her own religious education, clung to the ideals of the Church of Rome. Her mother had been a devout Catholic and Mary worshipped the memory of her. I think that her love and insistence on the righteousness of the Catholic idea of God was always influenced by her feelings for her mother. To her, her mother had been both right and righteous on all matters, so accepting the Catholic teaching as the only truth was merely another manner of showing her love for her mother.

Mary had accepted our father as Supreme Head of the English Church, but she still clung to all the old ideals in the nature of faith.

As I grew up and we came to discuss points on religion, Mary and I argued often. Although I had been taught to see argument not as a bad thing, but as a means to learn and hone one's views into logical shape, Mary saw my arguments with her at best as the overzealous passion of the young, and at worst, as heresy. She liked not that Edward and I were being taught religion as we were.

Mary was often at Richmond Palace these days and we saw less and less of each other. She was so much older and had a household of her own to run. As I grew older, the bond that had seemed so close between us when I was little seemed to evapo rate. We were growing less close and the more she pushed me on matters religious, the more I dug in my heels and raised an obstinate chin to her. When she did visit, we seemed to spend the first day smiling and all other days scowling. She did not like the fire in my temper.

Our relation, Lady Elizabeth Fitzgerald, a distant cousin of royal blood, came to stay with our household sometimes and often was thrust into the widening gulf between Mary and me. Poor Elizabeth was thrown at us by Lady Bryan and Kat whenever it looked as though we might implode. She was as in-between us in age as she was in arguments, but I liked my cousin and she was good company for me as I grew up.

Mary was concerned that Edward and I were surrounded by tutors that seemed only to be interested in teaching us the ways of heretics and dissenters. But Grindal, Asham and the others were great men, and the new Queen Katherine approved of each and every one of them. There were rumours that Queen Katherine was in fact much more interested in the new learning and in the religion of the Protestants than she allowed to be known publicly. That could become a dangerous interest.

My father was Head of the Church and had broken with the See of Rome, but our Church in England was still a Catholic one. Only the spiritual leader of the church had been altered. It gave the people of England a greater understanding of the word of God to have our father as their leader in spiritual matters, and under his mastery, the English Church allowed the people to hear the words of God in the vernacular. Our father was bringing his people closer to God by allowing them to hear the scriptures in their own tongue. The thought made me proud, more proud than I can say, to have such a man as my father.

But the break with Rome had also allowed new ideas to filter into the land. Even though our father punished Protestant heretics, he would also arrest and execute Catholics still loyal to the See of Rome.

Religion was a divisive force. I saw my father's way, with himself as the Head of the Church as a way to bring greater good into the country, to allow people to grow closer to God, but still retain control over the flow of ideas so that heresy could not walk freely about us. For not everyone was as wise as our father, or as able to understand the word of God as he. All men require leadership after all. That was what my father offered his people, both as King and Head of the Church, he was their leader.

Queen Katherine leaned very much towards the new religion. Towards a personal and close relationship with God that was not defined or clouded by Latin texts or by priests that sought to control the people. Our tutors also leaned in the same direction, but no one who had sense within them spoke publicly on their beliefs.

It was not safe to be either a Catholic loyal to Rome, nor a Protestant loyal to God only.

Growing up in my father's lands, we were loyal to him first, and to the will of God second.

CHAPTER 12
FEBRUARY, 1603
RICHMOND PALACE

To me, my faith has ever been a private matter between two souls; between God and me. Although I was raised in one faith and in that faith I chose to worship the Lord, to understand his meaning through those teachings, I have never thought that other ways of finding peace with God were necessarily wrong.

We all find our paths by different routes.

When I came to the throne as a young woman, I chose to unite the warring factions of the Christian faiths of England under one Church of which I was the Head. But I never sought to drill inside the minds of those I ruled. Should they be secret Catholics who could yet keep their manner of worship private enough to escape notice by the law of my lands, then I should have always allowed them to live in peace, even though their faith was different to mine.

But most men are not made of such acceptance. To me, the arguments over the manner of worship were insignificant compared to the glory of understanding God. To me, there is but one God; all else is merely the vanity of man arguing and dying... over trifles.

But my manner of thinking is clearly not as commonplace as one might have hoped. Men kill each other, and kill themselves to stand up for whichever method of worship they believe to be righteous.

No one likes to lose an argument, after all.

The stubborn manner of the spirit of man is such that countless thousands have sacrificed themselves for the honour of dying for their beliefs, and countless thousands have killed their fellow man, disobeying one of the first laws ever granted to us, in order to silence their different beliefs.

I too have killed, not by the act of my own hand; those deeds were done for me. But in all times when I took a life it was because I hoped for the greater security of my state and my people. It was not because I wished to alter the souls of the men who had disobeyed my rule and my will.

If men could only see that obeying the will of their country would have been enough for me, many less would have died for their faiths. I cared not for the manner in which a man chose to see God, as long as he obeyed me also.

But in my reign, and in that of my father, there were many who would not cast aside the outward representation of their faiths in order to live in peace. It is the greatest vanity of man when he is unable to worship in peace within himself and must make public show of his faith through word and symbol. If a man is secure with his own relationship with God then he does not need any trapping or garment to show his faith, it is at peace and rests within his heart. It is those who are unsure in their faith who seek to hide that truth from God by shouting their beliefs from the rooftops of the world.

God sees all within the hearts of men, and nothing can be hidden from the seeking of his eyes. And all the shouting and protesting in the world will not cover a craven, waving heart from the sight of God.

Trust those whose worship and faith is gentle and private, for those are the ones who understand and do not fear the searching eye of their God. Distrust any who proclaim their faith in shouting voice and raging blood, for they are the ones who try to conceal their true, cowardly and unsure natures even from God himself. They are the most dangerous of all people, for they will destroy all else in the world in the quest to hide their souls from God.

CHAPTER 13

HATFIELD HOUSE, 1544

It was in this year, when I was eleven that I dared to hope as I never had been able to before, that one day I might be seen fit to rule England. Our father, in his great wisdom, restored Mary and me to the right of succession in 1544.

After years of being held away from the succession, the stain of bastardry upon us, we were at last acknowledged as the daughters of Henry VIII and put into the line of succession behind our brother Edward.

But our father did not reverse our bastardry. We were still legally his illegitimate daughters. He would not accept either one of our mothers as having been his wife. Mary and I were still bastard daughters of the King of England, but we had been legally placed into the line of princes that would follow our father onto the throne.

Mary was joyous, but her restoration to the line of succession had been dependent on a condition she loved not, and one that sired a rift between us more serious than any we had previously had.

My father had decreed that Edward was his direct heir, and any children Edward should have would inherit the throne after him. In the event that Edward died childless, then Mary would inherit followed by her children. Lastly, should Mary also die childless, then I would take the throne. The possibility that I should ever take the throne was very thin, but the fact that I had been restored to my father's graces publicly was the important thing to me then.

Mary, however, was told that her restoration to the succession was dependent upon her acceptance and embrace of the new religion governed by my father. She must abide by his religious reforms if she was to be included in the succession. Otherwise *I* should supplant her and be put next in line after Edward. I did not have anything to do with this stipulation of course, but that did not mean that she did not hold me partly to blame in her heart.

It was a huge demonstration that my father's favour for Mary was as tenuous as ever, and entirely dependent on her obedience to him in every matter. If she did not agree then the uncompromising wording of the document said that I would inherit "…*as though the said Lady Mary was then dead.*"

Although Mary acquiesced to the demands of our father, she did so with great reluctance and a weighty conscience. Her religion was the same as that of her beloved mother, the last link that she had to preserve the love that had once been between them. To betray the See of Rome was, to her, to betray the mother she had loved, adored and now worshipped as a martyr.

I am sure that although she obeyed our father outwardly, she did not change a single point of her worship in her heart.

But it also brought up other things between Mary and me; picking the crusty head from an old wound and showing the infection that lay therein. Whilst I was a child she had loved and looked after me, she had made me dolls and taught me to make dresses for them. She had sung to me in her deep voice and written to me of the latest styles at court. But as I grew I sometimes saw her looking at me strangely.

She tried to hide it at first. But I would see her looking at me from the corner of her eyes. Her gaze was speculative, and it was judgemental. When we did argue, she would at times widen her eyes as though she saw a shadow of something awful behind me. Sometimes, she would not look me in the eyes when she talked to me at all.

I reminded her of my mother.

As I grew, the large, dark eyes and the little heart-shaped face in the mirror resembled more and more the faded images of my mother in my memory. When Mary looked at my features, she could see the woman she had hated more than anyone else in the world. I reminded her of all the pain and horror she had gone through as a child when our father and my mother had fallen in love and cast her and her mother aside.

The demands of the bill of succession, I believe, reminded Mary of all the anguish she had felt associated with me and my birth, all those nasty little cankers that had been hidden away whilst I was an innocent infant. Now that I was growing, now that my eyes and my face started to remind her of her most hated enemy, now that my father had threatened to remove her powers and give them to me.... now she started to see me less as a sister and more as the echo of her enemy.

She tried to hide it. My lovely Lady Bryan had raised both of us and I believe that she had done a good job in trying to remind Mary that I was not guilty of my mother's crimes. But I could see a change in Mary's eyes. She viewed me, even when I was only eleven, as a danger to her.

But, amongst all this, I felt joy in my heart to know that our father had restored me to the line of succession.

He felt that his blood could be trusted in the protection of the country he loved, and I was so proud to know that he felt me worthy of this.

I was still the Bastard Princess, but one day, Henry VIII had ruled, I could be worthy to be the Queen.

CHAPTER 14
HAMPTON COURT
1544

In July, I was sent word to join the household of Queen Katherine at Hampton Court. Mary and Edward were already there and we were to come together as a family with our new stepmother. Our father was away in France on a military expedition and he had entrusted Katherine with the regency of the country in his absence. Although I feared that my father had left to go to war, I knew in my heart that he would return. I had absolute faith that my father was invincible.

Katherine had written asking that I bring Kat and the other members of my household for a long stay. Our father had approved it and we were to be together for the summer and perhaps even for Christmas.

I had never known a time when my father was absent from the country and it was with a mind full of awe that I viewed Katherine, not in any way a princess born or educated to the role, yet still held worthy to preside over the court and the laws of the land with the greatest of ease and grace.

She was capable and resourceful, she took advice when she needed it and ruled absolutely when it was required. Queen Katherine was the only one of my father's wives I ever really knew well. She was really very special; he had chosen well in her.

She kept Mary and me in constant companionship with her, and I think in her own way she was trying to show us that a woman could rule, and rule well, when it was required. She had an eye for ceremony and never let the obedience due to her as Queen slip, even once. But she was also kind and merry, trying always to smooth disturbances.

I learnt a lot from Katherine.

We walked together most mornings after she had seen to the first round of dispatches and issues; she was fond of gardens as was I and she found them a comfort as she often required some time alone for thought in the bustle of the day.

"It is good to take a step to clear the mind," she said to me as we strolled. "I was not born to this role, Elizabeth, not as you have been, but your father placed a great deal of trust in me and I must seek always to make sure that trust was well founded. "

"I believed it was most well founded, your majesty," I said, looking out at the new walled gardens being built at Hampton Court. My father was a great builder of gardens and palaces; everywhere we moved I could see the touch of his hand on the landscape and the houses. It was as though he was as entrenched in the fibre of the land as God is.

She smiled at me. "You are so young to be such a skilful diplomat," she said, shaking her head. Those that are born to rule come to it with such effortless ease I think. I feel as though I struggle with every choice, for I do not want to let your father down by making the wrong one. But those are gifts *you* have taken from your father; he too was born to be a king."

"My *brother* was born to be the king," I said.

"Of course," Katherine paused. "But as a princess, as a woman connected to the King who will rule this land, it should ever be your duty and pleasure to learn all you can to aid and help the work of the ruler. You are placed in the line of succession because your father sees that you are worthy of that role. And should anything untoward happen, to rule in the stead of Edward."

"Mary is placed before me."

"Yes, but despite your difference in age, you have as great a wisdom as her, perhaps greater, for you are still willing to listen where she is not." She stopped and held my chin in her soft, perfumed hand. "You have learned well from the trials of your youth, Elizabeth," she said. "But I would see you enjoy life and smile more, you are grave for one so young."

I smiled and she looked pleased.

She looked around her; we were as alone as we ever could be... servants walked behind us, her ladies stood to one side of the grasses. Royalty was never really alone.

"I want to give you something," she said. "But you must promise that you would not tell anyone, not even your father, that I have done so."

I looked at her concerned. "My lady," I said "I would not want to disobey my father."

She shook her head. "It is not a betrayal," she said. "I inherited some items when I became Queen, and I want you to have them. I believe the knowledge would upset your father, but I understand perhaps more so than a man should be able to, of the great love between a mother and her daughter, even if the mother was judged as a traitor. I think you would like to have them, and I should like to give them to you."

I looked around me. The servants were far enough behind us, Kat was close by, but she would never tell if she saw or knew. I nodded to Katherine. Her hands reached into her dress and pulled out a little package, wrapped in velvet. It was rectangular in shape, and not too big. She slid it into my pockets before anyone saw.

I touched the package and felt tears jump into my eyes as I slid a finger over the soft fabric.

She smiled and nodded to me. "I did not meet your mother in life," she whispered, "but I do not think that she died in sin as was said of her. I will not speak against the rule and wisdom of your great father, but there are some taken to God who die for the right cause, for religious reform, and I believe she was one of those. A martyr." She looked around her again, her voice was little more than a murmur. "Be proud of her Elizabeth," she said softly. "But remember that it is dangerous to talk of her." She looked about her again and said *"Blessed are those who hunger and thirst to see right prevail."*

I nodded and we continued our walk. Our conversation was of the plants and the flowers, of fashions and of poetry. All safe subjects to be overheard by any.

I fingered the package in my pocket wonderingly… What could be in this little pouch of my mother's? What new secrets was I going to find this night?

CHAPTER 15
HAMPTON COURT
1544

That night I asked my serving women to sleep outside the door of my chambers rather than within it as was normal. They thought it unusual, but obeyed me. I did not want even Kat to be with me at the time I opened the package wrapped in black velvet. I wanted to be alone with whatever came from the soft wrappings. Whatever was in here had belonged to my mother. The woman all must have known once existed, and yet now all denied any recollection of at all.

Sometimes I felt as though she were a creature of mythology, so dark and mysterious that only garbled tales and half-truths remained of the woman who once held me in her arms and looked at me with love.

Who was she? This bright, intoxicating creature whom my father had risked so much for, and then had discarded so easily.

The package sat unopened in my hands as I thought these things. I wanted so much to believe those who said good things about my mother and yet there was every terrible thing I had ever heard whispered about her as well. I wanted to find something of her that would solve this riddle for me. It seemed that even in death, she was as fascinating as she was divisive.

Trembling hands undid the fastenings on the black velvet, slipped so secretly into my pockets. I felt my heart race with excitement; inside this little package could be the secrets unveiled to me of the truth of my mother, and her life and death.

I opened it.

Inside the package there were two small books, both rough volumes compared to some of the wondrous books of my father's library, and on top, tightly curled and coiled, were three long strings of pearls with a little golden decoration. The decoration was in the form of letters, *AB*. It had been my mother's own necklace.

I turned the little golden letters over, and on the back, engraved in tiny, elegant letters was an inscription: *HR loves AB and no other.* I stared at it for what felt like hours not knowing whether to laugh or cry; this had been a gift from my father to my mother. This proved that he not only had once known her, had admitted her existence in life, but had loved her once too.

The strings of delicate pearls were warm and shone like the moon in the light of my candle; their little lights awoke memories within me. I could remember my mother wearing something very similar to this on that last day I sat with her in the gardens, looking at the fish in the pond.

The golden letter winked at me too. I felt a warmth coming from the pearls and the gold that was not of this world. As though the love of my mother were seeping through the metal and pearl and wending its way into my heart, carried on the still space between me, and my memory of her life. As though these little tokens could contain and preserve the love that a mother might hold for her child.

I stared at my mother's necklace for some time, trying to recall from my memory all that I could about her; her face, her shape, the smell of her skin, the way she walked and moved, the sound of her voice. But even with the help of this lovely necklace, I could call only blurry images of the sparkle of her eyes, the sound of only the end of a word as it came from her mouth, the warmth of her gentle hands as she held my little body close. But still, despite the failures of my faded memory, there was still something that seemed to call to me from the treasures in my hand.

I put the necklace on my lap, not wanting to feel far from its magic and turned the little volumes over in my hands. They were simply bound in an old-fashioned style, with plain velvet covers that had been hand-stitched neatly and elegantly. Little heartsease and lily flowers sat faded slightly at the edges of the covers. Had my mother's long, elegant fingers done this work? I hoped so as I stroked the stitches. I opened the first one.

Inside I saw the title of the work. No wonder it had been bound with plain covers, without title.

The Obedience of a Christian man
and how Christian rulers ought to govern, wherein also (if thou mark
diligently) thou shalt find eyes to perceive the crafty conveyance of all
jugglers.

It was by William Tyndale. A man whom many of my tutors talked of quietly with some reverence, and many others talked of as though he were the devil. He had died in the same year as my mother, 1536, strangled and then burnt at the stake as a Protestant heretic. Tyndale may have died for his faith, but his works were not forgotten. The New English Bible, translated into the vernacular, was largely from Tyndale's own, also once banned, translation. A copy of that volume sat in almost every house in England rich enough to own books.

How could I, tutored by those so interested in the new faith, not understand the importance of such a work? My tutors might all say, for safety's sake, that they were committed to the Catholic religion with our father as the Head of the Church, but that did not mean they did not lean with an eye of favour towards the teachings of Protestants. Tyndale was a Protestant martyr, he had died for the faith they all secretly followed. *The Obedience of a Christian Man* was still largely a banned book, containing such ideas that had lit the fires of the new religion in our lands and in the hearts of its people. My father did not condone ordinary people reading such works, but I understood that he was not included in that sanction, being the King; he could read as he pleased.

The Obedience of a Christian Man had been seen as sacrilegious when it first appeared. And yet my mother had owned a copy, owned a book that the Catholic Church was opposed to, and had owned it even though the laws of my father said she could not. Obviously my mother had thought that rules she did not like did not apply to her. She had loved the new religion and the greater understanding of God so much that she had risked keeping such a volume in her own private collection. She had risked the displeasure of the Church, and of my father, in owning this book. Even now it was a volume no one would admit they owned; I wondered at her daring, back then, when this had been illegal to own or even read.

I opened the pages further; it was a simple edition, not overly decorated, but very well-read. Many of the pages had been annotated and as I looked further I found I could distinguish two separate hands writing tiny scribbled notes in this work. One, I recognised easily. The bold, black, often irritated looking script of my father's personal handwriting was clear to one who had been receiving his letters all her life. My father hated writing, he found it annoying, but that did not mean that he did not on occasion pen a word to me or my household himself.

The other hand was lighter, although at times often as rushed and messy as the other, and I realized as I read more, that this must be the hand of the owner of the book: my mother.

It seemed from the notes next to key passages that my parents had passed this book backwards and forwards to each other, noting interesting phrases and passages and highlighting those with their own comments. Tears started in my eyes as I saw the meeting of their imaginations and minds over the arguments and postulations contained in this work.

In one place the text read: "God therefore hath given laws unto all nations and in all lands hath put kings, governors and rulers <u>in his own stead to rule the world through them.</u>" This line had been underlined by one hand, my mother's, and then annotated in my father's bold hand with the words *"Dieu et mon Droit."* God and my conscience…

I understood that this volume had been one of the catalysts that had allowed my father in his wisdom to break from the rule of Rome, and to become the Head of the English Church. My mother and father, it seemed, had been interested and had *shared* in the truths of the work of Tyndale. The rules of the land had once not applied to either of them. My father had allowed my mother the same privileges and access to materials that he had himself. Once, he must have thought a great deal of the strength of her mind and the ability of her intellect. He would not have allowed this privilege to just anyone.

On another page, next to a passage on the obedience of children to their elders was written the following: "(God)…was present with thee in thy mother's womb and fashioned thee and breathed life into thee, and for the great love he had unto thee, provided milk in thy mother's breasts for thee…moved also thy father and mother and all other to love thee, to pity thee and to care for thee."

Against that, in little letters, was *"Semper Eadem" Always the Same*. And then, perhaps a later addition to the notes, was the inclusion of my own name: *Elizabeth*. It was written in the hand I believed was that of my mother.

I choked on emotions as they came rearing up in my throat. For a moment I felt as though I could not breathe. To see something that my mother and father had shared so intimately was moving, but to see the hand of my mother writing my name in her little book… it was like her voice was calling to me through all the years and the pain and the loneliness. It was as though when I had longed for her, she had longed for me too. She had thought of me, she had loved me. She *had* been real.

I clung to the volume, swearing to myself that I should never be parted from it. I should never show this to another person. It was my little repository showing that once my mother and father had been friends, and had shared the limits of their minds and knowledge with each other. This was proof that my mother had existed, and had been intimate on so many planes with my lord father.

For entirely different reasons to my parents, I decided that this was one of the most important books I had ever read. I placed this too in my lap next to the necklace. My fingers stroked them. These wonderful, tangible *things* that gave me parts of my mother back to me. I picked up the last object, the second book.

It was also very small. It was called *Le Miroir de l'ame pecheresse* or *The Mirror of the Sinful Soul*, a poem by Marguerite, Queen of Navarre and sister to the King of France, Francois I. Of course I knew of her. A patroness of reformers and free thinkers, many thought her a heretic only protected from the fires of death by her brother's love. As the King of France, he could protect her. The poem was something I was already familiar with; it emphasised the sinfulness of the human soul and how redemption could only be reached through faith, something that Protestants were keen to emphasise.

This volume, however, although neatly bound, was clearly much earlier and rougher than the finished, printed and polished versions I had read.

I realized with some sudden clarity, that this volume was a rough first edition of the book. It was a very early copy. Inside, being used to mark a page near to the end was a small note. It was addressed to my mother, and it was from Marguerite herself.

In French, the little note read:

"My dear friend,
I have missed your company and companionship since you left us for the English court. I miss your voice in our conversations,

*and your songs in our nights. When you were still with us, I men-
tioned to you this little volume which I felt moved to write. When it
was finished, I saw your brother at the court of my own brother, it
seemed only fitting that I send him to deliver a copy to you. Although
seas and lands or duty and family may divide us in person, the
love of God will ever join our spirits in harmony. Marguerite D'
Angouleme. Blois 1526."*

My mother had known the Queen of Navarre? This was new knowledge to me... and the date was too early to have been a letter to my
mother as queen. There must have been a time when they knew
each other even before my mother was married to my father. I
flicked through the volume, but although it had clearly been read
and thumbed well, there were no further notes made by the hand
of my mother in it, nor by my father.

I could not be disappointed in that, though. After all this
time... all this time with nothing of her... with only faded memory
and the words of other people. Now I had tangible, beautiful, wonderful, evidence of her life, of the words shared between her and
my father, and in the necklace, a gift with words of love from my
great father, to my mother.

All night I turned pages and stroked the words written in
my mother's hand. All night I lay awake and held her pearls and
gold close to my heart. I pondered the mystery of the letter from
Marguerite Queen of Navarre, and I cried when I read the lines
and passages my father and mother had shared; united once in a
common cause and goal, desiring and inspiring each other's opinion on Tyndale's book. They had respected each other's opinions;
they had shared so much.

No matter what had later occurred, I knew this now. Once,
there had been more than simple passion between my parents.

There had been more than just the lust that servants spoke of, more than even the great love Kat was so fond of relaying to me. They had been *friends*; they had shared opinions and interests. They had shared ideas. Whatever else had torn them apart, they had once been firmly together.

The thought made me as sad as it made me happy. I could not reconcile the two emotions. But I was happy to know that once... once they had truly loved each other.

I was never more grateful to any woman alive as I was to my new stepmother Queen Katherine. No gift could have meant more to me in the world, and the little bundle that I re-tied and stowed carefully under a loose board in a hidden part of my chamber was the most precious thing I ever owned.

CHAPTER 16
WINTER, 1544

I wanted so much to show Queen Katherine of my gratitude for her gift to me of my mother's bundle of possessions. For her gift this New Year's I decided to translate *Le Miroir de l'ame pecheresse* for her, and embroider a cover with my own hand for it. Katherine would approve of the text as she leaned towards the reformed faith, but also she would know where I had taken inspiration for it. It would be a little secret between us.

Although it had seemed a good idea at the time, I chose to translate the volume from French to Italian, a language that Katherine was attempting to learn at the time. My French was excellent, but the added trouble that translation into Italian gave me was frustrating. Perhaps I was trying a little too hard to show my own cleverness; the translation gave me much heart-ache and many headaches.

Kat was a little put out to see my growing devotion to my new stepmother. I think in her heart *she* was my mother, my best friend and my confidant. She was easily jealous of any who would steer my affections in another direction.

I spent time reassuring her that no one could mean as much to me as my dear Kat, and I think she understood and felt a little guilty, for she had wanted after all for me to get along with my stepmother.

But love is a complicated and jealous friend at the best of times. Even the littlest infraction can lead the heart of one who loves deeply to suspect the darkest of things. We are such fragile creatures, when we give our love to another.

I worked at Katherine's book cover when I could work on the translation no more. In blue velvet and silks I embroidered tiny forget-me-nots on the spine to symbolise memory, and in green, yellow and purple silks I embroidered heartsease flowers into the corners symbolising domestic harmony. In the middle of the cover I embroidered her initials *KP* in silver thread. With every stitch I felt as though I were saying thank you to the gracious woman who was now my stepmother.

When I sent the book to Katherine at New Year I had to rush to finish the translation that had given me so many headaches. I bound it in the lovely cover which I was very pleased with, and added a note saying I did not want her to show the translation to anyone, as I feared it was not as perfect as I had wanted it to be.

I got a note in return, along with the customary gifts for New Year from my father and new mother. Katherine wrote to me of her unbounded joy at receiving something that I had obviously worked so hard and long on, and had put much thought into on her behalf. She was deeply touched and had shown my work to my father who was pleased also. She wrote that the translation was "well done and with great thought," and that she hoped "soon we should be able to be together once more, to take pleasures of the court and gardens together." She had understood, as I knew she would, that this gift was an expression of gratitude for her bringing me together with the memory of my mother.

My new stepmother and I shared the best of things to bring together two women; as secret shared and safe, held and treasured between two hearts.

CHAPTER 17

HATFIELD HOUSE, 1545

The New Year brought change whistling with it, as though the two held hands and walked together into the future. My household was about to change.

Kat had been acting most un-Kat-like for some time. It was not in her nature to be guarded or secretive, and least of all to be quiet and thoughtful. I do not mean that she was stupid, for she was not, but Kat lived on the outside of her skin. I always knew what she was thinking. But I did not in the few weeks after the New Year. She was quiet, reserved and I caught her sometimes staring out of windows, looking at nothing. At other times we would be doing our embroidery, or walking in the park, and I would catch her staring ahead of her as though her mind had entirely left her body.

Something was going on.

"Oh, for Goodness sake, Kat!" I exclaimed finally as we sat by the fire one evening. I had watched her as her conversation had stalled and disappeared entirely, until she sat simply staring at the fire. In a sudden rush of both irritation and fear, I snapped. "For Goodness sake! What on earth is it?"

She looked at me with surprise, as well she might as nothing had been said to lead up to this outburst of mine. She had been as unaware of my growing temper as she was unaware of everything else. This showed how distracted she was, for generally, I was her sole care in the world.

"My lady Elizabeth," she said and hot tears sprung to her eyes. I was suddenly filled only with fear, my irritation dissipating as fast as the vapour of rain on a hot road. What on earth was she going to say to me? I went over to her and put my arms around her.

"Kat, dearest Kat," I said. "What is the matter? You have had this look on your face for so long now, that you need to tell me something, that there is something on your mind. Tell me, am I not your friend *and* your mistress?"

She burst into tears and hugged me tightly. Terrors swam around my head and my heart. Everything is always at the worst it could be, in that moment before someone tells you the real truth.

"Kat please..." I begged. "What is wrong?"

I pushed her away so that I could look into her soft brown eyes and sweet face. The fright on my face must have made me go white; I could feel all the blood in my body rushing to my heart. My skin went cold as my heart thumped within me solidly, as though trying to cope with the influx of every drip of blood in my heart. I thought she was going to tell me that she was dying, or leaving me. Kat drew in a shaking breath and wiped at her face and her eyes. Her nose was swelling with the pressure of her tears and her cheeks swelled under the torrent of her sobs. There are few women who look pretty when they cry, and my dear Kat was not one of the lucky few.

She pulled in another breath and wrenched her eyes to my face.

"I am in love," she said and burst into heart-wracking sobs. Her eyes streamed with tears and she sobbed heartily as though saying the words had sanctioned a release of emotion in her pent up for so long.

I stared at her, so relieved that she was not dying that I burst into laughter. "And does being in love usually cause this much anguish?" I said as she stared at me. My voice fell suddenly harsh as an awful thought came to me. "You are not in love with one already married?"

She shook her head and frowned at me. "No. My lady should not think so ill of me," she said frowning.

"What am I to think of all these tears Kat?" I said with a grin. "Is the man so awful, or so above you in station that there is no chance to marry him? Or he is too far below you?"

"Neither," she said. "None."

"Then what Kat?" I asked. "Have you fallen in love with the devil himself? For I never saw a woman so sad for having fallen in love."

"I love not the devil," she said crossing herself. "Nor one above or below me…. The man is John Astley my lady."

I knew the name, they called him both Astley and Ashley; he was a courtier of good standing, a good friend of Roger Ascham's. He was not far above Kat in station, and not at all below her. It would be a good match.

"As far as I know he is a fine man Kat," I said. "So, why are you so sad?" I asked. "He does not love you back in return?"

Suddenly I felt angry… As if anyone could not love my beloved Kat! If the man was fool enough to turn down a prize such as my Kat then he should hear of it from me! I would make sure he knew how lucky he was to be loved by a woman as wonderful as Kat. My eyes burned in their sockets as anger flowed around my blood.

If he did not want my Kat, then I should make sure that he would have no one else, ever! I should speak to the King on the matter. I would speak to the Queen. This fool would rue the day that he turned down the hand of my lovely Kat!

I was lost in my angry thoughts for a moment, and then noticed that Kat was shaking her head. "No," she said and sniffed loudly; quite an unpleasant sound as all the mucus in her nose retreated back into her head. "He loves me well… as I do him. He asked me to marry him and be his wife. But I was so scared to tell *you,* my lady. I did not want to have to leave you. I *still* want not to leave you. I would not leave you even to be the wife of the man I love. I did not know what to say or how to tell you, and I do not know what to say to him either. I cannot accept his hand if that hand leads me from you… but yet I do love him and I do want to be his wife."

She burst into further floods of tears; her shoulders shaking and her sobs becoming stuck in her throat as though she coughed them.

"I…do…not…want…to…leave…you…mistress," she sobbed at me.

I gathered her up in my little arms and held her. I did not want Kat to leave me either. But neither did I want her to be unhappy. She loved this man very much I could see; most of the time, when a servant married they would leave the house of their master. This was of course more true for women than it was for men, for men do not have to bear babes from their bellies. But there were exceptions. There had to be a way to do both, keep Kat at my side and have her marry her John.

I held her at arms length. "Kat," I said firmly. "We shall find a way to achieve both. We shall seek the advice of Roger Ascham on this matter and perhaps we shall find a role for your John Astley within my household? I cannot imagine that all the positions I should ever need are filled. Come Kat, dry your eyes, we shall find a way to keep your happiness and mine intact. I would not be separated from you either, so we shall have to find a way to make sure we are all kept happy. After all," I paused and threw my shoulders back, ruffling them at her playfully, "we Tudors have the blood of dragons in us, and dragons must be kept happy. Otherwise they breathe fire and flame."

She laughed and put her arms around me, shaking and crying into my crimson gown.

"I had been so afraid to tell you my lady," she said. "I thought you would be angry with me."

"Only angry that you did not tell me sooner to spare yourself all this pain and disquiet," I said laughing. "There is always a solution which can be easier found when two minds search for it." I wrapped my arms around her and held her close. "Always tell me all Kat… for that way we will always help each other to the best route to happiness."

I held her until the merriment returned to her eyes. When we parted and she went to find her John to tell him of our conversation, her eyes were soft with tenderness and love for me. Although she was still rather sniffly and wet, I think I had convinced her that she would not have to leave me.

When I met John Astley I was won over from the first moment. He informed me in a humble manner that he was related to my mother's family and was in fact a second or third cousin of my mother. He was handsome and straight-laced, quite serious and modest. I could see the devotion he had for Kat and I loved him for it.

Sometimes we fear having another person come close to the ones we love; we fear that their opening their hearts to another might make them love us less, as though love were something that was rationed.

But in truth, love is not in short supply; in fact it is one of few things to multiply the more it is used. And as Kat opened her heart to John, I found that her love for me did not diminish; it grew. And I had another heart who loved me for as John was able to take the hand of his pretty Kat, he was made ever-grateful to the mistress who had not only allowed it, but had ensured his marriage.

They were married and John was given a place in my household. It was the happiest I had seen Kat; her cheeks were flushed and she hummed merry tunes as she went about her business in the day. John and she read together with me in the evenings, we went out on picnics in the spring. He became a part of our lives at Hatfield.

Although Kat was not entirely mine anymore, she would never be lost to me. She cared enough for me to have thought about refusing the man she loved in order to stay with me. She had feared to lose me enough to give herself utmost pain in order to spare mine. I was not upset to learn of her devotion to me, just as I was not in the least displeased to welcome another loyal servant into my house.

CHAPTER 18
WHITEHALL, 1545

My father wanted a portrait painted of all the royal family. It was to show us as the new and united family we were, at least on the surface. There were still undercurrents of trouble as Mary strained to obey our father's dictates on her religion. I was sure in private she continued to worship as she always had, but in public she obeyed his word to the letter. Edward found Mary taxing even when we were young I think. Despite her outward obedience to our father's wishes, she still continued to send us Catholic works which contrasted sharply with the mostly Protestant teachings we received. Our father may have remained a Catholic to the core, but Edward and I were leaning much more towards the reformed Protestant faith than to the traditional Catholic one. Our tutors instructed us as closely as they could to follow the Protestant religion, even though it was still officially banned in England... They knew, I think, that we were the future of the kingdom, and they wanted that future to be at the least kind to those of their faith, and at best, a future England that was entirely Protestant, and free of the taint of Catholicism. Our sister wanted entirely the opposite, and so spent time still trying to convince us subtly of the truth of the Catholic faith.

Our father was under the impression that all we learnt was of his doctrine and will. But there were competing forces vying for our attention in the days of our youth. Protestants and Catholics who kept their heads down kept their heads ... and planned for the future.

"Our sister is blinded by her devotion to the old religion," Edward said to me one day as we walked in the gardens together. He had been sent a new set of clothes by our father, of striking gold and crimson, a new hat with a great feather for it. I have to say, my brother cut a dashing figure even as a young boy. He was almost eight then, and I was eleven. His face was rounded as his mother's had been, and like me, he had taken the eyes of his mother rather than those of our father. He was growing tall and liked to hold himself straight in order to appear even taller.

It frustrated him that our father would not allow him to take part in the more adventurous and dangerous pursuits that young men engaged in. Our father was too afraid that he would have an accident and die, leaving the country without a male heir again.

"Our sister is set in the ways in which she was educated and raised," I said "You must not blame her too much for her attention in this matter. She thinks what she does is right."

"Not all good deeds are sent from God," said Edward harshly. "Some are sent from the devil and are well-disguised. Our sister does not see that she walks a path that will take her only to blindness to the light of God... and she seeks to take us with her. I will speak to our father. She requires further disciplining."

It was not an idle threat. Our father would punish her most severely if he thought she was going against his will again.

"Please, do not, Edward," I said touching his arm. "Although I am sure that Mary would deserve such a punishment, let her try to come to the truth of God on her own. She was misled as a child as so many were. She will come to see the truth through the will of our father."

Edward smiled at me. "I will not report this to our father... to please you sister," he said. "But Mary must realise that her behaviour even in private is not fitting to the honour of her station. I hope in time she will come to see the truth as you say, but I wonder if the devil is too tightly entrenched in her heart to allow her to see the light of God's truth."

"Remember that our father is not disposed to favour the Protestant faith in full either, brother," I said. "We must ever walk the middle way with his governance."

Edward nodded. I could see that he was thinking that when he came to his full position as King, the Protestant religion would come firmly to the country.

But that would not be for a long while, I hoped. He was still so young and our father seemed invincible to me.

And so, despite the strains of the family in matters of faith, or perhaps because of them, our father had decreed that we should have this *united* portrait of our family done. It would show Mary and me, and Edward at the side of our father. In all ways would it show the honour and standing of the royal family... but there would be one striking variation from the truth.

The Queen who was to sit by the side of our father in the family picture was not his present queen, my beloved Katherine Parr. Rather it would be the long-dead, pallid wife who had given him

Edward. Jane Seymour was to be brought back from the dead to sit at the King's side in his idealized family picture.

If the idea rankled with Katherine's pride or honour as Queen, she did not show it.

If the morbid nature of resurrecting a wife, who died through *lack of care* as the common people said after the birth of the Prince, was difficult for my father, he said nothing.

If standing as equal with me, yet positioned outside of the *royal family proper*, made up of our father, Queen Jane and Edward, was difficult for Mary, she said nothing.

This was my father's *ideal* family. If you knew nothing of our history, you might think that Jane Seymour was the mother of all of us. You might think that we reached this moment as one seamless unit. You might think that there had never been a disruption in our lives, nor believe that each of us had lost a mother to the whims of our father. You might never think that other queens had existed. When the sketches were put together, we would become the perfect, loyal family born from one great King and one great Queen, the richness and fruit of the dynasty of our father.

I stood for the sketches willingly enough. But the inclusion of Edward's mother, and the exclusion of mine or Mary's, or indeed the lovely Katherine Parr, rankled with me. So I stood for the sketches. But around my neck I wore my mother's pendant and pearls.

Rebellious and foolish I may have been, but I was wise enough to ask the artist, Hans Eworth, who was sketching me, to ensure that the pendant was not clearly visible on the finished picture. If my father saw it then I don't quite know what he would have done to me. Hans smiled when I asked him to both *include* and *exclude* the pendant, and pressed a finger to his lips.

I had a way with people; I was friendly and that lacked that over-bearing pride so common to nobility. I liked to know about people, and that ease of friendship was something that served me well. It brought affection, *real* affection for me, out of people's hearts.

Hans Eworth promised to conceal the necklace in the finished portrait, but he gave me the sketches where my mother's necklace was fully visible. Hans was the protégée of Holbein, and one of his great-est students. Holbein had been a favourite of my mother's. Perhaps Eworth felt some loyalty to the woman who had helped his master's ca-reer, and thusly, his own. There must have been some reason for him to take such a risk, and although I am sure he liked me well enough, it would not all have been done in the name of friendship for me.

Why did I wear it? I can hardly answer the question. It was lu-nacy really. But I felt something within me cry out at the portrait. My mother's name was still banned at court. She was never men-tioned. Mary's mother too was not spoken of... and now our father wanted us to sit for this picture in which he was presenting Jane Seymour as the mother of all of us, the *only rightful* Queen.

It was another moment, another time where our father sought to exclude the past from his glorious present. Another occurrence where the mothers of Mary and I were cast aside in favour of the mother of Edward. The exclusion of Katherine Parr also hurt me... I could not bear that our father should value the pallid Jane over the beautiful Katherine as the wife that should be remembered for all time at his side.

Perhaps I just felt that something of my mother should be there, however quietly, however secretly concealed, to remind people that my father's vision of our past was not the only one that existed.

I wondered whether Mary thought the same. Her devotion to her own mother was something that she carried in her with pride and with sorrow. In accepting our father as the Supreme Head of the Church she had gone against all that her mother had believed in and would have died for, given the chance. I wonder how often she talked to God trying to convince him that she had done the right thing? How often did she talk to her dead mother as I sometimes whispered to mine?

It was many months before the picture was finished. When it was done, there we were, looking down on the realm of our father, the perfect, finished family.

Edward, looking as pale as his ghostly mother; Mary and me to each side with our fools behind us; our father in the middle next to his son and heir… and his dead pale Queen. The only one who had given him all he wanted, the only one of our three mothers to die in glory, still a Queen. Perhaps she deserved her place next to him, re-writing the history of the Tudors. Perhaps not.

But when I looked up at the portrait I could see the tiny **AB** around my neck; Eworth had kept his word and it was not clear enough to see it if you did not know it was there. But I knew that it was. It made me glad to see some remembrance of the woman who had borne me into the world, on the fictionalised account my father had created.

Every time I looked at the portrait, I could almost hear the distant echo of a pretty, merry little laugh from an elegant throat.

My defiance of our father's wishes would have made my mother laugh I think, and that thought made me smile.

CHAPTER 19

WHITEHALL, 1545

A young boy entered service in my brother's house at this time; a young boy who would one day become both my dearest and closest friend, and perhaps also the one great love of my life.

Boys were sent from every wealthy and noble house in the hope they would serve my brother, become his companions and one day therefore, the close friends of the future King. Much the same had been done when our father was young; the companions he had played with as a boy were those honoured when he came to his throne. Each family that was given a chance to place a child within Edward's house tried to choose the most promising of their children. Edward grew up a precocious boy surrounded by precocious boys. Some were strong and fast, and Edward admired their skills at archery and running at the rings practising the skills required for jousting. Our father would not let Edward do this himself. It was too dangerous. But my brother had the utmost admiration, in a slightly jealous fashion, for any other boy skilled at this sport. Some of the boys were intelligent and ready to argue Thomas Aquinas from the break of dawn. With those boys Edward was entirely the King already... ready and able to exert his intellect over them and prove his worth.

It was a lively household, full of young boys as eager to impress each other as they were to impress my brother. When I first met Robert Dudley though, he seemed even then to stand apart from the other young boys chosen to accompany my brother.

Robert, or Robin as I came to call him, was dark as a Spaniard, with soft brown hair and sparkling black eyes, and he had a hint of mischief about him that I liked. When we were younger children we had danced together at court when his family had brought him to state occasions, but as he entered the service of my brother, I saw him more and more. One day as I walked the gardens with Kat, we came across this young Dudley sitting in a grove and sighing in frustration over a book. His hands were pressed to the sides of his head next to his eyes; it looked as though he endeavoured to force his eyes and mind to concentrate on the book in his lap.

"What causes you to sigh, so, master Dudley?" I asked as we approached, looking and seeing one of my favourite versions of Cicero in his lap.

He rose and bowed to me in a fluid and graceful motion; Robin always looked as though he were dancing, even in the mundane actions of everyday life. There are some people who are gifted with such grace naturally that it comes to them without effort. He held out the book to me and I took the volume in my hands. "You do not find interest in the works of the masters?" I said with a faint notion of reprove in my voice. I loved this book. I was very protective over things that I loved.

He smiled at me; he was quite charming even when in trouble. "My masters say I must read it in order to advance my mind," he said. "But I must admit that I have little love for the work. There are other books I do love, but this is not one."

"And what other books do you love Master Dudley, that could best Cicero in his knowledge and wisdom?"

He smiled again and those black eyes twinkled at me merrily. He seemed to take a little delight in my riled temper; oddly enough, I found that more exciting than I did infuriating. The sudden thought that he was a handsome boy entered my thoughts, above the irritation at his dismissal of Cicero and then I tried to stop thinking those thoughts in order to control the flush that rose to my cheeks. He was a servant of my brother. Even though he came from a family that was riding high in the esteem of my father, their lineage was not as noble as many at court. It was not seemly for me to think such things.

"I love the study of mathematics," he said "Navigation, charts and geography. I would love to know the world. I love to see maps and see the different worlds and oceans."

I smiled, for our tutors were rather divided on the value of mathematics and preferred us to understand the worth of the classics, but I too liked to see charts and images of distant lands that bold men were discovering; strange and distant lands, brave new worlds, captivating new creatures and treasures from far away territories.

"I too would love to know the world," I said. "There is much to be said for the discovery of new lands, new riches and the expansion of the Christendom."

He bowed to me "You are a wise princess, my lady," he said. "Perhaps if your father marries you to a foreign prince, you will get to see many of the worlds that I dream of being allowed to see."

He must have seen my face fall a little. I felt my heart slump in my chest. There had been much talk over the past year of marrying me to one prince or another, each of them so far from the lush green of merry England that I loved so much. I had no wish to leave these shores. At least, not to leave forever.

Such is the fate of a princess; she must be ready to give up her native land in order to advance the interests of its people. I would have to be sold off to the highest bidder, or the prince with the best ships or silk trade. I would be gifted to a man to secure the friendship between his country and that of my father. My marriage would secure a friend for my people, secure safety for their lands. But if I had the choice, if anyone would ever think of consulting me, I should have wished to always be a princess of England, *in* England.

His face turned gentle as he saw the expression on my face. I knew well that he had wished to pay me a compliment and express that my fortunes were on the rise; being used as a pawn in the international game of royal marriages was after all an indication that I was again valuable as a recognised and legal heir to my father's throne. But he knew as he looked at me that I would not wish to leave here.

"Do not be sad, my lady," he said. "Perhaps if we ever get the chance, I shall discover such lands for you. One day I will bring you the golden crown of the kings of the Indias, and rubies from the Emperor of the New World. I will bring you new lands to name after yourself and emeralds from the lair of the dragon at the end of the world."

I laughed and Kat laughed too. He was a merry companion, a gallant boy.

"Such a bold adventurer!" said Kat admiringly to me as she laughed. I nodded and smiled at him again. Robin looked pleased to have the wrapt attention of us both. He always had that way about him even as a child, to fascinate women.

"I should like that Master Dudley," I said. "But perhaps you should stay closer to home. Your father may have many plans for you in mind, as my father has for me."

"And we should all do as our fathers wish," he said dutifully but with mischief riding all over his handsome features. "I have the advantage however, my lady, of being subordinate also to *your* wishes as well as to my father's. So if, one day, you should wish to travel the seas and see what treasures there are out there, I should be willing to be your captain. I would have no choice but to place your wishes above that of my father. You are after all, a princess of England."

"Should we be pirates together then?" I asked and laughed. "I had never heard a woman might be a pirate as well as a man."

He grinned and bowed again to me. "A gracious princess such as yourself, should be able to be and do anything she wishes," he said. "That is the gift that God gave you when he bore you into the royal family."

I smiled tightly. "Sometimes, God moves us in ways that we do not expect," I said. "But I do not think he placed me here to indulge in piracy."

Robin shook his head. "No, of course," he said. "I jest, but I do believe there is more in store for the princess Elizabeth than simply marrying and leaving our fair country. Your father in his wisdom would not marry such a prize off and lose you."

It was flattery; it was the way things were at court where men advanced through pretty words and less noble deeds. But I felt like he meant it in truth. Yes, easily and from the first times we spoke, Robin Dudley was my good friend, and later in life it would seem to me often, that he was the one person on this earth that understood my nature and my soul, as every good friend knows instinctively of another.

CHAPTER 20
WINTER, 1545

Katherine the Queen was becoming known at court for not only her intense piety and devotion to religion, but for a little circle or *salon* of women she was gathering to her. Meetings in Katherine's apartments included the Queen's sister Lady Herbert, her stepdaughter Mistress Margaret Neville and also the wry Duchess of Suffolk and Lady Lisle. I too was honoured to be often brought in to discuss points on religious texts. We would pour over scriptures, new translations of the bible and discuss matters of doctrine.

It was an intellectually exciting time for me, in the company of women who were as interested in learning, and were as well-read as I was. We found the blossoming of thought and word blooming in our minds and hearts and became devoted to the companionship that comes from a shared and loved interest in learning.

Katherine was noted at court for having more serious leanings towards Calvinist and Lutheran beliefs than the rule of my father as Supreme Head of the Church would have allowed. Katherine perhaps thought that she was protected by her position as Queen, but as we would find in the New Year, the position of a Queen was a fragile thing.

And it was perhaps my fault that we became so acutely aware of the dangers inherent in being the highest ranking woman in England.

It was in the New Year that I presented another gift to my step-mother. This year, I had chosen to translate *Prayers and Meditations*, which Katherine had herself written and published. It was a volume of five original prayers. I thought it was a wonderful work and chose this time to translate the original English prayers into French, Italian and Latin for her. The work caused me many hours of grief and left me with an aching head, back and brain. But I was pleased with the result. I hoped that my stepmother would enjoy once again seeing how she had influenced me. I also sent a letter to accompany the volume to my father, to let him know how Katherine, his gracious wife, had influenced me, taught me and guided me. I wrote to him that the study of theology was a proper study for kings, as he himself had shown, and also that I thought my father must have been proud of this work by the hand of his lovely and pious queen.

I could not have been more wrong.

I did not realize that my father *had not read* the works of his wife, nor that he thought her salons and groups were mere diversions for womanly gossip rather than the application of study into the theological paths of scripture.

I did not realize that he was tiring of her constant talk of religious matters, nor that he was annoyed by her drawing him into discussion on biblical theology and then disagreeing with him, debating him.

I had not realized that Katherine had enemies at court, those who found her devotion to Lutheran leanings disturbing. Enemies who would seek to once again change queens and place a Catholic wife in Katherine's place. They viewed our father's growing displeasure with his wife with baited breath, just waiting for a chance to bring her down.

I had never thought that a simple present, showing affection and love, could ever be dangerous. When it was delivered to her I felt no shiver of foreboding from the future, I felt no chill breeze ruffle the air of my chamber. I sat back happy in the knowledge that she would love the gift.

The queen, my beloved stepmother, was in danger....and just how serious this was to be, we all would soon know.

CHAPTER 21
JULY, 1546

My father was often ill.

An old injury on his leg made his life hard and gave him much pain. He had injured it when he was a young man, taking more than one fall from his horse in the joust. When he was young, the injury had healed fast and given him little trouble, but as he grew older, and larger, the wound returned and gave him grievous pain. The injury seemed to keep to a cycle of its own. It would heal and our father would be in the highest of spirits, taking to riding and hunting with zest and vigour. Then the injury would come back, stronger than ever, causing him to go black in the face with pain, stopping him from riding and hunting as he still loved to do. The infection would bring forth great quantities of pus and blood, pouring from his damaged leg. The smell that came from the rotten flesh under the bandages was pungent and only a few of his most trusted servants were allowed to dress the wound.

When it was at its worst, our father would shout and scream in pain, lashing out with his stick at his doctors as they tried to lance the wound and release its hold on the putrid pulp festering inside the swollen red wound. When the old injury was very bad, it would refuse to close at all, leaving the wound open to spoil further, like rotten meat in the sun.

When he was ill, we children were not allowed to see him. I think our father enjoyed the idea that he was invincible as much as we honestly believed in the fiction ourselves. He did not want us to see him as weak or broken, as capable of being laid so low by injury and illness. He wanted to look in our eyes and see the devotion of those who truly believe their father to be a God of old. If we had the scent of sour blood and puss up our noses, or glimpsed the horror of the wound on his leg, it would be harder to preserve the fabric of fiction of this, over his illness.

But even though he tried to hide it from us, we could see well enough the drawn paleness of his face when he emerged from a period where he had been too 'busy' to see us. We never spoke the words to each other, but we knew that he was a sick man.

Katherine helped to make his time easier, but he did not like to have her near him either when he was really ill, perhaps for the same reasons as he separated us from him. He wanted all of his family, especially his wife, to believe him indestructible. Katherine was more than aware of the pain he suffered and could have coped easily with him in his misery, having had several previous husbands whom she had nursed through illness, but his will was law. His doctors bore the brunt of his rages and bad temper in his pain.

It was like a magic spell in a fairy story; if he could stop us seeing the worst of his pain, then it was not real. But I suppose we all need the blanket of fiction to make the worst of times manageable.

When she *was* allowed near to him, Katherine would try to divert him from the pain by discussing scripture, writings or other books with him. His mind was still one of the best she had ever known, she told me, and she thought it did her good to learn from our father.

For me, the vision of my father was always preserved in majesty and might. He made sure that although the lines of his face might show some of the pain he had felt in his sufferings, when he appeared at court and with us, he was every inch a king and emperor. My father understood well that in order to be a king, one had to *look* like a king.

As I always said that my father's spirit was conjoined to England, it seemed I was right again. For there was a sickness which grew through our England even as the infected flesh of our father stretched and bloated under the weight of his infected load. As my father's spirit was tied to the land, so as he grew sicker, so did the country. The constant war against heresy flared into a rage even as my father's leg did, and this time it found new victims in a fashionable court preacher called Dr. Crome and a young woman of Protestant beliefs, Anne Askew.

The conservative faction at court, those who longed for a return to the Catholic Church, were fastidious in rooting out all those who took a stronger leaning to the Protestant religion than my father liked. If they could not persuade him to return to Rome, they could at least persuade him to kill those who tried to manhandle his country closer into Protestant belief.

My father was at heart a conservative Catholic. He may have agreed with my mother that the Church required reform, but I believe that if he had never been thwarted by the Pope on the matter of annulling his first marriage, he would have remained within the Catholic Church until the end of his life.

None of us Tudors have ever liked people telling us what to do.

The break with the See of Rome had seen him become the Head of the Church in England and even after he had disposed of my mother, who many saw as responsible for the break with Rome, he had retained the title. He could not do so without some change to the Church of England, and some of the ideas of Protestant belief had crept in to mingle awkwardly with those of the Catholic Church. This mixed rule had led him to tread a middle path between the faiths, where those of extreme views on either side of the religious gulf had to either tame their beliefs and follow him or disobey him and lose their heads. It was not safe to be either a Protestant heretic or a traitorous Catholic loyal to Rome. It was safe only to follow our father, and do exactly as he said.

Although I had been brought up in the faith of my father, much of my learning and many of my tutors, including my noble stepmother, leaned much more into the Protestant than the Catholic faith. But to say any such thing would mean death under the rule of my father. So, secret factions on each side of the religious war formed, and fought their battles underground, through word and thought and subterfuge. It was one of these underground and underhand battles that nearly took my beloved stepmother from me.

The Catholic, conservative faction at court disliked the Queen; they found her piety and her written works suspicious, sacrilegious. They liked not this heretic sitting at the side of the King and whispering in his ear in the bedchamber. They liked not her power;

they liked not her influence over other rich and noble women. They liked her not, they wanted to see her removed.

With the arrest of the young woman preacher Anne Askew came the first, and most horrific, interrogation of a woman for heresy. Askew had been outspoken about her belief in the Protestant faith, and had also used her divinely inspired beliefs to lecture and teach some notable women at our father's court. She had preached in public places; something that was held as scandalous for a woman. She was also acquainted with many of the women who attended Katherine's *salon*.

Askew was arrested. They had her taken to the Tower of London where she was put on the rack and tortured. They broke her bones and ripped her flesh, hoping that she would give them something they could use against the Queen. A woman had never been used in such a manner before, but this act was approved by the King himself, who believed her to be a most unnatural type of heretic. Askew's jailers used their powers well. They made her scream for them, they made her bleed. If they could get one snippet from Anne to incriminate the Queen, then they could remove Katherine and set up another queen in her place who could whisper conservative values to my aging father.

It was a method others had used before when they liked not the Queen on the throne at the side of our father. Katherine's enemies were sure they could make the pattern work for their interests too.

But Anne gave them nothing, brave woman. They broke her body, they tore her flesh, but she gave them nothing they could use against the Queen.

But that did not mean they would not try by other means to achieve what they failed to do through the torture of a remarkable woman.

One evening Katherine was dining with our father and his aide Stephen Gardiner. As usual, Katherine sparked a conversation on a theological matter. Our father was tired and sore, and when Katherine pursued the matter further he became sullen and annoyed. She argued against a point he made and when she left our father said to Gardiner that it was; *"nothing much to my comfort in mine old days to be taught by my wife."*

Gardiner was of the conservative faction, a devoted Catholic. He was well able to take advantage of such a situation. He had done so when the same fate befell my own mother. Some snakes will always hunt in the same grass. Gardiner suggested that the King might find some of his wife's beliefs to be not what he had thought they were, and suggested that she might be harbouring heretical tendencies. These things were not to be tolerated in any wife, he argued, not the least in the wife of the Head of the English Church. It may be that it was these ill *influences* on her which caused her to speak to her husband in such a manner, without respect for his intellect and his position above her. Perhaps it would be suitable to investigate the matter further, and see if there was anything within the chambers of the Queen that might confirm his suspicions?

My father was irritated, in pain and frustrated with his wife. It is easy to act irrationally when one is annoyed with one's husband or wife, but when one party is so much more powerful than the other, such displeasure can turn into real danger.

Our father gave Gardiner permission to search the Queen's chambers, question her ladies and also gave Wriothesley, another conservative, a warrant for the Queen's arrest… so that she might be questioned on her beliefs also.

Tremble all women in the absolute power of a husband!

The first we knew of any of these matters was when Lady Willoughby, Duchess of Suffolk came running to the Queen's apartments like a hind chased by wolfhounds, breathless and panicked, her beautiful face almost purple, waving a bit of paper as she fell to the floor in front of Katherine, weeping and gasping for breath.

We all stared at the lump on the floor that previously had been one of the most sophisticated noble women of the court. Lady Katherine Willoughby, Duchess of Suffolk was a noted beauty and wit. Her sharp tongue was famous as was her quick mind; but now here she was, a gasping, hysterical, slumped form on the carpet.

Katherine took the paper from her in astonishment, looked at it and then went deathly pale. Lady Willoughby grasped her shaking hands to the skirts of her mistress and looked up into Katherine's almond-shaped grey eyes. She looked as though she feared her mistress might be taken from her at any moment.

And this was in fact the case.

The paper was the warrant for Katherine's arrest; it stated that she was to be questioned on her religious beliefs. She was to be taken to the Tower to await interrogation under order of the King. At the bottom of the page was the seal and signature of the King himself.

Katherine sat down heavily on a chair, pale and shaking, staring at the warrant for her arrest which was authorised by her husband, the man she had gone to bed with only the night previous. She knew, as we all did, that if she went to the Tower then she would not come back. Our father did not bring his wives back. Once they were gone, they were gone. If she went to the Tower like my mother, like Catherine Howard, she would be released only by her own death.

Her enemies wanted her head and her husband, my father, had given them the tool they needed to remove it from her neck.

"It fell from Wriothesley's pocket," wept Lady Willoughby, still gasping for breath as she spoke. "As he walked, it fell out. I went to shout to him and give it back to him until I saw your name on it, read the... read it and then I turned and I ran to you, my lady."

Katherine sat, still staring at the letter and then suddenly she rose and began to take off her clothes. Her trembling hands pulled at the lacings of her sleeves and pulled the beautiful silks from her hair.

We all stared at her in some shock. I thought that perhaps the paper had unhinged her mind until she spoke.

"Come," she said. "Help me. I must undress. I am ill and must remain in bed. I cannot be moved. I cannot be moved *on pain of death.*"

We saw her purpose then. If she was ill and sent to bed, they could not take her willingly to the Tower. If she kept to her bed, perhaps we would have some time to find a way to save her. We all but ripped the fine crimson gown from her body and helped her trembling and shaking into her bed.

We were crying, many of us, as we did so. My cousin, the little Lady Jane Grey with her serious face and pale eyes collapsed in a faint and I had to take her to her own bed.

Jane was the granddaughter of my royal aunt Mary Tudor, sister to my father. She was my cousin. Jane was a little grave girl who loved to read and learn as I did. Her home life gave her not much in the way of affection or understanding, for her parents believed in beating an education into their children. They believed in beating their children for most things, it seemed. Jane did not talk about her home life, but I saw enough of her bruises and scars to understand that she withstood a lot of physical pain at the hands of her parents. This was not unusual; many parents beat their children, many tutors did so too. But I had been raised with limited beatings and so I tended to view them with an eye of suspicion. It seemed to me that beating one's opinion into a child was only likely to teach the child that was the only way to get anything done. We teach our children better when we explain the world to them, rather than teach them to cope with the world by hitting out at it.

Jane had come to love the gentle Queen as a mother, much as I had. Katherine was a woman who really understood how to draw people to her, and to love her with much devotion.

As my maids and I put little Jane into her bed, she clasped my hand and wept. "The King would not truly seek to hurt the Queen?" she whispered to me, begging. I tried to shake my head, but my obvious fear made my action meaningless; she could see the terror written plain on my face. I reached out and drew her to me, kissing her head and crying with her.

Every horrible emotion and fear that I had ever known came to me. I felt as though I *knew* that Katherine would be taken from us, in just the same way that I had lost my mother, and another stepmother before her. But this mother I had dared to love, perhaps more even than the dim memory of my own mother. I had dared to open my heart, dared to love and now our father was planning to remove another wife, to make way for another woman to take her place. He was ready and able to kill my beloved Katherine.

I dropped to the floor at the side of my cousin's bed and I wept tears of terror and loss. Fearing that I was to lose another woman from my life that I loved.

I had never felt so alone in all my life.

CHAPTER 22
JULY, 1546

Katherine was stunned into calmness at first when she took herself into her bed but later on that day, perhaps when the full force of her dreadful situation hit her, she started to become hysterical.

Weeping and moaning, shrieking and wailing like a banshee; we could not clam her, nor tame her restless cries. The good, sensible woman that I had respected and known was completely overcome with terror and became insensible; she cried out names, the various wives of my father and also the names of her previous husbands in between her fulsome tears. There was nothing we could do or say to make her rest. We feared for her mind.

Eventually, her hysterical cries came to the attention of the King. From his apartments, which adjoined hers, he could hear her crying. He knew not that she had found the arrest warrant. I imagine that by this time Lord Chancellor Wriothesley had found that he had mislaid the valuable bit of paper and was spending some time desperately searching for it.

We had thrown it into the fire. There would be no paper for him to find.

Eventually my father sent a servant to discover what all the noise was emanating from the Queen's apartments. He did not come himself at first, as he was still angry at her. We did not allow the messenger to enter and see Katherine in the terrible state she was in, but we informed the messenger of the dire illness of the Queen.

The King was in much astonishment to hear that the Queen was so unwell, having seen her for their evening bedding only the night before and finding her quite well and buxom. So he sent his own Doctor Wendy to see her and find out what was wrong with her.

When Wendy arrived, Katherine was sent into a mortal panic thinking that the guards had come to arrest her. The knock at the door was enough to send her retching with fear over the side of her bed. But when we let him in, good man, he brought peace to Katherine where we had been unable to.

Wendy was another who sympathised with the Protestant faith. He may have been a secret Protestant, and so having a lady on the throne who was of the same beliefs was important to him. Once Katherine had sobbed her fears to him of arrest and execution, Wendy advised her that he would send the King to her, and tell him that she was rendered ill because she thought she had lost the love of the King. He told her to mention nothing of the warrant for her arrest, and to say nothing of her knowledge of it. She merely needed to convince the King of her utmost devotion to him, and she would be safe.

"Be humble and womanly," he said clasping her hands in his. "Wash your face and look beautiful, use the charm that is *yours*, madam, and let the King know that you are his modest, mild and dutiful wife… Assure him that you seek to enliven his mind *only* to distract him from pain… that your thoughts are his thoughts, and you will save yourself from this fate. The King loves you, but his temper is a fragile thing in his great pain. Tempt him and soothe him. Survive to fight another day, learn to be more careful in your words, and you will be safe."

Wendy could counsel her where we could not. She started to breathe normally once more as the plan settled in her mind. We helped to wash her face free of the ugly stain of tears, to smooth her hair and freshen her breath, made bitter with fear. We changed her rumpled nightgown and dabbed perfume on her skin. She was still pale and shaking, afraid for her life, but she was calmed and prepared to plead for her life. My father was brought to her. He leant on his cane heavily as he entered the room, and there was an expression of such concern and love on his face that I could hardly believe this man was the same that had signed the warrant for Katherine's arrest.

Which man was my father? The lover or the tyrant? I would never really know. For all my life it seemed as though there were in fact many men who bore the title of my father. They all wore the same body and flesh, and yet they were as changeable as the weather on the shore.

We ladies bowed and left, only to gather at the door, our ears pressed to the wood, desperate to hear what was going on.

For my own part, I felt ready to defend Katherine to the death. I was no man, but I could fight if I had to. I felt then as though I had the strength to fight, the fear pulsing through my veins.

"How now, sweetheart?" we heard the King say. "What ails you? My doctors tell me you are sickened… but not *unwell*, what means this?"

Then we heard Katherine's faint voice through the door saying that she was much sickened in herself, thinking that she had done something to drive the love of her dread sovereign and most beloved husband from her, and that this thought had caused her to become lain low with sorrow and with devastation.

"For you are my *only* love and care in this world and if I have not your love then I have nothing. I would rather die than lose the love of so great a man and King," she said.

Our father's voice was soft as he asked why she thought he would have stopped loving her and she replied that she had marked when they had discussed some points at dinner that he had become angry with her, and in doing this she feared that she had lost his love. But she had only sought to argue with him, she said, to distract his mind from the pain he felt in his physical body.

"Not so, Kate," I heard the stern voice of my father say and felt my heart tremble with it. "You have become a doctor, seeking to instruct us."

Katherine denied it strongly: "My lord, I have never thought it the position of a woman to instruct her husband. Such a place would be beyond the realm of all that is natural. But in your mind there is such a wealth of knowledge that I have always benefited from the privilege of learning from you. If I have ever adopted a point of view opposite to your majesty's own, it was only so that I might better understand all the facets of the *rightful* argument, seeking through debate to better educate my own dull mind with the full weight of all your majesty's higher education and understanding. I have at times also sought to distract you with talk on scripture, so that you might be diverted from the pain that presently assails you in your body. I have profited from your gracious generosity in sharing your wisdom with me, but I would never want you to believe that I *ever* sought to *instruct* you. The thought would be inconceivable to me, for you are my better in every way."

It was very clever. In one fell swoop she had our father convinced that she saw him as her superior and only sought to argue with him for the betterment of her mind and to see to his greater comfort. She was fighting for her life, and she was doing it well.

She was a clever woman, Katherine Parr.

My father paused, obviously thinking about her words. Every one of us was holding our breath at the door, but then we heard him say, with gruff affection in his voice; "Is it so Kate? Then we are the best of friends as ever we were."

And she was safe.

I think I learnt a lot that day about how a person may be saved by words. They are our most powerful weapon, and can be used to incriminate or save a person's life at will. And she lied, of course she lied! She was fighting for her life... would you not have done the same?

A few days later, my father and Katherine were in the gardens together. Katherine was reading to her husband gently from a book of prayers. She had carefully chosen a volume that had been dedicated *to* the King. It was as they sat together reading in the warm sunlight, that Lord Chancellor Wriothesley arrived with a detachment of guards to arrest Katherine. He had a copy of the warrant with him. No doubt something he had made up and copied to make it look like the one we had burnt in the fire.

As he made his proclamation, declaring he was there to arrest the Queen and take her to the Tower, my poor Katherine paled and sunk backwards into her chair. Perhaps for a moment she thought that my father really intended to go through with the arrest after all. She had thought herself safe, and now she was to die.

But it was not so; my father had simply forgotten to revoke the warrant for his wife's arrest. It had slipped his mind.

My father jumped at Lord Chancellor Wroithseley in a rage and beat him around the head with his stick shouting that he was a *knave*, a *beast* and a *fool*.

Wroithseley was somewhat surprised and made a rather undignified exit, scrambling out of the gardens and out of reach of my father's stick. Wroithseley realised that the pale, shaking woman who had almost fainted when he arrived to arrest her had been saved by the changing tides of my father's thoughts and affections.

Anne Askew died in the fires of Smithfield, burned at the stake as a heretic on the 16th July that year. If she had any dealings with my stepmother she never mentioned them; the brave woman concealed anything that might have incriminated the Queen.

And if Katherine had known Anne, spoken with her, or respected her beliefs, she said nothing. But on that day, as Anne's flesh was melted from her bones by the licking tongue of the flames,

Katherine's eyes brimmed with tears as she bent her head to her embroidery.

Katherine had learnt a valuable lesson, and unlike my mother and many other wives of my father, she had survived it. The position of a queen is more dangerous than that of a common man. For there is farther to fall, and there are more people who would wish your destruction than any commoner could imagine.

Katherine had faced death, and escaped. She would be more careful from now on to ensure the love and support of the only man who could choose to either protect or destroy her... my father, the King.

CHAPTER 23
WINTER, 1547

When a woman gives her hand to a man, she hands him the power to do as he will with her life. This was a truth made most clear to me as I watched Katherine's close scrape with death at the hand of my father.

Her marriage to him had brought her wealth and prestige, yes, but it had also placed her in the greatest of dangers. If my father decided one day he did not like her anymore, she could still easily find herself without a head.

Our world, the world in which I lived was fraught with danger and one was all the more near to danger the closer one was to the throne.

The favour our father showed to Katherine after her near-arrest spoke volumes as to how deeply her absolute submission had touched him. This was what he wanted of a wife and queen; someone that was intelligent, beautiful and wise, but who would conform all her desires and will to his. Perhaps that was why he had loved the pallid, insipid Jane Seymour so much... her motto of

Bound to Obey and Serve spoke to his own need for dominance over not only the country that he ruled, but over the wife who was his partner in life.

Little, flighty Catherine Howard too, had understood his will for domination…her motto of *No other Will but His* had unfortunately turned out to be a lie, but as long as he had believed it, he had loved her absolutely.

My mother was not made of that kind of mettle. That was, I think, why she died.

I think in those dangerous days of 1546 I learnt the values of pragmatism; that even if Katherine did not believe that her husband was in all ways her superior, her survival and the continuation of her life was in his hands and therefore it paid to be humble before him. Through Katherine I learned that it was more important to be pragmatic and survive, than it was to die to defend one's own belief.

The world is not perfect, but it is the only one we have to live in. Sometimes it was better to keep the fullness of one's thoughts within, and share them only at a time when it was safe to do so.

Thousands disagreed with me. Many went to the executioner's block or to the fires my father used to rid the country of Catholic and Protestant extremists. Unlike the pragmatic Katherine, they would not hide their true feelings for the chance to save their lives.

Was it wrong of me to think they did the wrong thing, these martyrs? Would I have ever harboured the certainty of the martyrs who went to the flames in order to preserve their immortal soul?

The way I was starting to see the world was different to this steel-hard surety that some people seemed to have

To me it seemed God wanted certain people to be able to survive for a greater purpose than even they knew.

To me it seemed that God would not want all people rent apart by the technicalities of their Christian beliefs.

To me, it seemed, being able to survive, to live, to go on to greater things and help others, was more important than flying like a celestial comet, burning out and being forgotten as soon as the tail of your flight had left the skies.

The people knew and respected the reign of my father, and it had been long enough now that we understood the changes he had made to England for the betterment of its people. I was a keen student of history. It seemed to me that those who were able to reign well and for the most part peaceably, gave more to their people than those tiny, fragmented reigns such as in the civil war between York and Lancaster. War only causes the common people to lose all they have both the money in their hands and the blood in their veins. The rich lose little, the common man loses all. Although it is their place to remain loyal to their liege lord, it is the place of the lord to protect the common man's interests as well as his own.

My tutors often said that I had an uncommon understanding of the history of our country and the world. I found the lives of those who had ruled our country absorbing and often found myself musing on certain situations kings and queens had been placed in before... would I have chosen differently to them?

Edward and I often liked to discuss these ideas together when we had the chance. We were often together at our combined household at Ashridge if I was not with Katherine at Whitehall or Greenwich. Katherine had asked that Mary and I be often at court with her; our names often headed the lists of the gentlewomen of the Queen's chamber at court. It was a great comfort to be near to her; when I thought of how close we had come to losing this woman from our lives, due to a difference in religion or thought, it made me shudder and feel quite sick.

When I was not with Katherine however, I loved to be in the company of my younger, most serious brother. He was clever and although he took his position with the utmost of seriousness that gave him a great gravity for one so young, he had a sense of fun also. I was perhaps one of the few people he would ever show that side of his character to. Even in the journal he was starting to keep, he tried to remain as regal and as collected as he wanted to appear to the rest of the court.

Edward had been raised with the knowledge that he was our father's sole true heir and only hope for the country. That sort of pressure can come out in many ways when placed on young shoulders, but our father and our country I thought were lucky in that, rather than rebelling against the weight of his responsibility, Edward tried in all ways to learn all he could so that on the day he was to take the mantle of kingship, he would be ready, no matter how young he was.

And that day came so much sooner than we thought possible.

Death is always sudden, and it is always a shock.

Even if you have seen a person you love grow older, weaker and the knowledge that their passing is coming, it still does not prepare you in any way for the day that someone comes to you, and tells you they are gone.

You will never again see their face, laugh with them, or hold their hand.

You will never again walk into a room and find them there.

People we love pass from our lives so fast.

One day they are ours, a part of our family, our lives, as vital and colourful as every field and flower, and then one day they are a shadow, flitting at the edge of our vision, inconstant and wavering like a silhouette reflected in a sun-dappled pond in the spring light. Like my mother... like my stepmothers... they become just a memory in the minds and hearts of those who knew and loved them.

Our father, the Great King Henry VIII, died on the 28th January 1547. I was thirteen years old, my brother Edward was not quite ten.

News of his death was a closely guarded secret for some time. We were told later it was to ensure the smooth passage towards Edward's reign. But who can say what really lurks in the mind of some men?

Edward had been at Hertford castle, the seat of his uncle, Edward Seymour, Lord Hertford. When my brother left the castle, he was under the impression he was coming to London to be inaugurated as the Prince of Wales.

No one told my brother, the new King, that he *was* the King.

It was only when Edward and I were brought together at Enfield, where I was in residence, that Hertford fell to his knees before us, his small eyes narrowed as he watched us and declared;

"The King is dead.
Long live the King!"

Edward and I looked at each other. His handsome, delicate face went pale with shock. But he rose and extended his hand to his uncle to kiss.

I stood, my legs turned to jelly as the unfathomable thought of our father being no longer with us mixed in my head with the knowledge of death. I went to curtsey to my brother, but he pulled me to him and wrapped his arms about me.

With all the suddenness of fear and shock, we two, children of the royal house of Tudor, clung to each other and wept for the loss of the father we had loved, feared and admired. Edward, Mary and I were all now orphans. We had no living parents left to us in this world, and only relatives of our respective mothers or aunts, and each other to hold together the fiction of a family.

Perhaps it was not as Edward should have acted in his first moments as King; reaching out to weep with his sister. But I loved my brother all the more for reaching out to me during the first impact of our grief together; for giving me the comfort of his love in that first white shock of grief.

Hertford stood silently by as we held each other. He did not intrude on our grief.

Finally Edward released me and straightened himself. Long hours of thought and preparation for the weight of responsibility and kingship had brought him to the calm he now seemed to feel.

He nodded to his uncle, who bowed to him again.

"Where are we headed to, uncle?" he said. "The Tower?"

Hertford nodded. "Yes, your majesty," he said with all reverence, his eyes still narrowed as though he wished to pin Edward down with his glance.

But as they left to prepare the new king's passage to the Tower where all kings of England stay before their coronation, I felt as though there was a little chill coming to me from Hertford. Edward was the King, but he was still only nine years old. There was to be a Regent, an adult who would head a Council until my brother was at least fourteen, if not eighteen.

We were under the rule of my brother, Edward VI, the boy-king, but we were also under the rule of whoever sat in the chair of Lord Protector. Whoever was given that position would hold the power of the crown within their hands. It was something men had, and would, kill for.

CHAPTER 24
HATFIELD HOUSE, 1547

In the weeks that followed our father's death, Kat made a habit, more so than ever, of coming to sleep beside me. A princess, even a bastard one, is but rarely left alone. My ladies slept either on pallet beds on my floor, or in the bed with me. Kat made it her habit to be my bed-mate in the time after my father's death.

After my ladies had undressed me and combed my hair, after all the rich trappings were stripped off my skin and the glittering rings were taken from my fingers; when I was covered only in my little shift sitting in bed, Kat would come in so that I could weep on her shoulder for the loss of my father. Sometimes grief is easier to share when it flows freely from the heart of one friend to another. We spend so much time in our lives assuring others that we are alright; with a friend at least one can answer honestly, and tell the other that things are *not* alright, and all is *not well* with the world.

Remaining positive is a fine attribute, but that does not mean that at times it does not do us good, to accept and embrace the sorrows of life.

We talked of my father as the hours rolled on into the darkness of the early morning and the candle-light flickered with the drafts coming under the tapestry.

During the day I tried to remain stately. A letter from my brother had attested to the fact that this was what he expected of me in public. But during the night, and in the company of Kat, I did not need to be so guarded.

Kat told me stories of my father.

In my mind as she spoke I heard the ringing sound... the crash and the bash of jousts he had ridden and won. The figure of my father sprang into life with all incandescence and vivacity as she spun tales of his heroism and youth.

I saw him dance with my mother, spinning her dark-haired lithe figure as the two of them stepped together gracefully.

I saw him ride out on great horses, against the French in the battles long before I was born.

I watched the people cheer wildly at his coronation as the young prince full of promise became a king.

I watched him pick up the tiny figure of me and spin her as she gurgled baby giggles around the room as the court looked on and applauded.

I think Kat wanted me to hold only good memories of him in my head. But my mind was not like that. Although I remembered and cherished all those images of my father, I could not refuse the other memories that came to me...

Of the darkness of his face in anger, the way the atmosphere of a room or even a palace could be changed by his black moods. The way Katherine had looked as she held that bit of paper in her hand and saw his signature on it; the fear on my mother's face as she held me out to him, and he just turned from her and walked away.

Oh yes, there are always two sides to a person, and none more so than the figure of my powerful father.

How could I love such a man, who inflicted such pain and fear, such tyrannical domination and cruelty on so many I loved? And yet... how could I not love the man whose arms had held me in love, laughed with me and admired me as his daughter and who had given me the title of princess even after the disgrace and fall of my mother?

Do we ever really understand why or how we love someone?

I think not.

We only know that we do, and once we do love someone we do so forever.

My heart has taught me this in my life at least. I know not the hearts of other men or women, but I know that in my own heart, once I love I cannot un-love.

I can hate those I love and I can adore them, equally and some-times simultaneously, but I cannot un-love them. It does not speak for my pragmatism that I value so highly, but it cannot be helped, it is how and who I am and was made.

And I have always thought that God moulded my heart to this wish for a purpose. Whatever that purpose is, is still a mystery to me, but He knows better than I what the world needed. It was not the easiest path for me for sure, for it has given me little peace. But love in my life is a constant, irrefutable path that once started on, can never be abandoned.

I loved my father. And I had lost his presence from my life.

Kat held me in the night as I cried for the giant figure of the man who had given me life, just as he had taken it away, from so many others.

CHAPTER 25
CHELSEA, 1547

At the end of January, Edward and his council took up residence at the Tower of London. The will of our father Henry VIII was promised to be adhered to, and then almost immediately ignored as Edward Seymour was created Lord Protector against our father's final wishes. All the power of the regency was placed in the most-willing hands of Edward Seymour who later became the first Duke of Somerset.

Our father's will included provisions for Mary and me as well as for Edward. The money, properties and titles that we had been allotted were made known to us. Mary was able, as an adult, to take possession of the £3,000 income per year and her title as Edward's heir to the throne. She had become overnight one of the richest people in England and a powerful political figure. I was still too young, at thirteen, to live and manage a household by myself. It was agreed that I should go and live with my stepmother, the dowager Queen Katherine and my inheritance should be managed by the Council.

Katherine was well provided for by my father. Although she was not given the regency of Edward in his will, which she might have expected after he entrusted her with the country when he went to war with France, she was given money, position and lands as part of her dower, and she was still able to retain her regal state of life as one of England's premier noblewomen and a part of the royal family.

And however unlikely it was, the Council were keen to keep an eye on her belly in case she had another heir to the throne in there.

Katherine herself obviously didn't think it was a possibility when I came to her house in Chelsea; we talked of her great sorrow at never having had a child of her own despite being stepmother to many children from her marriages.

"And although I love all of my husbands' children," she said, reaching out and touching my arm, "I would love to feel a babe of my own in my arms too."

She looked downcast and I pressed her hand in mine. She shook herself and smiled at me. "Perhaps I am too greedy," she said. "Look at everything that my husbands and your own good father gave me... I have more children than any woman I know through marriage, and I have felt their loving influence on my heart through all my wedded years. Perhaps I ask too much to ask for one more child... even if it is one of my own blood."

"I do not think you would presume to ask too much, my lady," I said. "I think God would understand such a wish from a woman who has devoted herself to loving and protecting all her husbands' children and given up much of her own life to do so."

"You must not think that I do not feel privileged to be your mother, and Edward's, and Mary's... although she was already a woman grown when Henry and I married. But there is in all of us a desire to see our own blood continuing to live when we are gone."

I nodded. I understood her, of course I did.

Sometimes I thought of the day when I should be grown and be given in marriage. I understood all the feelings of which she spoke. But there was the other side of me which whispered of the dangers of becoming entirely dependent on a man in the state of marriage. After watching my father and his marital lives, there was a darker voice in my soul, which talked to me of the inconstancy of the hearts of men, and the danger to women who were dependent on them.

I was not present at my father's burial or my brother's coronation. Katherine was the only immediate family member at our father's burial next to Jane Seymour, and even she watched it from the Queen's Closet.

No one should imagine the death of the new King, or the royal family, so we could not be seen next to the hand of death.

Mary and I could only visit court, rather than stay there. Edward was unmarried, being rather too young at the age of nine. Without a resident queen it was not seemly for unmarried ladies to be present without a female household in which to serve.

Edward's court was therefore very male, and very lacking in fun.

Perhaps this suited my serious brother; for now at least there much for him to understand and do as the new King.

But it does not do to have no fun in life; I had a merry spirit and when I thought of nights at court with no dancing, for there were few or no ladies, I thought it sounded rather dull. Even though our company was limited at Chelsea and we were officially in mourning, Katherine and I talked, laughed and danced together as mother and daughter, renewing and strengthening our bond through the enjoyment of mutual company.

There was, in those months after the death of our father, a constant visitor to Chelsea in the form of Edward's younger uncle, the Lord Admiral, Thomas Seymour. Thomas was a new member of the Council, and was the same Thomas who had been sent away from court by my father when he sought to marry Katherine Parr and feared competition; but now he was back.

Thomas Seymour was a handsome man.

Bright blue eyes sat in a strong and playful face. His dark hair shone in the sun like the wing of a raven, and he was tall, graceful, and had an air about him that spoke to every woman in the depths of her heart. There are such men that come about through some accident of nature that despite any other failings will convince women to abandon all reason, religion and reserve in order to be admired and loved by them.

He was such a man.

When he came into a room, everyone turned to him. He was a star that shone brighter than any other around him. Men hated him for it. Women flooded to him, like wasps to jam tarts.

At first it seemed to me that he paid court to us as many others had done before, but I did wonder a little at the frequency of his visits. Kat was the first to tell me in whispered tongue that the younger Seymour had been inquiring about my personal property with Thomas Parry who managed my personal accounts, and it seemed that, despite my youth, he was interested in me as a potential wife.

At first the idea was quite shocking; quite apart from the fact I was little more than a child at thirteen years old, the provisions of my father's will ensured that I was ruled by the Council and my brother in the choice of my husband. It was their choice whom I should marry, not mine. My hand was of great value to them. It was unlikely, highly unlikely, that the younger brother of the Lord Protector Somerset would be given such a potentially politically explosive bride.

But I understood his ambition certainly. I was now second in line after Mary to the throne of England. Marrying me, even with only a slim chance for the succession, was attractive to those of lesser ranks seeking higher powers. But this would never be allowed to happen by the ruling elite.

But I also could not help but feel a little excitement in my chest when I saw his handsome face. Was all his interest for my position only? Or was there something in Thomas Seymour that desired Elizabeth of England for the woman she was growing to be?

Did he desire me as a man desires a woman, or did he view me as a piece of attractive property? A good investment for the future, or a wife to enjoy in the present?

In the secret places of my heart, I longed to be admired. I wanted to be seen, to be missed, to be wanted as a woman first. Perhaps it was a childhood of feeling overlooked which brought this into my heart, or perhaps it is simply the wish of all people; to be seen, to be admired.

I started to look at myself in the mirror, trying to see what parts of me were attractive for themselves. I was middling tall for my age, my waist was delicate and thin, my breasts were just starting to bud forth, but they were still small and round. My hair was thick, lustrous and a becoming shade of red-gold, but my eyebrows were almost non-existent. My eye-lashes were the same pale colour, and my face was pretty with youth. But there were prettier girls I had seen at court. My hands were lovely, long, pale and elegant with tapering fingers and looked dazzling with jewels on them. My eyes were dark and black, striking in my heart-shaped face, and my skin was pale and smooth, soft and white.

I was not unattractive, I knew, but I was not the beauty that some court poets extolled me as.

I longed to be admired and to be loved. Thomas Seymour was the first man I ever fell in love with, and risked losing everything for.

But Thomas soon gave up the idea of taking either myself or, as I found out later, my sister Mary as his wife. The opposition to his enquiries on Mary's wealth and mine were met with censure by the Council. He would never be allowed to marry either of us. I was not overly surprised that he had looked on my elder sister as a potential bride as well as me, but I was saddened to hear it. It made me feel less special.

I was though, surprised by what actually happened afterwards… Three months after the death of my illustrious father we found that my stepmother, who was known for her calm, wise decisions, had thrown caution and her position to the winds and taken the hand of the rakish adventurer Thomas Seymour in marriage. The man I had started to feel the first, sudden and powerful feeling of adult attraction to... was now my new stepfather. The lawful and legal husband of my stepmother, Katherine Parr.

Thomas Seymour moved in. This was eventually to cause all hell to break loose under at beautiful house at Chelsea.

CHAPTER 26
CHELSEA, 1547

Don't think for a moment that the marriage of the Dowager Queen of England and the younger brother of the Lord Protector went either unnoticed, or un-criticised… especially seeing as the marriage was conducted without the permission of the King, Council or Lord Protector Somerset and was carried out in what many considered unseemly haste, after the death of my father.

What a storm was to follow the discovery of Thomas and Katherine racing into this marriage together! Even though I was living in the same house, I had no idea it had gone on at all. Kat, whose nose was always pressed against some door or other to glean a bit of gossip, was caught unawares too.

And she was oddly upset by the news. More so than others.

I think now, looking back, that Kat was a little in love with Thomas Seymour herself. The idea that he wanted to marry me pleased her because she admired him and loved me. If he had married me it would have brought together all her fantasies in a convenient bundle. She could not marry him herself, but Thomas marrying me was I think to her, just as good. But in marrying Katherine, Thomas had acted against Kat's wishes and, she was sure, his own too. Kat thought that Thomas had merely settled for Katherine as a wife. Kat was sure he did not love Katherine, for she was sure that he really loved me.

To Kat, I believe that Thomas and I had become two star-crossed lovers separated by the cruel fortune of fate, and she was determined to be the one to bring our lives together once more, as they should be.

"He admired *you* first my lady," she whispered to me as we walked together in the gardens. It was summer, the news of the marriage had broken, everyone was in uproar and messengers ran back and forth from this house in Chelsea to the King at Greenwich. The house was full of a restless, watchful anxiety which was too agitated to sit in, so Kat and I had come outside for a walk. It is easier to deal with restlessness, after all, when one is moving.

The grim faces of the messengers and the shouts from behind closed doors were all signs that this news had not been well received. We were all wondering if Thomas and Katherine might be sent to the Tower for acting in such defiance against the Council and my brother Edward. As the Dowager Queen, Katherine should not have married for at least a year after our father's death to ensure no child of the King's was within her womb, and even when she did marry again, she should have had the approval of the ruling King. She and Thomas had played with fire here, and there was a distinct possibility they might both end up being roasted for their reckless, rebellious act of love.

"Shush," I said hushing Kat as we watched another messenger in Seymour livery almost fly out of the door and onto another horse. More wear must have been done to the roads today than any other time. I watched the messenger ride off and then turned to Kat and spoke quietly: "It is clear now that he admired my stepmother, not really I. It was Katherine he came to see, not me."

Even as I said the words I felt my heart rebel against them. *No!* said the little traitor in my heart. *He liked you better than Katherine, but he had to settle for her. He wanted you. You are young, comely and the second in line to the throne. He wanted you, not Katherine.*

I tried to quiet my rebellious heart. The ache that I felt thinking that Thomas Seymour might love Katherine rather than me was enough to keep me grave and reserved. Perhaps people thought I was solemn with the news of the clandestine marriage? If so then that was more to my favour than them thinking that it was jealousy eating at me. I found myself thinking ill of Katherine for the first time in my life. I was jealous of her. Jealous of the union she now had with the man I had looked on with interest, and angered, that I could be so easily set aside for another woman. I felt as though I had a canker in my heart, and it was growing in its childish, selfish jealous blindness over the love I had cherished for Katherine. I tried to swallow it, cast it aside and think of all my heartfelt admiration for Katherine; but anyone who has had to try and do this knows well enough it is a fool's errand.

"He likes *you*, my lady," Kat continued to whisper. "You know he did, I knew when I saw his eyes fall on you. There was never a man who could disguise a feeling for a woman when he felt it. It's as clear to read as the good book itself."

"Even if this were true," I said, "the Council would have never allowed it. They decide who I marry, and they would never let Thomas

Seymour have a chance to possibly be king one day. Besides, remember, he made a play for my sister Mary's hand as well as for mine." I sighed and pulled the daisy-like heads from some feverfew.

"He didn't want your sister's hand," said Kat with a wicked grin. "The only thing that made her more attractive was her closeness to the crown."

"And then how can you say that he loved me?" I asked. "A man who is clearly so interested in placing himself in the royal family by hook or crook is not looking for love but for power. He tried my sister and me and failed, so he took our stepmother."

"He *settled* for her," said Kat sullenly.

"And he might well thank God for his luck in securing the love of a woman of such infinite courage, patience and beauty!" I said, almost shouting at my friend and governess. "You would do well to think of her better than you do Kat, it would do more to credit your spirit."

Kat flinched from my rebuke, but my words were directed as much at my own self as they were at her. These traitor-thoughts, that Thomas loved me and I loved him and now we were separated by his marriage to my stepmother, these were not helpful. These thoughts were not worthy of me, I thought miserably, but I could not stop having them.

"If Katherine and Thomas are allowed to stay married and together… they will have a better chance of happiness in marriage together than he and I ever could have had," I said and threw my flowers into the hedge.

Kat crowed triumphantly. "I knew it!" she exclaimed loudly, almost shouting. I had to cuff her hard across the shoulder to bring her back to earth. "I knew you liked him my lady," she said quietly as she rubbed her arm where my fingers and rings had cut her.

"Whatever I felt or did not feel is irrelevant now," I said. "Thomas Seymour is married to my stepmother the Dowager Queen and I wish them all happiness together." I don't think my face was as convincing as my words.

Kat linked her arm with mine and we continued around the garden. She spoke no more on the subject. But there was a twinkle in that eye of hers that spoke to me as one friend's spirit will do to another. That although I might say it was over and done with, that this was not true.

She knew as well as I did, that the heart will not be ruled by the head, and certainly not when the head belongs to a young girl, little more than a child, in the first flush of attraction towards a man with more experience than she could possibly imagine.

I was in love; although I told my heart to contain itself and be quiet on the subject... I knew it was the truth.

Those first few days after we learned of their marriage were the hardest; I hoped Katherine merely took my quiet and solemnity as concern over the news, but I wondered if Thomas suspected I was heartsick for him.

Thomas Seymour moved into Chelsea. More than twice my age, he was a man of much experience with women. He only had to glimpse the flush on my cheeks when he entered a room, he only had to watch the faltering rise and fall of my chest to know that I strove to control feelings of a strength I had never experienced before.

And he did watch me; he enjoyed my faltering words at our first meetings. He teased me, he played with me. It did not take me long to understand that Thomas was flirting with me, the thirteen year old ward of his new wife and sister to his King. He only had to cast a dark eye over me to know that I was just as attracted to him, as he was to me.

Love and attraction are deadly games to play when one is not experienced in them. I felt as though I had no control over myself. I felt as though I might drown in his eyes. I was so much younger than he, but at the time I thought nothing of it. It was only later that I saw how reckless Thomas Seymour really was, playing with the hearts of a young girl and his own wife... playing with the power of the English line to the throne... playing with fire as he always had done.

I had never been in so much danger as I was in that beautiful house in Chelsea when my new stepfather moved in.

CHAPTER 27

AUTUMN, 1547

Katherine and Thomas were lucky. They did not get sent to the Tower for treason as many of us expected them to; luckily for Katherine, the affection that my brother the King still felt for her saved her and her reckless new husband Thomas Seymour. I think that his elder brother, the Lord Protector Somerset would have liked a much more severe punishment than the one the new couple received. He liked not his brother's new-found wealth and position. There were many others who found Katherine's haste to marry another man entirely disrespectful to our late father's memory and morally quite disgusting; Katherine herself however seemed to care very little for the opinions of others now that she had her husband. It seemed that she had loved Thomas even before our father has started to court her, and this ending was, for her, the completion of a fairy-tale love story.

The pair were fined for their disobedience and were in disgrace at court. My sister Mary was outraged by the affair and wrote many words to me in disgust at the tasteless speed in which our stepmother had abandoned the memory of the great King she had been so lately married to. Mary's letters seemed to imply that

Katherine was entirely overtaken by the sin of *lust*, and was obviously unable to contain or control herself. That such a woman should have been ever held worthy to marry into our family filled Mary with shame, and she thought that I was at great risk of corruption, being so young and housed with my immoral stepmother. Mary asked me to go and live with her. She thought it would be more fitting and less dangerous for me to go to her, rather than stay in the household of Katherine. She felt it was unsuitable for me, both as a princess and as a child, to be surrounded by the iniquity of such a woman as Katherine had turned out to be.

But I wanted to stay. Not only because of the love I still had for my stepmother and the thought of how boring life would be with my pious elder sister, but also, secretly and silently, because I desired to be near to the exciting, enticing figure of my new stepfather. I was hardly likely to admit this to my sister; the thought would have given her apoplexy.

I wrote to Mary and expressed, with what I felt was tact and delicacy, that I wanted to remain in the household of our stepmother, at least for now, as this was where the new King and his Council had decreed I stay. Until our brother and his advisors spoke otherwise, I should operate in accordance with their wishes. Every prince, I wrote to my sister, must show duty to the King of her country.

It was just helpful in this case that the wishes of my heart and the old orders of my brother were in concordance.

My little cousin Lady Jane Grey also joined Katherine's household in short time. She was around eleven at the time. Thomas Seymour with his infinite ambition had secured her as a ward, seeing the value in having two princesses of the royal line guarded under his roof with the Dowager Queen. Thomas had convinced the

Greys that if Jane was left to his care, he could advance her greatly. I believe the plan was to attempt to marry my little cousin to my little brother in time, and produce a great English line of Protestant Tudors. I don't know if anyone ever mentioned this to Jane. She was quite young although she was very clever. I would not have minded if my serious brother had married my solemn cousin; they were a good match, almost the same age, and Edward would have to marry someone when he grew older. Why not a girl from our own line?

Jane was not exactly pretty, but she was not unfortunate in any way either. Her hair was blonde with a tiny hint of the Tudor fire which was so striking in my own hair. Her eyes were a dark blue and her skin was pale and clear. She was little in build but her mind was strong and eager. She had not been treated well by her own family, and this made her eager to please others, and grateful for the slightest hint of friendship. It was a winning mixture. She was easy to overlook because she was so slight and little, but you would miss a great deal if you did overlook her.

When she was tempted from her general reserve into conversation, Jane was an able debater. Her mind was sound, her arguments convincing and I found her the perfect person to resolve any point against, for no matter what subject I was learning, she could find a point to argue against me on. Despite the slim difference in our ages, she was as able and willing as I to make and prove her point. It does much more to advance the strength of a mind when it is made to argue and to justify its points.

One thing no one remembers about Jane though, was that she was really quite funny. She did not play with people and their humour unless she knew them well; her home life had made her shy on that front. But when she knew you, you would find that her humour was dry as salt.

With Jane's arrival at Chelsea, we became like a little family; Katherine and Thomas with their two royal wards settled down as the scandal died down.

At Chelsea with its gracious, fashionable gardens and warm red-bricked walls we all settled into a life together. Jane and I settled into our lessons together and took walks together. Katherine shone; a woman released from all the terrors of a royal marriage, and seemed to love and respect her husband to such an extent that she saw no wrong in anything he did.

Kat continued to look on Thomas as being my property and every night she helped to inflame my foolish and unguarded heart with the possibility of his love and devotion to me.

And like every fool in love, I listened to her.

And like every fool in love, I had no compunction in taking every look, word and deed of Thomas Seymour as a sign of his returning my own childish flutters of love.

CHAPTER 28

AUTUMN, 1547

When I first entered the household of Katherine at Chelsea, I sat for a portrait commissioned by the King. Edward requested a portrait of his *dear sister* to keep beside him when he could not see me, which was more often than not.

Since Edward had become the King, we had barely seen each other, but I resolved to keep in better contact with him through letters. As the portrait was finished, I wrote him a letter to go with it.

"Like as the rich man daily gathers riches to riches, and one bag of money layeth a great sort until it come to infinite, so methinks your majesty, not being sufficed with many benefits and gentleness showed to me afore this time, doth now increase them in asking and desiring where you may bid and command, requiring a thing not worthy the desiring for itself, but made worthy for your highness's request. My picture, I mean, in which if the inward mind toward your Grace might as well be declared as the outward face and countenance shall be seen, I would have tarried the commandment but prevent it, nor have been the last to grant but the first to offer it. For the face, I grant, I might well blush to offer, but the mind I

shall never be ashamed to present. For though from the grace of the picture the colours might fade by time, may give you weather, may be spotted by chance; yet the other nor time with her soft wings shall overtake, nor the misty clouds with their lowerings might darken, nor chance with her slippery foot may overthrow. Of this although yet the proof could not be great because the occasion hath been but small, notwithstanding as a dog hath a day, so may I perchance have time to declare it in deeds where now I do write in words. And further I shall most humbly beseech your Majesty that when you shall look on my picture you will vouchsafe to think that as you have but the outward shadow of the body before you, so my inward mind wisheth that the body itself were oftener in your presence; howbeit because both my so being I think could do your majesty little pleasure, though myself great good; and again because I see as yet no time agreeing thereunto, I shall learn to follow this saying f Horace, 'Feras non culpes quod vitari non potest'. And thus I will, troubling your majesty I fear, end with my humble thanks. Beseeching God to preserve you to His Honour, to your comfort, to the Realm's profit and to my joy. From Hatfield.

Your Majesty's most humble sister and servant.

It was a long way to tell someone that you missed them and loved them, but I was often wont to get carried away in my letters. It wasn't something I ever grew out of, in fact, I became more loquacious in my letters as I become longer in years.

There was a sorrow for me some months after I joined Katherine's household when my excellent tutor William Grindal ailed and died. For four years, this quiet and clever man had taken the fabric of my mind and helped to fill it with all the sophistication and love of learning that he had. My poor master Grindal was so anxious even at the last stages of his illness that I should continue my studies that he asked that his great friend Roger Ascham be brought on as my next tutor. The dear man was more concerned, even at the last, with the continuation of my studies than he was with his own death.

We, all of us, remember best those who taught us well. Their names remain etched in our hearts for the rest of our lives. They were the first people we looked up to and who sparked mere learning, into love. I mourned for Grindal, and I never forgot him.

Ascham was interested in me. It was quite a prize, after all, to tutor the girl second in line to the throne, and he was delighted to find my mind was as inquisitive and as logical as his friend had told him in our lessons. There is something deeply ironic that during the time I was so taken with all the irrational feelings that a first infatuation brings to a girl, that Ascham wrote of me:

"Her ears are so well practised in discriminating all these things and her judgement is so good, that in all Greek, Latin and English compositions there is nothing so loose on one side, or so concise on the other which she does not immediately attend to and either reject with disgust or receive with pleasure as the case may be...She has no womanly weakness....her perseverance is equal to that of a man."

I am thankful that my new tutor, who had such faith in my abilities, could not see the secret pondering and aching of my heart as I bent my head dutifully over Cicero or Aristotle. Thank goodness that Ascham had so little idea of my flighty sensibilities.

It was also at this time that my stepmother brought a young man, older than I of course, but then most people were, into my household.

William Cecil was a young and highly ambitious courtier of moderate background but with an immense amount of promise in his abilities. Katherine brought him into my company and we got along well, even from the very start. Cecil was likeable, affable, clever and assiduous, all things I liked well in people. Cecil became responsible for the management of my many estates and revenues. As a princess of the realm I had a great wealth which needed tight control whilst I was a minor and not in charge of it myself. There needed to be someone of impeccable credentials to care for my money and my land. When the day came that I should come into my inheritance as an adult, I wanted there to be plenty there to greet me. Cecil was clever with numbers, and with detail, he was moral and dedicated to my family; all things that a good manager of a princess' estates should be able to do, he did with care and with devotion.

Good Cecil, one of the best and longest lived friendships that I should ever know came about through the offices of my stepmother. A woman I loved so much, owed so much to... and yet soon enough was to betray shamefully, and disgustingly.

CHAPTER 29

AUTUMN, 1547

It started with so many little things; as many events of importance often do. A glance here and there, the way his eyes roved over my young body when he greeted me in the morning or the afternoon. The way he would draw me into his arms for a fatherly hug, and then hold me for a moment too long... the way he would linger at his customary kiss of my lips every morn....

In all outward appearances it would seem that Thomas Seymour was but my devoted stepfather; but in all the covert ways, in all ways unseen and felt, there was another purpose to his growing friendship with his "dear daughter" as he called me. Katherine could see no wrong in Thomas, at all. She adored him, and in that infatuation she was blinded to the manner in which he was approaching me. She thought it was beautiful that her chosen new husband should not only please her so much, but also be so openly loving and affectionate to her stepdaughter, the Princess of England. She thought that his ways of being around me were playful, innocent, fatherly... but my father was never to me as Thomas was. I understood his purpose well enough.

Thomas desired me.

I was more than just a sparkling match for marriage, a young heir to the throne, just turned fourteen, although that was enough to make me attractive to most men with ambition. But for Thomas Seymour I think there was also the heavy, hedonistic attraction of the danger that came associated with me and my body. Legally I was the *property* of the country, Council and the King. I could not marry without permission. Therefore the idea of a clandestine affair with a princess so forbidden, so untouchable, was irresistible to a man as adventurous and reckless as Thomas Seymour.

I look on this now with the eyes of a woman who has seen much of the world, of men and of love. But then, then I was little more than a child; un-trained in the arts of love and un-used to having to restrain my feelings. God forgive me! I was not prepared to defend myself against such a man! When his dark eyes rested on my waist or hip, on my budding breasts or my neck, when I saw the path of those eyes across my body it would make me shudder with a feeling that I was not prepared to control... nor yet to reject.

There was in my heart for him the simple love that a first love always is; you know so little of the person you have fallen for, and yet you will never forget them, nor relinquish the affection you have for them... the first person that awoke such strong feelings in you.

I did not know what I wanted, but I knew I wanted him.

I was fourteen when he started his advances to me in earnest; a woman grown I thought, educated, the finest princess in the land, learned, wise so some would say... and yet when he came near me I would lose all my wisdom under the force of feeling he woke in my body. I would blush and he would smile; I would go quiet and he would touch my chin to raise my eyes to his, I would talk to Katherine on religious matters and he would pull me into his arms to dance around our chambers as Katherine looked on laughing. She saw nothing that he did as wrong, nothing as having any meaning other than that of an affectionate stepfather.

But that was most likely the thought farthest from his head... becoming a father-figure to me.

At night I dreamt he was my lover, sweeping into my chambers like one of the knights in the romances I was not supposed to read. He would grasp me by the shoulders and kiss me, tell me we should run together and rule in a foreign land as one... and then I would awake, pressing my hands between the wakened ache between my young legs, hardly understanding what it was I ached for. Although I understood what passed between a man and a woman in the marriage bed, I understood it technically after it was explained to me by Kat. Until I met and was courted by Thomas, I had had little idea of why people were eager to engage in such activities with one another.

But when I felt his body against mine as we danced, when I felt his hand brush my breast as though by accident, when I looked into his sparkling black eyes, I understood suddenly all the urges and compulsions that one may feel in the grasp of an attraction so strong, so sensual and so sexual, that it caused the breath to be punched from one's chest.

Sometimes at night, I was doubled over, half in pleasure and half in agony, feeling the burning ripples of *want* for him pulsing through my chest, my lips and my loins. I tried to be quiet when I wanted to scream. I tried to hide everything I felt from the ladies who shared my chambers. Sometimes in the day I had to excuse myself just to press my cheeks and forehead against the cold stone wall of the outside of the house at Chelsea, just to cool the passions of my blood.

I was not armed for a battle against a man like Thomas Seymour. A man with huge experience of the female conquest, a man with twice the years I had, who covered all he did with me under the mask of a respectable married man.

It was not long before his little daytime games were worked into other hours of the day and night too. Early one morning, before the servants or any of the house had risen, Thomas came suddenly into my rooms.

Kat and I were in bed. The morning was a little chilly and it was often our habit to warm each other in bed before the fires were lit. We happened to be whispering about Thomas himself when the curtains were thrown back and there, in nothing else but a night-shift and a bed jacket, was my handsome stepfather himself!

No man came into the bedchamber of a princess, especially not before she was dressed. I struggled up in shock, trying to arrange my own night shift that was quite sheer around me so that he would not see my naked body. My hair was loose around my shoulders and I was half-awake. I raised a hand as though to smooth my hair and saw him smile. He was delighted with his own appearance in my rooms. I, however was pale with shock and surprise, then went red with the thought that he could, and did, see through my shift, and was enjoying the view. Kat screamed a little and then giggled a bit, half in shock and half in admiration of the bold man. She stared at him with her mouth open, her eyes devouring the half-naked man before her.

"What are you doing here, my Lord?" I asked struggling to pull the covers around me as his hungry eyes roamed over me, catching glimpses of pink nipple and smooth skin. I blushed again, a deeper, shameful crimson.

Half of me was terrified that he had dared to jump into my rooms; half of me was enchanted with his daring.

Kat suddenly remembered herself, she was after all supposed to be my guardian and thus far a man had invaded my rooms and was standing half-naked at the end of my bed, a swinging shift not quite covering all there was to cover.

"My Lord Admiral," she said, her voice quavering with the notion of having to tell her favourite off, "it is not seemly for you to enter the Princess' rooms at this hour."

Thomas laughed, a merry sound, his laughter bounced off the walls and thrilled me to the tips of my toes. It sounded so like the laughter of my own father in some ways.

"Can a man not come to wish his good daughter a good morning?" he said in a booming voice. The servants were rising, and I could hear their feet outside of the room, stopping to listen to the unusual sound of a man inside my chamber. I flushed again.

"Not… at this hour, my Lord…" said Kat, rising from the bed with a shawl around her and moving to herd the errant knave towards the door. Thomas just stood, resisting her harrying and smiled down at me again. His handsome face was flushed with pleasure and excitement. I could not help but smile a little back at him.

"Hah!" he said, seeing my smile, and he pulled Kat's hands from his chest where they fluttered like nervous birds. He raised her fingers to his lips and kissed them gently and then, as Kat flushed as red as I, he laughed again and strode towards the door.

"I had thought the *morning* would be a good hour to wish my daughter a good *morning*, but I have been corrected by a learned woman such as Mistress Astley," he laughed again. "The next time I wish my good daughter a good *morning*, I shall do so in the *afternoon*... would that suit you better?"

Kat laughed, as did I. He was so disarming, standing at the door, his hands on his hips in mock indignation, laughing at us.

"Oh... my Lord," giggled Kat, looking at him with eyes that shone with admiration. She did not look on her husband with such eyes.

Thomas strode out the door, boldly, laughing to himself about the proper hour in which to wish another a good morning as the servants came past him ready to light fires and tidy as they did every morning.

And yet this morning they were greeted by the sight of me, still abed, half-dressed and with the bedclothes pulled around me like a protective shield as the half-naked form of my stepfather strode out of my chambers. My face was flaming red and my eyes were shining with both fear and with desire. I could not still the restless rise and fall of my breasts as I sought to control my breathing. I could not decide if I was terrified, or enchanted.

God knows what they suspected. But even if my stepmother had no idea of what her husband was getting up to, the rest of the house surely did.

CHAPTER 30
WINTER, 1547

K at's husband John was far more worried about the scene in
my chambers than Kat was; this he made plain to Kat and
then to myself. He said that we needed to take more care when
it came to the Lord Admiral. Kat, although she loved her husband, had been used to being independent for so long that she
did tend to follow her own instincts rather than her husband's
advice in life. So, whilst being a good wife when he was in the
same room and agreeing with him, she effectively and resolutely
ignored his wishes and spent most of her time giggling, gos-
siping and in all ways she could, encouraging me to flirt with
Thomas.

I wonder now that she never worried for her position, or for
the real danger that Thomas might actually take what he wanted from me. He was after all much stronger than I, and had he
forced himself on me, I would have had little power to escape
him. But I do not think that my dear Kat actually thought that far
ahead. She, like Katherine and like me, had fallen for the Lord
Admiral Thomas Seymour and all his charms. She could see he
admired me, and short of having your own love-affair, it is sometimes nearly as satisfying to be able to encourage that of a friend.

Besides, as she said so often to me, Thomas was *mine* first. He had just *settled* for Katherine.

It is so easy to believe what you want to in the words of your friends. But it was dawning on me that this situation was getting more and more out of control. I felt entirely as though I might fly apart at any moment, as though the skin on my body and the blood in my veins might burst through the pent-up excitement of all that was occurring in this house. But I was also afraid, afraid to lose control, afraid of what might come of these visits from my stepfather.

Over the next few weeks, Thomas appeared regularly in my bedroom in the morning. I took care after the first couple of times to go to bed with two shirts on so that he could not see through one to my naked skin. But when he saw this trick it only seemed to encourage him to further intimacies; he started to jump onto the bed with loud cries and shouts, grab the bed clothes and wrestle them off me. As he pulled off my sheets he sometimes managed to pull of one of my night shifts, and he would tickle Kat and me into weeping hysteria, jumping around on the bed with us.

Screaming, giggling, and fighting off a man twice my size and power was both exciting, because I believed myself in love with him, and fearsome, when I felt the power really behind that lithe body. He was outrageous, but I started to get an edge of alarm in my mind each time he did something more shocking than the last act... where would he stop? Would he stop?

I did not know, and I had no one eager to help me rein him in.

Kat loved every second of it, screaming and running from him in her nightshift, throwing herself in between me and him as he pounced across the bed growling at me. Just feeling him near her was enough to make her glow with excitement. John Astley and his friend Thomas Parry, were becoming increasingly aghast at what was becoming a daily romp in my bedchamber, John tried to caution his wife on what would become of my reputation should this become public knowledge.

Kat, again, ignored him.

Katherine, my stepmother, was almost blissfully unaware of anything untoward going on. She had found out that she was pregnant, carrying her beloved's child in her belly, and in this state that she had so longed to be, she had found a kind of peace and a marked refusal to see any ill in her Thomas. Her face was calm and beautiful at all times and she hummed to herself as she wandered about the great house. Later, the thought came to me that most likely Thomas' restless pursuit of me in the bedchamber was most likely fuelled by his inability to lay with his wife in her pregnant condition. But I did not know such then… and since I could barely reconcile the two emotions of terror and desire within me as he came on his visits to me each morning I was in no position to give much thought to anything.

One morning Katherine followed him to my chambers and found him pulling the bedcovers off me and Kat as we screamed and giggled. Katherine stood in the doorway and when I looked up I saw a look of pallid shock on her face at the scene of her husband wrenching the covers from a screaming young woman, looking for all the world like some raping knave in a legend.

And then Thomas saw me staring at Katherine and he bounced towards her laughing. The look of adoration, of relief, that swept over her face as he turned his visage to her was as pathetic as it was empty of all thought. The woman I admired so for her fine brain and clever words was a *fool* for this husband of hers. He had only to smile at her, and she was entirely within his power.

"Come, Katherine!" he said, pulling her to the bed. "I come in here to wish my good daughter a merry morning, and she and her serving woman tell me that I am to leave! Well! I shall have none of that from a little snippet! Am I the Lord of this house or no? Am I the girl's father or no?"

Katherine started to giggle and shake her head. He was just so outrageous, so over the top and foolish, you could not help but think he was as innocent as he seemed. But it was all a trick. Thomas Seymour knew how to work women well. He knew how to lie.

"Thomas..." she said giggling at him. "You are such a boy... look, you are scaring our daughter."

"Scare her! Hah!" he said and started to prowl around the bed, his hands raised like an animal as I screamed, half in terror and half in pleasure as he stalked around the bed.

"This one is not scared, Katherine," he said laughing as I scrambled up from the bed and ran behind my stepmother. "This one needs scaring some *MORE*!" he shouted, and ran at me.

Katherine laughed and danced in between her husband and me, as I screamed, trying to get away and he growled, trying to catch me. Katherine was placed in between us like some human shield. She was laughing, holding Thomas off with her little hands as he leapt around her, frenzied, like a mad beast growling and yowling at me. I was shrieking, laughing, gasping for breath, flushed and excited. So *glad*, after all, that Katherine was there to protect me and yet knowing that she thought there was nothing to protect me from.

When finally she managed to tame her wild husband and lead him from the room, I fell backwards on the bed, my face red with excitement, exertion and with growing pleasure in the attentions of a man that I admired and loved.

Kat threw herself on the bed with me. "What a man he is!" she said and dodged the cuff I playfully aimed at her.

It took some time before I could go out into the day, some time before I could control myself, some time to take the redness from my cheeks. This was getting out of control. And the more it did, the more I wanted more.

CHAPTER 31

AUTUMN, 1547

I t took a dress to make Kat aware of the dangers I was in from my amorous stepfather. The new dress I had ordered some weeks ago was the catalyst for Kat to become very afraid for me.

When the seamstress brought it to us I squeaked with pleasure at the beautiful black velvet that I had picked so lovingly. I was eager to try it on at once. Stripping down to my undergarments, Kat and my ladies helped me into the fine fabric and I pranced around my chambers in it, well pleased, for the deep black of the material was as expensive as it was becoming to my pale skin, and when I looked into the mirror, I saw that it gave me a bearing that was older than my fourteen years.

I looked older, like a woman grown, rather than a maid still. When we have youth in our cheeks we wish for maturity, and when we have maturity, we wish for youth. The human is an inconstant and giddy thing.

It pleased me to see that I looked so much older; I could have been eighteen in this garb. Kat, however, did not like it so much. I think she would have loved to keep me as a child for herself forever, but I did not care as I was well pleased with the look.

As I was admiring the dress, we heard a gay laugh from the courtyard below. Looking out I saw Katherine, her body now starting to swell with the blessing of her child in her belly, and at her side, gambolling and dancing like a little dog for treats, was her husband. The man I adored and feared in equal measures.

"I will go and show them my dress," I said blushing, and Kat let out a little, excited laugh. I knew that she saw the workings of my mind; I wanted to show to Thomas that I was more of a woman than he had thought. I wanted to show him what he had missed out on, by rushing into marriage with Katherine. These petty thoughts were not nice ones, but we are none of us nice people all the time. I left my apartments and walked out to meet them, Kat stayed behind in our chambers to watch from a window. As I walked down the stairs, I stopped myself from running at them like a girl; I wanted him to know that I was mature, grown... that I was an adult, not a child any longer. I reached the entrance to the gardens and adopted a strangely un-casual casual air as I strolled as if by accident into the gardens.

I sauntered nonchalantly towards them, and then bowed in the presence of my stepmother and father. I saw Katherine crease her brow as she looked at me in my dress, and Thomas' eyes lit up as he took in my lithe form. He raised an eyebrow at me; it was out of Katherine's sight.

I blushed slightly and felt my heart beat with that familiar mixture of anxiety and pleasure; I was happy to see the little lights of desire that lit in his eyes for me, but with Katherine there, this could not go too far. I was safe to be admired, and I so longed to be admired by him.

My black dress was cut low, brought in tightly at my waist, with crisp lace at the sleeves and at the chest. It was simple, elegant and it brought attention to my slim figure, budding breasts and graceful hands. Its darkness contrasted and accentuated my pale skin, my red hair and my fine eyes. Thomas looked me all over, as though I were meat to feed well from at a feast.

"A new dress, Elizabeth?" said Katherine and I bowed to her smiling.

"Do you like it my lady?" I asked, feeling through my velvet layers the hot eyes of her husband as his view focused on one part of my body, and then the next.

"It is most becoming," she said although there was a note of hesitancy in her voice. Perhaps she had noticed the interest it had raised in her husband?

"What think you my lord?" I said, turning to Thomas. "Does my good father like my new clothes?"

Thomas breathed in, as though finally realizing that his wife was actually there at all. If she had not been, I think he would have thrown me over his back and taken me in the shrubbery. Such was the heat and recklessness in his eyes.

"I like it not," he said abruptly and quickly, too quickly for truth.

What a lie! He knew it and so did I, but still my face fell with his words.

Katherine saw my countenance drop and touched her husband's arm. "Thomas," she said gently, scolding lightly. "You are too blunt; see how you have made our daughter sad now from your clumsy comments?"

She turned to me and smiled. "Your dress is very nice, Elizabeth, but it is… perhaps more mature than your wardrobe previous to this. It has surprised your father, that is all. It comes as a shock to all fathers to learn that their daughters must grow into women." She smiled with affection at Thomas.

He grunted. "Ha!" he said. "I still like it not, it is too grown up for our little girl, the colour is not suited… she looks like an old matron, whereas I would have our good daughter stay young for as long as she can."

Katherine laughed. "You cannot keep her a child forever Thomas," she said.

I pulled myself up a little, pushing my pale chin into the air. "No indeed," I said haughtily. "For I will be a woman grown soon, it is not up to *you* my lord to halt the passage of time for such as I."

His face widened with mock surprise and he started to back away with his hands at his chest as though in pain. "See Katherine?" he exclaimed and leapt forward at her, grasping her arm. "See! One dress… one dress! And already our sweet daughter is turned from our will as though she were a woman with no loyalty or sympathy to those who raised and nurtured her! This dress is an evil thing! I am sure it is a work of the devil and I will have no other master in my house! I will answer to no piece of cloth! Come, I will have away with this evil influence!"

Then, he pulled his dagger from his side. A bright shining blade winked at us in the sunlight. Its hilt encrusted with rubies, as red and deep as blood. I stood an involuntary step backward, my hands raised before me as Thomas Seymour walked towards me with a knife held level with my throat.

"Thomas..." said Katherine with a wavering of alarm in her voice. "What are you...?"

She did not get to finish her question for at that moment he sprang towards me like a cat on a mouse, wrapped his strong arms around me and pulled me backwards, my body flat against his. I froze in shock as his strong arms banded about me like a vice. For a moment I went weak. I could feel the blood pouring from every part of me and rushing to my heart in panic. For a moment I thought he was actually going to kill me, but his knife sought another victim.

Holding me still with one hand, his other reached down and slashed the fabric of my beautiful dress from the hip to the bottom of the skirt in one sudden, quick gash.

For a moment, both Katherine and I were so surprised that we did not move. Then, Katherine suddenly burst into giggles.

"Thomas..." she said giggling with tears coming to her eyes. "You are such a boy, what have you done to Elizabeth's dress?!"

I started to laugh a little with relief. His arm still about my neck he held me in his arms. I loved to feel the closeness of him; I could see the curling hair at the back of his neck and smell the musk and sweat of his skin. But I was also afraid, excited, overwhelmed. This man was more than I knew how to handle. I was never in charge of these encounters; I was never in control.

He laughed. "Come, Kate," he said to Katherine. "Hold her!! I shall be master in this house and no other, come! You are my wife and promised to obey me at the altar before God! Do so now, and hold our daughter whilst I teach her a lesson!"

Katherine laughed and jumped forward at his command, gripping my arms behind my back as I struggled and shouted in surprise at her. She held me as he slit my dress all over, bolts of black velvet and silks flying this way and that as the frenzied man slashed and stripped my dress from me. Where his knife was not fast enough, he used his hands to rip my gown off me. Tiny strips of my skirts flew past bits of the bodice; bits danced along the cobbled paths and clung to the trees. Before long Katherine was weak with laughing and I fought my way free, to find myself standing in the gardens of Chelsea, in nothing more than my undergarments, with tiny bits of my glorious new dress clinging to me as though they alone wanted to preserve my modesty. I stood shivering in front of Thomas and Katherine. She was laughing, and he was admiring.

"My lord," I said, pulling myself up to my full height whilst still trying to shield my young breasts from show. "You have ruined my new dress; you will have to buy me another."

He bowed and saluted me with his knife. "Gladly," he said. "But it will be one of *my* choosing."

Katherine giggled more, and then seemed to suddenly realise that her stepdaughter, her charge, a princess of England, was standing in the gardens almost naked.

"Go on in Elizabeth," she said, suddenly looking a little worried. "You'll catch your death of cold. Go and put your crimson gown on, your good father should have nothing to complain of in that one."

I turned and started to trot back to the house. It was cold outside and I was almost stripped. I looked up at the windows and flushed bright red.

There was hardly a window of the house where there was not a servant's face staring out at us in the gardens.

I looked up into a sea of shocked faces that suddenly disappeared as though they were birds flying from a field.

I looked up into my rooms and saw Kat. Her face was not the usual mask of admiration and desire that she had when she saw the Admiral. Her ghostly face in the grand window was white with fear.

I flushed deeper and ran into the house. There was not a person in this house who had not seen Thomas and Katherine stripping me for fun in the gardens, or who would not hear of it by the night. When I reached my chambers Kat ran at me and caught me in a great blanket and put me by the fire as though I were an infant. She said little, but in the fear in her eyes I knew that even she thought Thomas Seymour was treading too far... taking too many liberties with his desire for a girl who was not only his legal daughter, but was an heir to the throne of England.

CHAPTER 32
WINTER, 1547

The incident with the knife had seemed to sound an alarm with Kat that Thomas invading my bedroom or casting his eyes on me had not. Perhaps it was the very public nature of the assault in the gardens. Perhaps it was that he and Katherine had held me and all but stripped me naked before the watching eyes of the house. Perhaps it was Thomas' repeated assertion that he was the "*master of this house*" and would have his way done. Perhaps it was my obvious inability to control myself around him; or perhaps it was simply watching her charge, a girl she was inordinately fond of and loved, partly as her own child and partly as a friend, stalked with a dagger.

For whichever of these perhaps-es, Kat was suddenly much more disturbed by the increasing attentions of my step father. For my own part, and as usual when it came to this man, I was a mass of confused feelings and desires. I feared him, but he excited me; I was drawn to him, but repulsed by him... I longed to feel his arms about me, to be helpless with him, and yet I wanted him to admire me as an equal and an adult; to respect my rank, of which I was prodigiously protective.

And then there was the matter of Katherine.

Her belly swollen with Thomas' child, this should have been the happiest time of her life. She was finally to have her greatest wish, her own babe, after countless marriages to old men long past planting an infant in her pretty body.

But I got the impression that a sneaking suspicion was entering her mind that these games were not as innocent as she would have liked to believe they were. Was she fooling herself to retain the perfect image of her marriage to the man she loved? I thought so. I wondered how much she suspected of Thomas and me. Did she have an idea of my feelings for him, and his for me? Was she jealous as I was of her? Was she afraid for me as Kat was, that I might not be ready to withstand the amorous approaches of a man so much older and stronger than I?

I do not know what she allowed herself to suspect at this time, but since the incident in the gardens, she had become more dogged in her watch over me. Whenever Thomas invaded my bedrooms, she was there; she was holding me as he tickled me, standing between us as he hunted me around the room like a wild beast. Whatever new game my stepfather had, she was always there, which meant that Thomas was less able to accidentally stroke me or touch me as he did when Katherine was not around; he could not very well actually molest me in her company after all.

But this also meant that in the few times she was not there, his intensity, his desire to touch and be near to me increased three fold in its strength. When he found me alone without her, the shining of his eyes turned to a flame.

If he came upon me when I walked in the gardens, he would try to sneak kisses from me. If he found me with lesser company such as servants in a chamber, he would soon be hugging and stroking me. He would press himself against me and run his hands over my back and buttocks, caress my hair and try to kiss my neck. I found myself watching the space behind me in fear when I walked down a corridor. I found myself trying to hide in the gardens. Even as I desired him back, I was becoming more and more aware that he was the one with the power in our little dance, and it scared me.

It felt as though things were coming to a climax; this man would not be stopped in his pursuit of me.

I stopped sleeping and my eating became sparse. I was nervy and jumpy about the house, unable to concentrate on my studies, unable to find rest and refuge in my books. I could not reconcile my contradictory feelings for him. I lived in fear of him as much as I longed to see him.

But then you must remember, I was only fourteen years old. Those who are few in years are always more convinced than those long in them, of their maturity and ability to cope with the adult world. It is a fiction born of lack of experience. The older we are, the more we understand our lack of ability, the more we see the flaws in our rationalising. When we are young we may be resilient in many ways, often courageous to the point of idiocy, but we are no match for an adult who is a predator. We think we are the mongoose to his snake, when we are in fact the mouse.

Kat was worried enough about me that she went to Katherine to talk to her about Thomas and his behaviour towards me; his visits to my chamber in the morning had become almost daily. I had started to rise early to stop him finding me abed in my night shift, but this meant that he was also rising very early to try and surprise me again. As I tried to hold him off, he just kept coming at me. My nights were starting to be dogged by the fear that he would simply come to me then instead of waiting for the morn. Sleep was a stranger.

But I wanted him to come to me too. In so many ways I was fascinated by him. I managed to convince myself that none of the servants would notice he and I loved each other; that his advances to me might soften and become romantic rather than physical. But if I thought the servants did not know, or that this man pursuing me had any intentions that were romantic, I was a fool.

Katherine told Kat that her fears were foolish. Thomas' regard for me was but the sign of an overly-boyish fatherly affection. He had never really been a father before, she told Kat, and he did not realize that his actions were slightly over the normal bounds of affectionate display.

Kat, however, pressed that I was a very young girl and my reputation both as a princess and as a maid, were things that I had to keep intact should I wish to remain unstained and pure, as every maid should be, in the eyes of the public.

"The incident in the gardens was seen by all the household, my lady," Kat said to Katherine. Katherine sat serenely sewing clothes for her imminently expected baby. "And whilst it may have been all innocent, you know as well as I that a royal princess cannot be too careful in protecting her reputation with the common people. There were many in the house who saw the… game and whispered of it abroad. "

Katherine looked at Kat carefully and said that she was thankful for Mistress Astley's comments, and would speak on the matter to her husband.

Whether Katherine did or not we never found out; but Kat came back to relay her visit and conversation with worry in her face.

"It goes too far, my lady," she said. "*He* goes too far... A little flirtation was light and harmless, but that thing in the gardens...," she shuddered and crossed herself. "I thought he was wont to kill you with that knife."

"And he jumping into my bed every morning was entirely proper, I suppose?" I said in a strained whisper. "You did nothing all those times but laugh, and now you think you stand on the moral high ground as though we are below you? It is not only the Lord Admiral and I who deserve a bit of censure here, Kat Astley."

She flushed and stammered, "I saw no harm in his silly habits. And I tried, you saw I tried my lady, to get him to leave your chambers when first he came in. But then... you seemed so happy and he was so *charming*, and later even Katherine came in and joined in, it was not out in the open like that thing in the gardens. It was private, just a little fun. Nothing could happen when I was with you. It was not like that in the gardens when they stripped you. Everyone saw..."

I flushed, remembering my run into the house. I wondered if I had looked like a common country whore caught in the act in a field with a farmer-boy.

"Well there should be an end to it now," I said. "I've been a fool as well as you. He has done enough now, he needs to pay attention to Katherine. She'll soon be handing him this little knave, his child he talks of all the time and that should keep him busy."

But even as I said it, I knew I didn't want him to stop, I didn't. I didn't want the attention of his handsome face to wander back to

Katherine; I didn't want to stop feeling his hand on my side or my breast. I felt so lonely when he wasn't there. I wanted him to treat me gently, to be kind, stop jumping out at me from like dark like a monster… but I didn't want to be without him. My heart was a traitor to my head. They both urged me in different directions.

But it must stop! I thought. *It must! This is no way for us to behave.*

CHAPTER 33
HANWORTH HOUSE
SPRING, 1548

The household moved to Hanworth House in the spring of 1548 to await Katherine's lying in and take some pleasure in the cleaner airs of a new palace. It was necessary to move from house to house on a regular basis so that the old residence may be cleaned, cleansed and made ready for use once more. A prince needs many palaces, mainly because staying in one would become intolerably and entirely smelly after a while.

So it was we packed up from Chelsea and wended our way to the lovely house of Hanworth. Katherine rode in a litter due to the advanced stage of her pregnancy. Thomas went on ahead with his men, whipping their horses and screaming into the distance like wild savages. Katherine watched him go with a smile of affection and a shake of her head. She thought him entirely a boy in all ways.

Kat and I rode with Katherine and her servants. We kept an easier pace than Thomas and his rampant men and although I was happy to be at a distance from him, I also regretted not being able to ride as I wished to. I loved to gallop on my horse, and I was becoming an excellent horsewoman. I could feel the temper of my mount as surely as I could see fine weather in the skies. Kat told me that my father was a master of horsemanship and that I was growing to be just like him. This pleased me and made me feel closer to his memory. I wished we could have ridden together more, my father and I. It seemed we might have enjoyed the mutual experience.

Although it were a thing impossible, I wished I could have known my father in his youth. I feel that he and I could have been great friends in our youths.

We reached Hanworth by the fall of the night and I was taken to my new chambers there. I was glad to settle at the fireside with Kat and speak of unimportant things. My mind was too busy these days. I felt tired often; my nights were not easy to sleep through and I was not eating as a growing woman should. Thomas was still invading my rooms and it was now every day. Kat's warnings to Katherine had had little sway on the behaviour of the Admiral. If Katherine had talked to him on the matter, he had ignored her.

Kat had become as close to me as my own undergarments in a bid to rescue me from the advances of my stepfather. She now tried to persuade him to leave when he came to my chambers where before she had joined in his reckless games. But all that this did was to infuriate him further. If he could not bend us to his will, then he would find a way to break through.

It was one day as I was reading alone over my newest chapters for translation from Master Ascham. My tutor himself had gone to bed, feeling suddenly unwell in the afternoon, and I had not sought out further company. I had relished a moment of peace to myself to draw together my thoughts, so whirled and confused my head was lately, that I had decided to refrain from calling Kat to me, or any of my other women. For a moment, just a moment, I would be alone and I would try and draw some order to this mind which spun with confusion and desire.

I did not hear his step as he came into the room, but he must have been there for a little while, just looking at me, as I stared out of the window into the gardens.

I looked up and he was staring at me. His handsome face was half-hidden in shadow and for a moment, when he smiled at me, he looked like a wolf rather than a man.

I jumped and stood up when I saw him. "My lord Admiral," I said, taking an involuntary step backwards. "I did not hear you come in." I dropped to the customary curtsey, and in that short moment of time he crossed the floor and took my arms. Raising me to standing before him, he reached out a hand and stroked softly the skin of my cheek with the back of his hand. I felt as though I had frozen in place. The wild banging of my heart was such that I knew not whether I was terrified, or aroused. The feelings were each as powerful as the other for this man. His hungry eyes roamed my face, and then, sliding a hand to the back of my neck and head, he pulled me to him in a long and lingering kiss.

There had not been a word from his lips. He had just seen his opportunity to kiss me, and had taken it.

For a moment I froze as his soft lips and their whisper of whiskers came down on mine. And then it was as though all the world and its confusion had melted away, and all there was, was the feel of his muscular body against mine, the feel of his hand on my hair and the sensation of his lips against mine. Flashes of untamed desire flooded through my young blood, and I unfroze, as though his kiss had shown me all that I had really wanted from him in truth, and I melted into him, my body pressed against the contours of his, my hands reaching up, my fingers running through the soft dark curls at the back of his head.

I felt his body shudder as he felt me respond willingly to his touch. He broke from our kiss to murmur my name in my ear as he pushed me gently back, against the wall, where he could press more of his hard body to mine. I was lost in a sea of passion, feeling nothing but how much I wanted him and I stumbled back willingly, pulling him to me as we bashed against the wall together barely breaking apart in our kissing.

His hands were everywhere now, pulling me to him, over my buttocks where he squeezed hard, bruising my skin. He groaned as he felt my curves under his hands. His hands covered over my face, where he pulled back from our kissing, only to grin and plunge at me again with more force. His eager fingers pulled at my bodice to release my young breasts, and he moaned as he pushed his face into them.

All I could feel was the coursing of desire in my body and my blood, as I allowed him to take any and all pleasures of my body; I was as soft as honey for him, moaning and whispering his name, willing him on, willing him to take anything of me, but just to never stop touching me.

He pulled at my skirts, pushing them up as I moved my legs apart. He looked into my eyes, and when he saw they were dazed he smiled at me. "I knew you loved me too..." he said, and I nodded, unable to talk, pulling his lips back to mine. I wanted so much to feel loved by him, to feel wanted. His hands were pulling at his trousers with anxious impatience as I murmured, "I love you Thomas..." and he groaned against my neck, one hand over my breasts, and one moving himself into position to take me, there and then, as ready and wanton as any alley-way whore.

Then there was a gasp, and a short strangled shout.

Thomas froze. His back was to the doorway, but I had a clear view over his shoulder of the woman standing, pale in face with shock as she looked on the sight of her beloved husband and her beloved daughter caught, almost in the very act, against a wall in her house.

Thomas dropped my body and quickly tried to sort out his own clothing, as I turned red and shamefaced to the wall, fumbling to try and rectify my own. My bodice was unlaced; my breasts were on show for all to see. I started to cry in shame as I pushed them back inside my dress and tried to pull the silk of my gown over the bruises his eager fingers had made on me. I pushed my skirts down. I was hunched over in my own infamy, my face as red as sin. I did not want to look at Katherine, but I could not stop myself stealing glances at her.

He had not pierced my virginity, I was a maid still, if barely, but he may as well have taken me completely, for the horror on Katherine's face. I could not believe what I had just done, or almost done. I could not believe what had just happened.

I heard Katherine break into tears and walk away, her heels clattering along the corridor in the unsteady steps of the distraught. Thomas pulled himself together quicker. Perhaps a man such as he, was more used to amorous encounters where clothing must be replaced quickly, and without a word or glance to me, he ran after his wife.

I was alone once more. I could not stop crying as I put my clothes back in order. I did not feel as though I was in the throes of desire any more. I felt sick, dirty and ashamed.

As soon as my clothes were back in order I went out into the private gardens. No one but Katherine had seen us, and no one should know of this but her, I was determined. But would she keep me in her house? I did not know. I kept seeing the horrified look on her face and my cheeks jumped into shameful flames once more. I had betrayed a woman I loved as a mother and a friend, with her husband, in her own house.

I had never, and have never since, been more ashamed of myself, nor more felt the pain that I had inflicted on someone who loved me.

As it started to rain, I stayed outside and lifted my flaming, shameful face to God in the heavens. Where was all my wisdom now? Where were my advanced skills and learnedness? I had never been so unprepared for anything in my whole life as the force and feeling that his touch had arisen in me. In the first trial that God sent me of true temptation, I had failed.

The rain may as well have sizzled as it landed on my heated cheeks. I felt like the devil himself.

CHAPTER 34
RICHMOND PALACE
FEBRUARY, 1603

We all want people to think the best of us, to like us.

That is why when we tell them of us, of our lives and our adventures, we often omit that which does not show the best in our character. We do not lie, but we tell a half-truth. We conceal those parts of ourselves we do not like, and others will not like.

For in every person there is the light and the dark. There is the bold and the craven, the great... and the shameful.

We pick what parts of ourselves we share with others, and we leave the other parts to the darkness, where dreams may whisper what is true into our ear only.

Though we think that everyone may somehow see through our skin, be able to see the truth past our lies, this is not true... we are creatures made of paint and water.

We are but portraits of ourselves, painted by our own words and actions.

That truth is even more true for a prince.

For when I stand before my people I am not a woman, nor a person, but an embodiment of their hopes and dreams, their aspirations and their values. To learn that I am a woman, with all the flaws of my sex and my human nature, is an affront to the image of my people, an affront to England and to the crown I wear.

I am an emblem, I am a banner. I am the warrior pennant of my people. I must be to them all they want me to be, and to hide my failings and faults behind a covering of paint and plaster and words.

We, all of us, if we are wise, learn to mould the inner character to the one we most want the world to see. We are creatures of such habit you see, that sometimes when we take so much time emulating something of greatness, we become great.

But when I was a young girl... I did not know this. When I was young, when I was but a fool who thought herself wise, I acted wrongly and I hurt someone I loved.

More than any other incident in my life, I have regretted this one. It was the first time that I really understood that there was a world of feeling outside of the prison of my own skin and flesh. Other people had souls that could be damaged by my actions, and the repercussions could be more harmful than I ever thought.

Shame is an unpleasant emotion because it contains truth. We know, when we are shameful, that we have done wrong, and that truth hurts more than all the others.

When I appear before my people, I do not let them see the weaknesses of my nature, of my soul within. I am their *Gloriana*, their Queen, their Saviour, even their beloved *Bess*, but I am not the Elizabeth that I may be here on this page.

These recollections, these words will not be shown to anyone, and therefore I do not have to omit who I truly am now, who I truly was... then.

To you, and only to you, these pages on which I recant my life…. I lay my soul bare to tell you of this time, so terrible in my life, when I realized I had taken part in breaking the heart of a fine, kind woman who never wished anything for me but good.

CHAPTER 35
SPRING, 1548

Kat's mouth was open so wide I began to wonder if bats should take up occupancy there, hanging from her teeth. Her silence and her horror infuriated me.

"Do not look at me so!" I exclaimed. "You knew well enough what was going on in this house, do not pretend the innocent to me... that you thought all he did was but in jape. You knew what he pursued me for!"

Her mouth opened and closed like a fish out of water. She ran a hand over her face as though seeking to bring forth clear thoughts by that mere action Trying to pull the tattered threads of the situation together again.

"My lady," she said, her voice low and shaking slightly. "Did anything go aught further between the Admiral and yourself? Are you... Did he...?"

"I am a maid," I said blushing furiously.

I was angry with her. It was not justified. It so often happens that when we are filled with shame at an action we have done, we seek to assign blame elsewhere, to place it on others near us. To mitigate our own sense of shame we try to dilute it by giving cups of it away to those near us, as though it were wine.

"You should have tried harder to talk to Katherine. You should have tried harder to keep him away from me," I said bitterly. Katherine's pale face covered in tears kept revolving in my head.

Kat looked at me aghast. "What more should I have done?" she asked me. "I am not responsible for my *Lady Princess' own arms* should they lock around a man's head and *beg* for kisses."

My hand lashed out from my side before I knew it, and slapped Kat hard about the face. One of my rings did not fit my finger well, it moved around on my long tapered digit. As I slapped my friend full around the face, the diamond on the ring slipped and caught her skin, ripping it open. A thin, red slit appeared on her cheek and a droplet of blood, like a tear, emerged, as Kat clapped a hand to her cheek in pain.

I stared at her in shock. I had not meant to hurt her. I was hurting everyone around me.

"Kat..." I said softly and held out a hand to her cheek. She looked for a moment as though she might move away from me, but she did not. Beneath the pale worry on her face, I saw the softness of her love for me move once more in her blood.

"My mistress is too easy with her hands," she said wryly, using the old stock phrase that I knew so well. I smiled at her without any real happiness, but with love for the woman who understood me so well.

"Yes," I said. "I am sorry Kat. My temper, it always gets the better of me."

"The red hair of the Welsh dragon," she said, taking a bit of cloth and soaking it in a goblet of wine. "Dragons are not patient beasts I have been told." She pressed the cloth to her cheek and winced as the sharp wine flowed into her cut and bruise.

I slumped down on a pillow on the floor. I felt miserable, awful, guilty, and tired. I was young and tiredness usually came to me as it always does to the young, in sudden and irrepressible torrents that force the active mind quickly into restful slumber. But now, I felt the first strains of what an adult feels when they are tired; a slow weariness born of frustration and exposure to the ills of the world. Today, *I* was an ill of this world. I was one of those that caused people to lose faith in human goodness. I was the craven whore. I was the bad seed that turned the crop to pestilence.

I could try and assert that Thomas was much older than me, that he was more powerful than me; that his actions were those of an adult and mine those of a child. But I had little resisted him. I had not screamed out or ran when he touched me. I had played his games and whispered for more.

And we, together, had hurt a good woman. A good woman who had given me a mother, a home and a family.

"What am I to do?" I asked Kat.

She peeled the cloth back from her cheek and looked ruefully at the line of smeared blood, purpled by the wine on the cloth.

Her cheek was dark red, already turning a little mauve at the edges. I had hit her hard. Another wave of remorse washed over me. My heart flopped inside my chest, weakened by the guilt weighing on it.

Kat sighed. "We must mitigate any effect this may have on your reputation," she said. "Although you say that no one saw this...encounter... we must ensure that no one hears of it. Katherine must understand this, even though she is hurt. You are the Princess, and it is *your* reputation we must protect."

Kat was all governess then. It shocked me sometimes to see her when she became her title, rather than my friend.

I nodded. Her words were wise enough.

"And if Katherine sends for me?" I said, feeling like a small child, wanting others to face the anger and sorrow of the woman I had hurt.

Kat looked at me sternly. Her warm brown eyes clouded slightly as she thought. She was in just as much trouble as I... perhaps more as she was supposed to be my guide, my governess, who would ensure I was taught the rigours of good behaviour. This incident reflected very badly on her ability to control me, and on her ability to teach me right behaviour from wrong.

To err with an heir to the throne could be considered a matter of treason.

I believe both of us at that time, suddenly felt much less removed from the court; it was as though all eyes in the world had suddenly turned up on us.

"*When* she sends for you," Kat said. "You must ask her to mitigate this scandal for the sake of your reputation as a princess."

"And if she is angry with me?" I sounded plaintive, begging like a little girl for Kat to protect me. But I saw in her face that she would not.

"Then it is up to you to moderate that anger, my lady," she said. "There is nothing I can do or say as a servant that will help sooth Katherine's anger. That is up to you. You have entered into an adult game with Thomas Seymour. Perhaps it is fitting that you see the consequences of such a game."

Anger leapt into my sad heart as I heard that. "But you encouraged me!" I said. "You too did not stop him, or me!"

Kat bowed her head. "I did not say you were the only one to blame, Elizabeth," she said softly. "But you were also, like me, a player in this game, not a pawn, but a queen."

My anger stopped abruptly. It was true enough.

I would have to face Katherine.

CHAPTER 36
SPRING, 1548

Days passed.

There was a silence about the house as though someone had died. There was that same strange air of stillness, as people shuffled in and out of rooms on quiet feet, where people fear to put a spoon in a bowl lest it ring with over-loud sound.

I kept to my rooms. Kat with me, we stared at books without reading the words, stitched at embroidery without seeing the design. My tutors were concerned, thinking I was coming down with an illness. I left my meals to congeal on their plates, feeling hunger, but having no appetite. I felt sick every time I thought of Katherine, or Thomas.

Still there was nothing from Katherine but a marked silence. She did not send for me to keep her company, she did not send for me to take meals with her, to walk or to read with her. She did not send a little message at the end of the day to let me know she was thinking of me as she had done before. There was nothing but the silence. Deep and reproachful. It was as though the emotions of her heart had been so intense they escaped to form a mist about the house, a ghostly presence that floated around me and prodded me in the side and in the heart wherever I went. Her ghostly accusation pained me. I could not see her, but I could feel her at my side all the time, sharing her pain with me generously, and increasing my feelings of shame, and disgust at myself.

In the end, I was longing to see her, just to stop this long and unending silence and guilt. But still she did not send for me. My cousin Jane Grey was sent for. S*he* sat with Katherine. S*he* read to her and stayed with her. I saw them walking together in silence in the gardens through my window.

So, I thought with jealousy, Katherine would have the pallid little Jane with her rather than me! My head answered my petty jealousy; *Of course*, it said... *Jane did not try to seduce her husband... Jane did not take the love she offered her only to spit it back in her face... Jane did not betray her.... but you did.*

Of Thomas, I saw nothing. Perhaps he was in the house, perhaps he was gone. He did not seek to see me, nor contact me since our little tryst. I knew nothing of him. I was miserable, alone and drowning in my own guilt and self-pity. I wanted to run from the house, to escape. My mind went over various fantasies about living on the road, or running to my sister, begging my brother for a place at court. But in each of these cases I would have to, at some time, explain why I could not live with Katherine.

I bowed my head over my lessons and tried to study the words of wise others, who would never have fallen into such disgrace as I had here.

And then, finally, after more than a week of silent shame, I had a message that I was to go and see Katherine.

I walked to her chambers, hearing every bounce my heart made and every shaking breath I took. Had I thought I wanted this over and done with? I was wrong. I wanted to turn back. I did not want to face her. I did not want to face my own shame.

I stood at the door and I stared at it. The servant to my side took my hesitation as a command, and pounded on the door with an insistent fist himself. I turned to shush his hand; the last thing I wanted was to enter with a pernicious air of arrogance. He stared at me when my sharp words burst from my mouth, and apologised, although frowning slightly at me. Clearly he did not understand why I was so keen to appear humble before Katherine.

Katherine's voice, low and sweet, called me in and I found her standing at the window, looking away from me. The gracious room was otherwise empty. I felt a little drop in my heart. Uncomfortable as it might have been, I had wanted to see Thomas. I bowed to her.

She turned to me and inclined her head. "Sit, if you wish to," she said indicating to the floor cushions. I shook my head and stood. I did not want to feel any lower than I already did.

"As you wish," she said, looking back at the window where she stood. Her voice was calm and soft, reasoned and… dull. I almost wished that she was raging with anger; I did not really know what to do with this lifeless voice that came from my usually lively stepmother.

"My lady…" I started to say, but she held up her hand. She was looking straight ahead of her, out of the window, rather than at me. Could she not bring herself to look at me? I flushed crimson as I stood not knowing what to say. Words usually came so easily to me, but not on this day.

"My Lady Princess," she said slowly. "I have loved many people in my life. God has been good enough to me to give me husbands whom I have loved dutifully for their goodness to me. They have given me children, not of my own blood, but dear to my heart nonetheless, and I have striven in all ways to become a good and loving mother to those children I was chosen by God to care for. When I accepted Lord Seymour's offer of marriage I thought that I was accepting something that had been my reward for many years of loving those who were given to me by duty, but whom I had not *chosen* to love."

She stopped and ran a hand over her huge belly. "Perhaps I was sinful in that respect; I should have accepted that this was another love that *was* chosen for me, and as such, perhaps I have received punishment here for my arrogance in presuming I understood the will and the want of God."

Sadly, she stroked her belly. Her son, her *little knave* as she called him, was well-grown under her skin, close now to the time when he should emerge. This should have been the happiest time of her life. The reason that it was not, was because of me. I said nothing. I did not know what to say. Being lost for words was an unsettling experience.

"When I felt my son quicken under my heart, I thought this too was reward for a life of service done to the will of God," she said. "But I should not have presumed again. Perhaps this was just the course of my life and God was not showing me special favour with this marriage any more than he was with the others. For my husbands loved me as I loved Lord Seymour, so what is so different in any of these cases to differentiate them from one another? Nothing. It was my own arrogance that allowed me to think this marriage was special not only in my eyes, but in the eyes of God. I should not have assumed that I was being looked upon by God with a special eye or favour. We are all sinners in his eyes, and we should remember that in the hours of both our pain and our pleasure. "

She sighed and turned around to me. Her face looked older, much older than it ever had done before. It is strange how unhappiness can make a person seem to age so easily. Joy causes youthful bearing in a body, but sorrow causes us to grow old. Her skin was grey and her eyes were dark with shadows. She looked as though she was sleeping little. That merry mouth, usually so playfully curved in a smile, was as straight as the horizon, and her demeanour was as distant. Her lovely grey eyes looked like two little lights shining doubtfully in thick sea mists. Her manner was sad, dignified and restrained.

It would have been better if she had raged and shouted. I felt worse and worse.

"My lady..." I said, trying to push some words from my mouth. "I never meant for anything to happen."

She held up her hand again. "Nothing *did* happen Elizabeth" she said sternly. "You would do well to remember that *truth. Nothing happened.* That is what you should say if anyone enquires or dares to ask. But I would also here give you some words of advice for the future. Men are adventurous. They long to explore, to hunt, to discover the foreign shore. If they do not do this on sea then they will do so on shore and it does not have to be a new sight that attracts them, sometimes it just has to be a new *adventure,* in whatever shape it may come. Do not become a mere *conquest* for the desires of men; for anything of that sort, if not accompanied by lawful marriage, will ruin the reputation of a woman, and in a princess, that reputation is all important. The people of a country serve the crown, but the crown also serves the people. If they lose faith in your moral abilities, then you will never be a valued leader in their eyes. If you allow yourself to become a subject of slander and gossip, then you will never be respected. "

She paused and walked to the fireplace; her hands reaching out to stroke the marble slowly, sadly.

"It is especially important for *you* to remember this, as the charges put against your mother, which brought her to her death, are the first things that most people are likely to know about you. However unfair it may be that we are judged by the reputation of our parents, it is the sad truth of the world. Even if you and I do not believe ill of your mother, you must understand that others *will* judge you based on your association with her. Being the daughter of a woman executed for adultery, incest and treason, it is of even greater importance for you to appear before the people as a *model* of morality and goodness. You have less room for mistake and human frailty than any other person. You had much better seek *in all your actions* to remind others of who your *father* was; for in that comparison they will have no censure for you."

There was a silence. Anger bubbled within me; I liked not the manner in which she talked of my mother. Had I been calm, I would have heard that she was trying to tell me this is what *others* would judge me for, rather than hearing that this was how she judged me.

"It seemed as though you approved of his play with me," I said, my bottom lip protruding like a sullen child. "You joined in often enough!"

She looked around. In the firelight that danced over her face, I saw tears shining in her darkened eyes.

"I believed that those I loved were above reproach," she said with a catch in her voice. "I believed in their innocence. I was wrong."

She turned back to the fire.

"I am sending you to Cheshunt," she said. "You will live with Sir Anthony Denny and his wife, Joan, your governess' sister, for a while. Soon I will have to go into confinement for the birth of my son, and you would not see me a great deal anyway."

"I could attend on you… " I said.

She shook her head and looked at me sadly. "I do not think so. Before, I would have been honoured. Now…." she trailed off, wiping at her eyes and turning her face from me.

"My Lady… Katherine… your Highness… I am so *sorry* for the hurt I have caused you!" I said desperately, tears bursting out from my eyes. All my sullenness was gone and all I wanted was for this lovely woman, this friend, to turn and take me in her arms and tell me all was well.

I wanted my mother back.

She sighed, and made no move towards me. "I am sure that is true, Elizabeth," she said. "Sometimes you seem so much older than you truly are, and sometimes it is easy to treat you as an adult where in truth you are still a child."

My arms dropped to my sides. Tears ran down my cheeks and onto my crimson dress. I did not seek to wipe them with my fingers. I just let them fall as I sobbed.

"You will take Mistress Astley and her husband, your accounts officer Parry, your household, and any servants you need," she said after a pause. "You will maintain written contact with me as your guardian, but you will not visit this house unless you are expressly invited by myself." She looked up and straightened herself. "I cannot command you to have no contact with my husband, should he initiate it, but I would ask you, for any thread of the love that you once professed to bear for me, that *you* will not try to contact my husband once you have left. I want to trust you, Elizabeth, but I do not know how to unless you adhere to these requests."

I nodded dumbly at her.

Satisfied, she nodded. "We will say that you are gone as the rigours of my childbed are too much for one so young. Jane also will not be attending me and I will have my own ladies, such as Lady Tyrwhitt and the court doctors to attend me instead." She looked at me and gave a small, tight smile. "Perhaps after the birth of my son, we will be able to see what arrangements can be done for the future."

I nodded. Tears were still flowing freely from my eyes and I wiped them with my sleeve. Katherine stepped forward and handed me a cloth with the very edges of her fingers, as though I was a leper. I slowly wiped my eyes and nose with it.

"Go now, and prepare for your departure," she said. "And when you get to your chambers tell Mistress Astley that I wish to have a word with her before you depart for her sister's husband's house." She paused. "If I should hear that anything is said of you, Elizabeth, in this matter or any other, then I shall send warning of it to you, so that you might defend your reputation. I myself will say nothing of what has occurred here and I will impress on my husband to do the same."

I nodded, curtseyed awkwardly, and then turned and fled.

Arriving back in my rooms and throwing myself on my bed, I fell into a torrent of weeping. Kat went to Katherine, and came back grim-faced. She set about packing for us with the other servants in silence and anger.

I lay on my bed and cried until it was time to sleep, and then I sat at my window and stared out at the moonlit gardens. Kat was already abed on a pallet on the floor. She did not, it seemed, wish to share covers with me that night.

I was being sent from this house in disgrace. I was being sent away from the woman whom I had loved as a mother and the man I had fallen in love with.

As I watched the moonlight trip over the manicured hedges and herbs, I saw on the far side of the park a shape moving in the undergrowth. As the shape moved closer, I saw the outline of tawny red as a little vixen came into view. Her crimson coat glinted in the silver moonlight, her black nose sniffed at the air, sensing if there was danger ahead. Quietly and quickly she moved, pausing here and there to sniff once again and to feel any hazard that moved ahead of her.

As she slunk away through the undergrowth, I thought of the cautious vixen, and her wily way of moving without being discovered. She was master of her own little space, without need for any other to protect or restrict her. She was free within her world, free because she was careful and cautious. I must be careful and cautious. I was not a child anymore, and I was, in truth, as alone and as vulnerable as that midnight traveller skulking through the undergrowth in the pale moonlight. I must learn to sniff out danger before I saw it, too.

CHAPTER 37
SUMMER, 1548

By the time we reached the house of Sir Anthony Denny at Cheshunt, I was low in both mind and body. The guilt that lay on my heart had so crushed the spirit in me that my body seemed to take up its sorrow. I become ill.

I took to my bed almost immediately upon entering the house, and I allowed no one but Kat to come and tend to me in my chambers. A chill and a fever was enough for my new guardians to bring a doctor to me, and I swallowed his bitter potions along with the acid taste of my own disloyalty to those who had loved me.

I was brought low; entirely humbled by the recognition of the wrongness of my actions. Removed from Thomas, I could not now even recall why his face had been so pleasing to my eyes, nor why his attention was worth the loss of a friend and mother.

I wrote to Katherine, my letter humbled and asking for the continuance of our friendship even though I knew I had done little to deserve that from such a lady as she.

"I am replete with sorrow to depart from you highness," I wrote from my bed, *"and although I answered little, I weighed it deeply when you said you would warn me of any evils that you should hear of me, for if your Grace has not a good opinion of me you would not have offered me friendship in such a way."*

I sent the letter within days of arriving at the house of Denny and his wife Joan, Kat's own sister. Kat was silent for the most part. She had lost the merry giggles and ready gossip which had so defined her nature until this time. We were, I think, both lost in the thoughts of what had happened, and what might have happened had this liaison continued with Thomas Seymour. If any had found out of the breadth of the liberties he had taken with a princess of the realm, it would not only be his head in danger of the axe. Kat, Katherine and myself could have also been placed in great danger, should the Council or my brother the King, ever come to know what had happened.

The worries that brought me to bed stole restful sleep from me and the fever replaced much-needed sleep with fragmented images of both the past and present. It warped friendly faces into those of rabid demons, and made me cry out and weep with fear of them. My father loomed in my half-sleep; his visage no longer merry and mighty, but monstrous. Through the gardens at Hever and Greenwich I ran from him, his great hands looming out of the darkness to catch me. And when he was gone, I chased a phantom of a laugh through those same gardens; running on legs that were slow and heavy as I sought to catch the green silk of a gown that was always out of reach, always slipping around another corner. The echo of my mother's laugh sounded in my ears but it was distorted, eerie, strange… and I could not catch her. She disappeared at my footfall.

For days I battled against the fever, the strength of my youth drained by the fearful images I saw. I barely drank and could not eat. My body was taken with its sickness and my mind was lost in its dreams. Until one day, the fever broke and I awoke to the grey fingers of dawn stroking my clammy skin. It was more than a week before I could rise, I was so weak and feeble; but with the end of my illness so came the revival of my guilt.

Even once the fever was gone, I kept to my rooms. I had other demons to face than just those of my fevered dreams. My face was drawn with the strain of entering the adult world for which I had been unprepared, and my skin pallid with the lack of sun. I went to my lessons and to my books, escaping the present in the words of those long dead, and far wiser than I should ever be.

I bent a dutiful and guilty head over my work, and I tried to forget the tingle of feeling when a stray remembrance of Thomas' touch entered my mind. I tried to shake him from my head. But some images and feelings are too strong to be denied. I would admit to myself that I had done wrong and sinned against my own conscience and my own sense of right. But in those memories of his whispers of love for me, in dreams where I felt his hands move over my face and my body, it felt so right, that it was almost like a sense of coming home.

But I tried to put him from my thoughts. I wanted to be good. I wanted to forget. I wanted to be forgiven above all other things. I was a child, and for all my wisdom, I had been a fool.

When I received Katherine's response to my letter, I could not help but pause before I broke her seal. I dreaded what lay beneath the cream parchment. I breathed in, and I read.

But her letter contained none of the reproofs and recrimination I had expected. The black ink spoke of love, friendship and how much she missed me. It was the warm letter of a mother to her daughter, and it spoke of nothing that should make me feel worse.

I was heartened by her tender voice, which spoke through the letter to me. It was a measure of her love for me, that this awful experience had not mitigated that love. Perhaps she could not trust me entirely, but she still loved me.

I wrote to her again and again whilst we were separated. Letters of love and loyalty, professing gratitude and affection, and they were heartfelt. During those first few months at Cheshunt, we restored the bounds of our love together using only the ink and pen, the parchment and the seal. Such is the power of words and distance, to bring two hearts back together once again.

She had been wise to send me away. In the miles between us there was enough distance to remind her of her love for me, and to take away the sourness of betrayal.

It was a surprise to me when another letter arrived, this time carrying the seal of Thomas Seymour. I quaked as I opened it in private. In his bold, thick hand he wrote to me that Katherine had asked him to write, to assure me that all was well between the two of them, and that his feelings of loyalty to me as a daughter had not wavered *"in this late season of our parting."*

I replied, answering him and thanking him for his letter, but assuring him that I was well-served where I was, and that I was glad for his coming happiness as a father. The letter I wrote was quite clear that I wanted and needed no further correspondence from him. There were two reasons for this: the first, to ease the guilt in my heart, and the second, to protect me, in case Katherine was using this as a test to see if I was truly loyal to her. I did not want to be tripped into further disgrace than I was already.

In late August, Katherine removed herself and her household to Sudeley Castle. It was late in her pregnancy to move to another house, but perhaps the memories of me with Thomas proved too much for her to endure in the latter stages of her pregnancy. In the last days of August her pains began, and after a short confinement, she gave birth not to the expected boy, but to a little girl; christened *Mary*... for my own sister. But for this turn of events, but for my betrayal of her, would her child have been named *Elizabeth?* I wondered, but I did not know for sure. Katherine made it through the trial of childbirth well enough; we were told the news of her safe delivery by letter of her steward. Thomas rushed from meetings with the Council at court to her side, to see his daughter and his wife.

But then, barely two weeks later, we had other news.

Katherine was dead.

A few days after the birth, after her safe delivery, she had taken childbed fever. She tossed and sweated in her birthing bed. She cried out that she had been evilly treated by those she loved. *"I am not well handled, for those that be about me care not for me, but stand laughing at my grief and the more good I will to them, the less good they will to me."*

She was delirious, they said, clinging to her attendant's hand and saying that those she loved only wanted her out of the way *so that they could be together.*

When I heard that, I flushed with shame all over again. Was that what Katherine had really thought? Brought low, sick unto death of childbed fever and thinking that her husband and beloved step-daughter wanted her dead so that they could be together?

The messenger said that the more Thomas tried to pacify and placate Katherine, the more she rounded on him with feverish anger and rage.

After days of being in this state, she fell into a stupor where the doctors could not calm her fever any more. She soon passed away, her body shaking with pain and roasting with the heat of her delirious blood.

Katherine Parr, wife, stepmother, mother, Queen and most learned author, was buried on the same day she died at Sudeley Castle with my little cousin Lady Jane Grey brought to be the chief mourner. Thomas Seymour shut himself up in the castle and mourned for his wife. In his way, he did love her after all, it seemed.

It was he who sent the messenger to me, with all the news of Katherine's last hours, and recriminations also. Was Thomas seeking, as I had before, to mitigate his own guilt by offering a portion to me? If so, it worked. When I heard of Katherine's death, I fell once again into sickness. It seemed that my body, only so recently recovered from the fever that had struck when I left Katherine's household, could not sustain itself against the onslaught of grief that losing her brought to me.

Death is always sudden, and it is always a shock.

CHAPTER 38
WINTER, 1548
CHESHUNT

In the weeks that followed the death of my stepmother, I was ill and kept to my chambers. Perhaps it was not the thought so much that Katherine was forever gone from this earthly world, but the thought that she had left this mortal life thinking ill of me that made me so low.

I thought, as one often does when one loses another person that made life richer, of all those I had loved and lost in this short life. My great father, my mother, my father's other wives, and now Katherine. Would time render the memories I had of Katherine, now so sharp and distinct into ones like those of my mother…. Wispy… ghostly?

Were all memories of those I had loved and lost bound to fade from my mind whilst the pain of losing them did not? It did not seem fair that we should be left with the pain of losing someone and fail to keep the image of them in our minds.

My appetite was poor after Katherine's death. Kat worried after me all the time, trying to feed me up. I succumbed to her hen-like flapping around me as a grateful child falls into the arms of a parent to sleep. I needed someone to care for me, to treat me like a child again, to defend me against the onslaught of the world. My hosts at Cheshunt, Sir Anthony Denny and his wife Joan, Kat's own sister, were kind and thoughtful to me. They did not pry into the nature of my illness, but must have seen how low I had been brought by the events of the last months. I was sure Kat would have informed them of what had passed at Chelsea; my loose-tongued governess could never be trusted to keep a secret from those she believed to be her intimates. So, within the understanding of the house at Cheshunt, I started to settle into a routine once more, and to think that perhaps with time, I could find peace within me once again.

That was, until Kat started, with unseemly haste, to question where Thomas Seymour might marry again, now that his wife was dead.

"The dowager Queen is not yet cool in her grave, Kat," I said grimly. "And yet you make plans to marry off her husband? Besides, this is and always has been; a matter for the Council and King to decide."

Kat shook her head. "The Lady Katherine would not want him to be alone," she said. "All men re-marry if their wives have left them for the arms of God. It is not unheard of.... And *now*, mistress, he is in a position to make an honourable offer for your hand. There will be no scandal attached to such a match, after all he is a great lord and you a great lady. Why should it not come to pass now? After all we have been through before... this could be the happy ending of the tale."

I shook my head and refused to enter the conversation. I knew where it was headed. Since she had recovered from the sudden shock of Katherine's death, Kat's mind had been clanking away like a little water wheel with thoughts of the future. She once had been unable to realize her desire to see me married to Thomas... Could this not be an opportunity to see it fulfilled and without the stain of adultery?

I wanted none of it. Tempting though the thought of Thomas Seymour still was, I was sickened by the loss of Katherine, saddened by the gap she left in my world. I wanted no talk of marriage to her husband, especially after all the things she had said at her deathbed about Thomas and me.

Eventually, as things spoken are wont to do, comments and musings such as Kat's spread, and servants talked. There were rumours abroad in the countryside that I had indeed had an affair with Thomas Seymour, and even, that I had been delivered of his child whilst at Cheshunt. When these things were relayed to me gently by a most reluctant and embarrassed Denny, I wrote immediately to the Lord Protector, Edward Seymour to ask that these allegations be refuted by parliament. That I be brought to court, so that all could see I was a maid who had borne no child. It was scandalous and ridiculous. I wrote with an indignant fury to him, but no such proclamation was made, and no such refutation.

Even though I felt nothing like it, I had to ride out, through the countryside and into the towns, to let people see me, to see that my maiden's waist was still thin as a whip; to bare myself to the people to show that I had borne no child to Thomas Seymour.

I was starting to learn that my actions, however private they may feel to me, were not private, and never would be, in truth.

Kat, however, would not leave the matter alone. She talked to me of Thomas as she had once before, extolling his virtues, his handsome face and his love for me. It was not long before my turn-coat heart started to listen to her instead of my own head. Kat persuaded me that whilst I could not write to Thomas, nor be seen to contact him, *she* could go and find out in truth if he was interested in my becoming his second wife.

At first I denied her this. "The Council and the King will never approve of such a match," I said. "And besides, he is in mourning for Katherine, as I am… and as *you* should be too!"

Thomas Parry, my chief accounting officer, or Master of Coin, relayed to Kat that Thomas Seymour had once more been enquiring by letter as to the lands and properties that would come to me when I became old enough to inherit them. It seemed, for Thomas Seymour, that marriage was as much a matter of business as it was romance. But Kat was only encouraged by this to believe that Thomas was in love with me still. She sent messengers to him without my permission. Some of those messages were written down which I raged at her for when she told me of them. "You should never have committed those thoughts to paper, Kat Astley!" I said, wringing my hands and looking at her with horror. "For then people will think I know of this insane proposal. They will see *me* as part of this plan!"

But when those messengers came back, I could not but help ask them of Thomas… How was he? Did he look well? What was he doing in his days?

My head was talking to me of dignity and reason, as my heart spoke to me of want, of love … and of an end to loneliness.

It was getting out of hand all over again. By Christmas 1548 there was a new rumour that seemed to have grown out of the land like a beast, roaming the country and dropping hints everywhere like pellets that I was going to be the wife of Thomas Seymour. It did not help that Thomas had not yet dismissed the ladies that made up the household of his late wife; he said they were there to take care of his ward Lady Jane Grey. But now that this rumour was abroad, everyone suspected he was keeping them in place to wait on me... when I became his wife.

And then, in the middle of January 1549, amidst all these rumours, Thomas was arrested and taken to the Tower of London, upon the orders of the King.

Charged with High Treason, and of conspiring to marry the King's sister without permission of the King, or the Council, Thomas was in peril of his life. He had got wind of the impending charges before being arrested, and he had broken into my brother's chambers determined to take Edward into his power. Perhaps he could have persuaded the King to be on his side, had he not killed Edward's favourite spaniel in the process. The valiant hound had barked, alerting guards to the intruder in the King's rooms, and Thomas had killed the little beast; hardly something that was going to endear him or his cause to Edward.

Once the guards got there, he was overcome by force, and was arrested. The King, enraged and sorrowed by the loss of his favourite hound, would hear no pleas of his uncle as they took him away.

All of this would have been enough to scare our household. We had been often in contact with Thomas' house, and to be considered affiliated in any way with one under arrest for treason was bad enough. But then, on the same morning this news arrived by messenger, a company of the King's guard arrived at Cheshunt.

They took Kat, Thomas Parry, and several other members of my household.

They took them to the Tower.

I was to be taken by armed guard to Hatfield. As Kat and Parry were led off to face the royal prison where my own mother and many others had entered and never left, Kat was in hysterical tears as they pulled her away from me. "I will say nothing," she said.

"There is *nothing to say*," I reminded her grimly as they led her off. I hoped she understood me. We were all in the greatest of dangers now. My governess, the closest members of my household and the man I loved were imprisoned in the Tower. I was under house arrest. If they could find me complicit in the plan to marry Thomas Seymour, then I and my servants were at risk of being also accused of High Treason, a charge punishable by death. My body and my marriage were the legal property of the crown, and I was not allowed to offer or promise my hand or any other part of me to a man without the consent of the Council and King.

If it was true that Thomas Seymour had plotted to marry an heir to the throne without permission, he could lose his head. If they could find any of us complicit in this plotting, then Kat, and Parry, and I were in danger too.

As I mounted my horse to leave, Anthony Denny came softly to my side and pressed his hand in mine. "Say nothing more than what you have to," he said gently. "Remain true to the fact that you authorised nothing, and agreed to nothing. Stay strong my lady, that is your best defence." I nodded to him and squeezed his fingers gratefully, feeling little surprise that he knew my affairs so well. I hoped Kat would guard her tongue better within the prison they took her to now, than she had when she was at liberty with me.

"You have been a good friend to me, Sir Anthony, in this time of sadness and trial," I said. "It will not be forgotten."

We rode out that day.

Sir Roger Tyrwhitt, officially my escort and guide, unofficially my investigator, took me to Hatfield. He had served in the household of Katherine Parr as her Master of Horse; his wife had been one of Katherine's chamber ladies during the time I was living there. I was well aware that he and his wife, like the others in that household, would have heard all the rumours there were to tell of me.

As Hatfield loomed before me I looked on it for the first time not as the house of my childhood, or a place of safety, but as a jail.

I was a prisoner.

CHAPTER 39
HATFIELD HOUSE, 1549

I was so afraid.

Hatfield was a familiar house, I had spent most of my childhood divided between here and Eltham Palace, but it had never felt more unfamiliar and strange as when I was brought to it under armed guard. I was not a princess, I was a prisoner first and foremost, and that was on everyone's mind as they saw me.

I stuck my pale chin in the air and held my head up high. I faced all the glances and glares with all the courage I could muster.

I had done nothing wrong. I had not agreed to marriage with Thomas Seymour. I had taken no vows, made no promises. I had refused to consider the idea when it was set to me. I had said all along that the Council would not approve of the match. But in my heart, I feared deeply what my beloved Kat might say when scared and alone at the Tower. I feared too what my slack-tongued governess may have said to Parry, which might allow him to incriminate me as well.

They had separated us to strike fear into us this I knew. To weaken the courage within us that might have been bolder if we were together. Together, Kat and I would have stood more of a chance at standing un-quailed before them. Removed from me and taken to the Tower, a place that held fears for all in this land after my father's reign, would be enough, they hoped, to quell her into submission and to incriminate Thomas Seymour... and possibly me.

I hoped I was wrong.

The only member of my household they allowed to stay with me was my old bedroom and riding attendant Blanche Parry. I don't know why she alone was allowed to remain with me, but it was of some comfort to have her there.

Tyrwhitt questioned me. What was the nature of the relationship between Thomas Seymour and me? What was the reason I was sent from Katherine's house? Was it true that Thomas had visited me in secret when I was at Cheshunt? Had marriage ever been discussed or offered between us? Had Kat ever passed messages between Thomas Seymour and me, before or after Katherine's death?

They were endless... The questions went on for hours and they went in circles. When I had answered one, another would come up and then after four, the same one would come in again. He was trying to trip me up. Confuse me into saying something incriminating against Thomas, or against myself. I was still unsure which of us they were really after. But with the Lord Protector Edward holding the strings of power over the Council, I felt fairly sure they wanted Thomas. Perhaps this last, rash, bold move to invade the King's apartments had convinced them that he was too much of a liability to leave alive.

After all, he had jumped in and married the Dowager Queen without permission. Was he now seeking a claim to the throne, through marriage to me? This would not be something his ambitious brother would want to see occur. Even amidst the overwhelming feelings I had for Thomas, I too had wondered if it was me he truly wanted, or my titles. These men clearly thought only the latter.

I stood firm. In those rooms where I sat pounded by Tyrwhitt's questions I found strength by staring at the wall just past his ear and imagining what my father would do when so confronted. I remembered too the calm and collected advice of Anthony Denny. I spoke out loudly and coolly; I was innocent of all they accused me of. Kat had not spoken to me of marriage to Thomas Seymour. It was well known that I was too young for such a state and that my person was the property of the country and the King. I spoke of my love for my brother and tried to impress on Tyrwhitt that none could understand love as we Tudors could, for loyalty, for family and for the crown.

"My brother is the sole owner and commander of my person," I said. "In all ways as he is my King and my kinsman, this is as right, and I have never overstepped the bounds of loyalty to him."

I stood up to his questioning with courage and spirit, but I knew nothing of what was happening to Kat, Parry or Thomas within the Tower. Were they singing the same song as I?

Later, I was told that Kat had been moved to the darkest and most uncomfortable cell they could find in the Tower. It was enough to make her suffer, but not enough to make her talk. She refused to speak against me, even though she was wet, cold, hungry and left in the dark for days. But she refused to speak against me.

It could not last. Everyone has their own breaking point.

They beat Parry, they threw him around his cell, they deprived him of sleep and of food and after a month of constant abuse, it was enough to soften his tongue.

Kat had confided enough in my senior household members when we had all been at liberty and this had all been a game. So Parry knew enough of what had gone on at Katherine's house, and of Kat's ideas and ambitions for me and Thomas, to give them a rich and tasty story. He told them all he knew, including that Thomas Seymour had enquired about my property several times… but there were more damning stories to tell than just that… The bedrooms romps, the incident of the dress in the gardens, the blushes, the dances… and the final awful tale that Kat had told him, unbeknown to me, that Katherine had found me in Thomas' arms, and had sent me from her house for it. When they confronted Kat with Parry's confession, she broke down and although she cursed him, she did the same.

The first I knew of this was when Tyrwhitt came to me with a look of triumph on his smug face as he sat down before me. I crossed my hands in front of me, ready for another barrage of the same questions, and he informed me that both Kat and Parry had betrayed me, and had told *all* to those questioning them.

I looked at him steadily, though my heart shook within me at his words. "Since there is *nothing* to betray," I said coolly, "I would think that you say this in order to bring forth some lie you think I hold. But I hold none."

He laughed. "You are as full of lies as *Jezebel*!" he said. "And as brazen! It is time to confess. You have been betrayed now by your own servants; things will go easier for you if you speak."

I pushed my chin up and eyed him again. He held out a paper to me. I took it and read Kat's confession which had followed on that of Parry. I blushed when I read of the encounters between Thomas Seymour and me and I looked up into the smug face of my interrogator who was almost dancing with glee.

"I will neither refute nor confirm anything written in this report," I said holding it out to him and rising to stand as though I were at court. "For I believe this *confession* as you call it has been drawn from the mouths of two frightened and abused servants, who never otherwise would have stated such salacious words against a beloved mistress." I paused, feeling my thoughts and my heart race.

"I will tell you that I talked with the Lord Admiral, Thomas Seymour, sometimes, and that when his wife, my honourable stepmother the Lady Katherine Parr died, my governess did mention the idea of marrying the Lord Admiral to me, to which I said that nothing of the sort could be suggested *without the approval of the King and the Council.* That is all I have to say on this sordid matter, in which my own reputation has been so laid out for all to abuse that I can scarce believe this is the land that my own father once ruled and made a Godly kingdom. Were he alive today, he should never have stood to see his daughter treated with such contempt."

Tyrwhitt did not believe me, but despite the confession and betrayal of Kat and Parry, I stuck to my own words. They would get nothing more from me.

It was the inclusion of my insistence that nothing could be done on a matter of marriage without the approval of the King and Council that saved me. Thank God for my own mouth! Kat and Parry's confessions both agreed that I had repeatedly said this, and no matter now far our other versions differed, this fact remained true.

However improper they chose to believe my relationship with Thomas had been, I had refused to consider the idea of marriage without consent of the King and Council, and therefore I had not committed treason.

Kat was dragged in front of the Council itself and roundly shouted at and abused for her part in all this: for not protecting my reputation as she should have done; for encouraging a young girl and older man in a fantasy that meant treason in the outside world. She was stripped of her position as my governess. Lady Tyrwhitt, an awful woman, as humourless and colourless as a dead fish, was appointed as my governess.

When I heard of this I took to my chamber weeping… for Kat to be removed, for my last and greatest friend to be taken from me was awful punishment. It also meant that the Council and there-fore everyone else, believed the very worst of my conduct. Despite my own protestations of innocence, they all thought me a whorish harpy.

Roger Tyrwhitt was horrified that I should be so upset at losing someone whom he thought had been a terrible influence on me. I said to him, "if Mistress Astley is removed from my service then all will believe me culpable of all the ills that have been put on me in this matter, and I say to you that I am not! I will accept no other mistress but my own governess Katherine Astley!"

It did little good. I had no real power here and now; no power to command or chose my own servants or order my own life. Kat was lost to me, at least for now. I was a prisoner in a house guarded by a cold fish and her horrible husband, and I was branded a traitor and a slattern to the outside world.

In March the two Tyrwhitts came to me to tell me that Thomas Seymour had been found guilty of treason; guilty of trying to marry me against the knowledge of the Council, of interfering with my person, and of trying to take the King into his own power by force. All of these actions were judged as High Treason.

He was executed at the Tower of London one cold morning. His own brother, Edward Seymour, and the King, his little nephew, signed the death warrant.

The Tyrwhitts watched me carefully as they told me the news, still eager to report my words and anything else incriminating to their masters. I listened to them tell me that the first man I had fallen in love with was dead, that his handsome head was cleaved from his body… that another person I had known and loved was lost from my life.

I breathed in and looked up at them, my face still and my voice calm.

I said, "on this day died a man of much wit, and very little judgement." Then I excused myself, rose, and left the room.

My tears would be saved for the saving grace of the night, not to be crowed over by the servants of my enemies.

CHAPTER 40
HATFIELD HOUSE, 1549

I hated Lady Tyrwhitt.

Even if the woman had been a loving and warm person, learned in the ways of books and history, I would have disliked her. Replacing my dearest Kat was not something that anyone could do, but Lady Tyrwhitt was just horrid.

She was everything I hated in a person; she was dull, stupid, without wit or understanding... but thought she knew everything. She thought that her limited and stunted understanding of the Bible and all matters spiritual were without question, that her moral compass, as cold and unfeeling as it was, was righteous, and that her word was law.

She was rigid and unmoving on all matters. She hated discussion and seemed to like only the Bible. Whatever affection I had for that good book aside, I felt this was rather limiting in life.

She was in all ways the polar opposite of a woman like Katherine Parr. Both Tyrwhitt and Parr were of the new religion, both were pious; but there the similarity ended. Tyrwhitt was cold, dead and flat where Katherine had been warm, gracious and lively. Tyrwhitt was solemn, forever atoning for some sin or another, whereas Katherine had understood that God loves us and does not call for us to suffer every day in order to understand his greatness.

It is a great sadness of this life that those who are dull of wit and understanding are sure enough of themselves to be confident in their beliefs, whereas those who are intelligent and wise know only too well that they can never know everything. Trust better the wise person who tells you that something is complicated, than the fool who says it is simple.

Kat was taken from me, Katherine was dead. I was in the custody of these dull-witted, puritanical fools, and I was alone. Blanche Parry was the only friend left to me in this household where I felt constantly spied upon. I asked Blanche to teach me Welsh, so that we might converse in secret without the Tyrwhitts understanding.

And… Thomas Seymour was dead. They had taken that handsome head and cleaved it from his body.

My life was in ruins. I had nothing left to me but my own self, and the chin that I had to keep raised high against the Tyrwhitts and their constant, nagging presence.

If I ever again achieved my liberty, I swore to myself that I should never treat it as childishly nor as lightly as I had done before. Just being able to order my own day became a struggle against the tyranny of the Tyrwhitts who wanted to control every aspect of my life. Punishment for my sins, they seemed to think, although I had been convicted of naught.

But perhaps I had them to thank for some things, at least. The grief that swallowed my heart when I was told of Thomas' execution was mitigated by my constant annoyance at the Tyrwhitts. Fighting against them for everyday privileges took my mind from the sudden death of my first obsession, my first love. And after all, the dead have no need for the living to fear for them, they are in the hands of God. It is the living who have greater cause to fear for each other.

I spent a lot of time worried for Kat and Parry, for the other members of my household who were still locked in the Tower. What were they doing? Were they treated well? Were they eating? Did they blame themselves for betraying me? Did they think I loved them not? I hoped not. For all their flaws and betrayals, I loved my servants dearly and Kat was the greatest and longest-standing friend I had ever had. Parry had betrayed me, Kat had betrayed me, but how could I blame them for that when I thought of all they had been put through on my account? I wanted them to know that I was not angered at them, that I loved them still... that I missed them.

It was worries like this, and everyday battles to be treated with the respect due to a princess that enabled me to put Thomas Seymour and all my confused feelings for him to the back of my mind. When I thought of him, my heart felt weighted and heavy, so I tried not to think on him. He was lost to me now as so many others had been before him.

I hoped he had found Katherine in God's kingdom, and that together, there, they should have happiness.

Lady Tyrwhitt was always calm, always cool and always spoke in a monotone. She was a religious obsessive, given to the trend of puritanical Protestantism that was starting to take hold in Edward's reign. There were many advocates of the severe and joyless in the realm now. But it was too extreme, too fanatical for my blood. I did not hold that God would not have wanted us to laugh, or dance.

"Not *all* those things are creations of the devil," I said when she informed me that dancing was the work of Lucifer. "Who are *you* to say you know the truth of God? Is not that great arrogance? To presume you know the heart and will of the Lord alone?"

She eyed me coldly. I think that her extreme brand of religion may have been one reason she was given as my new governess in the first place, perhaps to teach me a more reserved manner of seeing the world than my dear Kat was prone to.

"None of us can know God's mind," she said in her dull mono-tone. "But we can seek His truth for our betterment, and it is easier to seek when one looks *in* the Bible, rather than throwing oneself around a floor like a whirling fool."

I grumbled. She did not allow dancing, or music, and I loved both. She *did* allow me to ride out with Blanche as company though, and so I fled the house as often as I could; escaping the confine-ment and the tedium, the constant lectures on life and God in the free and open air of the parks, riding hard across the moist earth and breathing in the cold air of the late Spring.

I was a captive still… but this would not be the last time, nor the closest I ever came to danger.

CHAPTER 41
HATFIELD HOUSE, 1549

I wrote to Edward Seymour, Duke of Somerset, Lord Protector, and the Council, on the matter of Kat and Parry and my other servants. Still prisoners in the Tower, they weighed heavily on my mind.

It was an important letter; I worried for them a lot. Worried about the conditions in which they were kept, how they were, how they looked, how they were treated. My Kat was not good at looking after herself in many ways. I feared for them.

Edward Seymour had finally issued a proclamation of my innocence in the affair with Thomas Seymour, and although I knew this would not convince everyone in the country, it made me happier to see it made public. I did not want the common people thinking I was a vulgar stave. I knew that the rumours about Thomas and me had damaged my reputation in some minds, but I was determined to alter that once more. I did not like to think that the people of England should think badly of me.

But that matter could wait a little. For now, I had my friends to think on.

I started my letter to the Lord Protector by thanking him for his proclamation, and then I turned to the matter of my servants. I acknowledged that Kat and Parry had been at fault; they had erred in their duties of care to me, but I asked the Lord Protector to consider the pains that Kat had taken to bring me up with honesty and learning. I pointed out that Kat would have thought that any undertaking Thomas Seymour had planned with regards to me would have been taken to the Council *by him*, for he had been a member of the Council, albeit a rather transitory one. And as a gentleman a-wooing a lady, the office and responsibility to approach the Council would have been *his* to do, not that of a governess. Kat therefore, had erred, but she had been fooled by the actions of a man we all now knew to be guilty of treason, and who had endangered the life of the King. I pointed out that other people too, had been fooled by Thomas Seymour.

My first love became my first scapegoat. But there was nothing I could do for Thomas now… and there were things I could do for my living friends.

I further expressed in the letter that continuing to detain members, or ex-members, of my household in the Tower would mean that the common people would continue to see me as complicit in this scandal, whereas the Lord Protector, the King and the Council had proclaimed my innocence and restored my reputation.

Keeping my servants as captives was not conducive to the restoration of my character.

It was not a letter written lightly, for it put me at risk again. The stains on my reputation had only just been scrubbed clean by the Council's proclamation, and the scandal was still close enough to tarnish my name. But I could not leave my servants imprisoned in the Tower without friend or hope of freedom.

It was never in my nature to abandon a friend.

I went over the letter again and again, writing and revising and re-writing until I was sure it hit the right notes. Then I sent it, and held my breath.

My gamble paid off. Luckily the Lord Protector Somerset and the Council agreed that the continued incarceration of my servants could be seen as proof of my guilt in the Seymour affair. All they had really wanted was the troublesome head of Thomas Seymour removed from his bothersome body; they were not, as a whole at least, after my removal from either my position or my life, although I do not hesitate to believe that some of them would have sacrificed me quite happily, if Thomas' death had depended on it.

As it was, Thomas Seymour was dead and they were quite happy to be seen now as gracious and generous to the Princess who had been abused by such a man as he. Their own safety in their positions made them magnanimous to me. The Council released my servants as further proof to the people of my innocence. They were not allowed back into my service, and we were not allowed to meet, as it seemed the Council and my brother still thought them bad influences on my person. But they were free, and they were not left rotting in the terrible place where my own mother had died.

I breathed easier after their release. I found more peace within me… became calmer. I continued riding. I read, I learned lessons with Ascham who was allowed to tutor me under the guidance of the Tyrwhitts… and I thought much on the lessons I had learnt outside of my books in the past year.

For a while they brought my young cousin to keep me company, Lady Catherine Carey was the daughter of Henry Carey, who was the son of my mother's sister, Mary Boleyn. Some whispered that Henry Carey was in fact the son of Mary Boleyn and my own father the King, which would make him both my cousin and my half-brother. The similarity between the features of my father and Henry Carey were quite striking, and Mary had indeed been the mistress of my father, before he set eyes on my own mother, so it was possible. But Henry Carey had never been acknowledged by my father as being his son. I would never know if he was in fact my half-brother.

As it was, in law, Catherine was my cousin, but in reality she may very well have been my niece *and* cousin. Such are the complications of life at times.

To me it mattered not. She was blood of my blood whichever way you looked at it, and there are times in life when connections made through the veins of one person to another, are the most important.

She was young and sweet and I was thirsty for company, for some talk and song, for some giggles and friendship. She was brought to my household as a princess should have friends of an age with her who were of noble birth. She became a close friend and confidant… although I shied away from revealing anything of the scandal that had passed.

I had learnt to be cautious. Like my friend the little vixen in the dark night.

Our time passed in peace. Blanche taught me more Welsh and my tongue stopped tripping over the words she spoke to me, and started to lilt with their turn and inflection, but I stopped trying to talk in code near the Tyrwhitts.

Perhaps it was just that I learned to know them better, or that they came to believe in the proclamation of my innocence, but they started to soften towards me a little. Neither of them laughed much; they thought jokes and plays, music and dancing were frivolous things and did not approve of them. Whilst I liked this not, I started to remember the joys of merely reading and being alone with my own thoughts without interruption. Perhaps they brought me back to a sense of gravity and dignity that I had been lacking in my education under Kat.

I even started to understand Lady Tyrwhitt, and although I could never take on her joyless version of religion, I did like one stock phrase she used over and over at me. That it was of benefit to *"be always one…"* I translated this into Latin - *"semper eadem"* – it was the same phrase used in my mother's precious books, given to me by Katherine Parr. The phrase grew on me, perhaps for both connections to my life which it now had, and I liked it so much, that I adopted it as my own personal motto.

Where men and seasons change, where people die, betray and leave, it is of value not to waver from the truth of your own soul, and never to betray the values that you hold dear.

With the Seymour scandal I had allowed my heart to rule my head; it should never happen again. That, I swore to myself.

Semper eadem meant that one should be the master of one's own emotions, no matter what life presented you, or challenged you with.

In the house of my own body, I should be the only master.

CHAPTER 42
HATFIELD HOUSE, 1549

M y days at Hatfield became routine. I would rise early, take some small exercise in the gardens, or the long halls and gallery if it was raining, then settle into hours of studies with Roger Ascham, who was restored to me. Kat and Parry were still not allowed to visit or communicate with me, but there was a slow trickle of my old servants wending their way back to my service, somewhat secretly as I doubt the Council would have approved. Loyalty and love from servants are telling of the spirit of a master. I regarded my household as being my friends as much as they were my servants and the love I showed them was returned to me threefold in the loyalty they showed me at this time and others. True loyalty is not something that can be bought; it is only something that can be given.

Ascham was good for me too, showing me the peace that could come with diligent study. We started our lessons with translations and discussions on the New Testament in Greek, followed by orations of Isocrates or the tragedies of Sophocles and devoted the afternoons to Cicero, Livy or to learning modern languages. By this time in my life I could speak English, Italian and French all as though they were my first language,

and Latin with some degree of fluency. I could read and translate Greek and was learning Welsh and Spanish. In the late afternoon, there would be time for musical studies, or practise in
handwriting which I found took my mind into a place of great
artistic beauty and concentration.

On good days I would ride out with Blanche, wither to hunt, or
just to feel the fresh air rushing over my face and body. We would
stop to talk to the common people we encountered along the way,
and to take whatever gifts of apples, cakes, cider, or flowers that
they or their children offered to us.

The more of the common men and women I met, the more I
loved them. I was convinced at an early age that England has the
best of all peoples in her borders. A race who rise early to make the
best of all they have, work hard for all their pleasures and survival,
and fall into bed, worn and tired from their days in the field or at
the plough. I knew their lives were not easy, and yet whenever I saw
them they offered me their wares and their hearts. I loved to be
with them, away from the confusions of my own life.

I remembered how my father would play cards late into the
night with the workmen who built his most beautiful palaces, how
he had reached his arm about both noble and common shoulders
alike and engendered their friendship. I too wanted to nurture a
relationship with the people, so that they could see that the spirit
of my great father lived on within my own blood. Perhaps I wanted
to honour his memory; perhaps I wanted them to say I was like
him. But whatever the reason, I longed for the love of the people
of England.

During those months of incarceration and despair I had
found inside myself a new strength, and a new awareness. The
affair with Thomas had been the last vestige of the child in me;

a young girl led into betraying those she loved, by the foolish desires and inclinations of her own traitorous heart. I had been tempted and I had fallen. I had been tested and failed. It would not happen again.

As I stepped aside from my first love and looked back at it, I was ridden with guilt for the pains I had caused my good stepmother, who now lay in the arms of God. I mused on the actions I had taken during that time and felt ashamed of myself for having so betrayed all that I held dear. I hoped that surely, in the depth of punishment that I received in this matter, the separation from my beloved Kat; the arrest and abuse of my servants; the deaths of Thomas and Katherine; the forced incarceration with the Tyrwhitts; the damage done to my own name…surely, in those punishments was the hand of God trying to show me what my own selfish desires and actions had led to for myself, and for others.

I had sinned, and I had been punished. God had taught me valuable lessons in this matter and I would not forget them.

But still, despite this reasoning within me, I mourned for Thomas; when I thought of that handsome head lying on the block, it made my stomach churn and my head hurt. But though I mourned for his death, I could not excuse our actions taken together, to act on desire of the body and to forget all other loyalties and duties because of that desire.

After the first few months with the Tyrwhitts, after I had got used to the indomitable Lady and the stoic Sir, I started to appreciate some of the unchanging stability they were offering to my life. Perhaps after all the rush and confusion I had felt whilst held in the arms of desire, this was the tonic I needed to recover myself. Even so though, I missed Kat desperately, I thought of her often since we were not allowed to write or visit. I hoped that she was also taking time to ponder on her own sins for this affair, and to make peace with them, as I sought to.

Over time, I found comfort in my religious studies and in the Protestant state that my brother was creating in England; I started to lean towards the simple and un-glorified. I dressed plainly. Although my dresses were still of the best materials, I wore simple colours, garbing myself in black and white and leaving behind the adornments of rings or necklaces that had previously covered my necks, fingers and wrists. I wanted to show that I was no longer the same frivolous person I had been when Thomas Seymour chased me screaming around the bedchamber. I wanted people to know that I had learned and changed for although I had been exonerated by the King and Council, I knew there were still plenty within this world who doubted my innocence.

It is ever the practise of the young adult to try to show inward character through outward clothing. I was no exception.

Eventually, I started to be invited to court, sparingly at first, and only on formal occasions when seeing my younger brother; and then, as the Council and the King found that they approved of the 'new Elizabeth' in plain Protestant styles, I was invited to court more frequently. Although the start of 1549 had been disastrous, as the months wore on towards my sixteenth birthday, I started to breathe more easily.

It was rare that Edward and I were free to act as true brother and sister together. He was the King, and he took all his duties with the utmost of seriousness. We were little left alone and our conversation was often formal and serious. I worried for him at times as the strain of so much responsibility and power at such a young age did seem to take a toll on his strength. He was pale and thin in body, and often distracted and thoughtful in his mind. But Edward had always taken his position most earnestly; it was not in his nature to abandon himself to the pursuit of pleasure over the demands of responsibility. But he responded to my gentle friendship as a flower turns its face to the light of the sun, and began to request my presence at court more and more.

His Councillors, the Lord Protector amongst them, seemed to see that my presence at his side cheered him, and they were happy in this. I was now the model of what a modest Protestant maiden should be; demure, learned and gracious in my humility to our King… the paragon of the virtues they admired. They liked me and my influence at court now a vast deal; certainly more than our sister Mary. Edward and his Council got little joy from our older sister, who by now was barely ever invited to his court.

Mary was a thorn in the side of both Edward and his Council. She was making trouble for them. The problem between my brother and sister was that Mary was much older than Edward and I, and had been raised as a Catholic. All the practises that she loved and clung to belonged to that faith and she refused to convert to Protestantism. Edward and his Council had made England fully a Protestant country, but here was the present heir to the throne not only refusing to bow to their will, but actively promoting the Catholic faith in defiance of their laws.

Mary loved the Catholic faith. I think, not only because it was the faith she was raised in, but because she associated her loyalty to that religion as synonymous with her loyalty to her long-dead and beloved mother, Katherine of Aragon. When our father had become Head of the Church, Mary had been forced, under pain of death, to proclaim that her mother's marriage to our father had been unlawful, and to revoke her loyalty to the

See of Rome. These had not been things that she would ever have abandoned lightly, and I doubt very much if she would have done so had her life not been in dire danger. When our father died, and our younger brother took his place on the throne, Mary saw no need to continue in pretence of her true feelings and loyalties. She made quite clear that she was a Catholic, loyal to Rome and she did not fear our little brother as she had done our father.

Her refusal to convert her religion was bad enough, but her household also encouraged Catholics to flock to it, making it a base for dissent against the King and his Council. Not everyone in England was ready or willing to convert from Catholicism to Protestantism. Mary was making herself a dangerous enemy to the peace of England... and she did not seem to take Edward at all seriously when he threatened her.

The trappings and ceremony of the Catholic faith were all the religious practises that Edward and I had been raised to see as false, heretical and vainglorious. The Protestant religion that Edward favoured was simple, stripped of all its pretensions. It allowed one a closer, personal relationship with God. Mary may have thought that Edward was simply led by his Council in matters religious, but she was entirely wrong. Our little brother was as set in his faith as she was in hers, and he was enraged at her defiance of his will.

With the coming of Edward's reign, the religious changes brought about by our father became solidified into a fully Protestant religion for the country of England and her territories. It was only to be expected, since both Edward and I had been raised in the Protestant faith, and even under our father's time, it was clear to which side of the Christian conundrum we were being placed into.

Mary and Edward were at odds with each other. Every religious decree that he or his Council installed in England, Mary ignored. She was told not to have High Mass; she was told that her preachers should speak in the English tongue; she was told not to waste money on idols... and she ignored him and his Council totally, carrying on exactly as she wanted to.

I think that Mary had never come to see Edward as anything more than her little brother. She did not see his decrees and demands as anything more than childish tantrums.

To have his wishes and laws flouted in his own realm was unbearable to Edward. The Tudor pride ran deep within his veins, as well it might. He was our sovereign lord and his age did not make it acceptable for Mary to ignore his position. Each and every time she did ignore that position, she made herself more and more a lodestone for those who liked not the new religion or the changes in the country. She was becoming a beacon for opposition to his rule.

I commiserated with Edward on the subject of our rebellious elder sister, but what could I tell him to do? Neither Edward nor I wanted to come to an argument with our sister that would have sent her to the Tower, which is where any other noble that showed such flagrant disregard for the office of royalty would have gone.

I am sure that many of Edward's more righteous Protestant Councillors would have much approved of sending our Catholic sister to a nice dark cell in the Tower. But for now at least, Edward refused to send his sister to prison.

There was dissent forming in the country. Any change will not be approved of by all, and when you ask a man to change the method of his faith, that is not something done easily or lightly.

For those of us, like my brother and me, who were brought up understanding the Protestant faith, the answer to the battle of the Christian religions was an obvious one.

To those who had had to change their faith due to the pressure put upon them by their rulers, the lie of the land was very different.

To force a man to change the bend and set of his heart is something that every ruler should shy from. For my part, I thought that as long as my countrymen were loyal to me and never outwardly disobey my laws, I should not seek to make windows into their souls. But my brother and sister were not made of the same mettle as I; they wanted to *own* the souls of their subjects as well as their bodies, to not only have all men obey them, but also *think* the same as them.

But all men, no matter how simple or humble, no matter how educated or rich, think for *themselves*, even if they sometimes hide it well. That is the gift and the curse God gave to us all. A sovereign may have the right to make laws and tell their people how to live, but they will never be able to stop those people forming opinions themselves.

Edward was Protestant, Mary Catholic. Neither would convert and neither would yield. The people now had two opposites to choose from and two possible futures to live in. I watched as the battle lines were drawn between the heir to the throne and her brother the King. For now at least, Mary seemed to refuse to take action of all-out rebellion against her little brother and Edward would not arrest his older sister for her continued disobedience of his laws. So the fight continued in letter and missive. Angry words flew back and forth from one to the other and all of the court and country were keeping one eye on the ongoing argument between the King, and his heir.

As Edward and Mary fought with bitter words on cream parchment over who was right and who was wrong. I dressed in simple clothes and came to court to see my brother; I spent time thinking and studying. I spent time mending a heart and a soul that had known sorrow, love and destruction.

And I kept my head, down, even as I kept my ears very much open.

CHAPTER 43

1549

I t was in the latter months of 1549 that the rule of the Lord Protector, Edward Seymour, First Duke of Somerset... came to an ungainly end.

To take a life is something most grave. To take the life of a kinsman, let alone one's own brother, is something that all men should quail from.

With the execution of his younger brother, Thomas Seymour, the Protector had become deeply unpopular. Perhaps, like me, the common man admired the buccaneer in Thomas Seymour enough to distrust and hate his elder brother on whose orders that handsome, reckless man had lost his head.

No one can trust in a man who murders his own brother to advance his own ends.

But it was not just the execution of his own brother which spelled the end for the first Duke of Somerset.... Somerset was greedy; he piled his name with titles and estates, and always ensured the best pickings were kept for himself. His wife acted as though she were the Queen and people hated her for it.

It is a mistake to grasp on to more than can be ably carried, for the man who seeks to hold too much in his hands, will surely drop it all.

Incursions into Scotland, as the Council, led by Somerset, tried to force the Scots to marry their child-princess, Mary of Scots, to Edward, thereby adding Scotland to the lands held by England, brought more trouble. At first, early victories brought pride to England's people, but later incursions with the Scots seemed increasingly directionless and full conquest of that neighbouring nation became unlikely. The Scots, with their usual skill for cynical humour, called the whole process, "the rough wooing" and Mary of Scots was sent, for protection, to France where she became betrothed to the dauphin Francois. The fight to take Scotland as part of England's territories, with the hand of Mary of Scots bonded to that of Edward of England's, became a fantasy and now the little Queen of Scots was promised to our old enemy of France. The venture was classed as a failure, and Somerset was blamed for it.

Unrest had broken out already in England in 1548; small pockets of resistance to the actions of Somerset sent men piling from their houses to protest and rise up against the King and Council. War, especially when it is unsuccessful, is unpopular, and the common people had been taxed hard to pay for soldiers for the march on Scotland. Taxes are never popular especially when the people see that hard-earned money has been wasted.

In early 1549 two rebellions rose in England; one from the south and one from the north. People who were opposed not only to the war with the Scots, but also to the imposition of the

Protestant religion on their churches, started to take up arms and march on their lords and masters. The rebellions were put down, but it was clear the ruling elite were in danger from the people it governed. Everyone was looking for a scapegoat... and Somerset was the man in charge of the kingdom.

The rest of the Council and courtiers resented him already. If he had sought to share his wealth and gain more friends, it would have aided him. But some men are so blinded by their own authority that they forget the transient nature of power; the moment you think you are in control of it, is the moment you will lose it forever.

Perhaps his greatest mistake though was in trying to hold his nephew the King under his heel. Edward had come to the throne as a young boy of only nine, and the Protector's hold over him then had been strong and true, securing his own position... but Edward was growing older, now past his twelfth birthday, and tiring of being told what to do with his own kingdom.

The over-possessive father-role that Somerset was trying desperately to maintain, began to crumble under his grasping fingers.

The Council seemed to scent the King's increasing opposition to the Protector and hardened their wills against that of Somerset. Many hoped that with his removal, they would advance at court, and were eager to join in the plotting against him.

At court, there are few men who cannot be bought with the promise of power, and fewer still who will not turn to the excitement of intrigue to escape the boredom of privilege.

Finally, in October of that year, Somerset panicked and tried, much as his brother had, to hold power by holding the body of the King. He took Edward to Windsor Castle, claiming the King was in danger from his own Councillors. He brought my brother there under armed guard, but Edward refused to cooperate with Somerset any further than he had to, complaining of the dingy apartments and the cold he was suffering due to his incarceration at the hand of his uncle. The guards Somerset brought with him became nervous at the dissatisfaction of their young King, and worried on the motives of the Lord Protector... there had been another time in English history where a young King was taken prisoner by his uncle and it had not ended well. They liked not the similarity in these events. Even Somerset's own men were starting to turn against him.

The time was ripe for a change in power, and it came through the hands of one of the most politically able and personally untrustworthy men of those times. John Dudley, Earl of Warwick, emerged as the leader of the Council. Warwick was father of Robin Dudley, the charming boy I had befriended in Edward's household. The Council published details of Somerset's mismanagement of the realm, stirring up more bad feeling against him with the people of England. Volleys of guards were sent to infiltrate Windsor, and did so easily with the willing participation of Somerset's own guards within the castle. Overcome by superior force, Somerset was arrested, stripped of his position as Lord Protector and taken to the Tower of London. Accused of negligence, entering into vainglorious wars, enriching himself of the treasury of the King and doing all by his own authority rather than that of the King, Somerset wallowed deep in his own troubles within the confines of the Tower. He was not sentenced to death, as yet.

Edward was recovered and rode back into London at the head of Warwick's men and we rode out to meet him. I never saw my brother look as handsome as he did on that day riding at the head of those men, waving at the people of the city with a great smile on his face. It was as though he was finally able to become the King in truth; set free from the bonds of childhood by the able Warwick. They made fast friends, Warwick and Edward, and everyone could see that a new day was dawning for the future of England. I breathed easier to see my brother released from the hands of Somerset. I don't know if he ever really considered doing anything mortal to my brother, but I had feared as others, what a man might do in desperate times.

It was the first time in many hundreds of years that we had seen power shift without blood spilt... at least, not *right* at that time.

Warwick forged alliances to gain power, not only amongst the Council, but amongst the Catholic faction that was present in the nobility; most notably, with my sister Mary. Who knows what he promised them so that he could be taken into the arms of power? But he managed it with ease. Such is the brilliance of the Dudleys and their line; their charm and capacity for effortless lies made friends... and also made enemies with ease.

But those who charm easily, are often more dangerous than they seem.

As I retired from court for the country once more, after assuring myself my brother was well, rumours came to me... that as one man fell from power and another took the reigns, *Mary* would be made *Regent* for my brother during these last years of his youth... she could be made Queen in all but name, ruling on behalf of Edward the boy-king.

I could scarcely believe the rumour and spent many hours musing on it.

Were *these* the things that Warwick promised as he bargained his way to power as head of the Council? To replace my brother with my sister on the throne? To go against the will of our father and bring back the religion of the Catholics over our newly Protestant country?

At Hatfield we could but watch and listen. My household was almost fully restored to me, though without my beloved Kat, it would never be complete. Parry had returned to me, throwing himself unnecessarily to my feet to beg forgiveness for his betrayal of me. When he swore to serve me with loyalty for the rest of his life, I believed him. A man who can admit his faults and promise to change them, is a man worth keeping. I knew somehow that he would never let me down again.

On hearing the unsettling rumours about Mary, I called my advisors Paulet, Denny, Parry, Cecil and Ascham to talk over the events that were coming to us on whispered breath from court. They advised caution, as ever. What could we do but sit, watch and wait?

As it came out, none of the promises made under cover of secrecy were to be fulfilled. The Protestant rule was never going to submit willingly to the power of the Catholic faith and the rule of the See of Rome again. Whatever promises were made to Mary... Regency; the return of the country to the Catholic faith; or her own freedom to worship as she pleased without interference... these were not upheld.

Often the practise of those on the rise to power is to promise much and yet perform nothing when the time comes... some things never change.

That Christmas, the bonds and offices of power held neatly in his hands, Somerset removed, and Edward the King happy in his friendship, Warwick announced a continuing resolution to make the country of England a Protestant state. And in this, he had my brother's absolute approval and faith.

Edward was held within the charming gaze of Warwick, and his heart seemed entirely won by the magnetism of the Earl. Many of us Tudors were enchanted at one time or another, by the magic of the Dudley family.

Mary was discouraged from coming to court that Christmas, whilst I was sent an invitation that positively glowed with encouragement to attend. It was another sign to the Catholic factions that the Catholic faith was on the way out, and the Protestant in. With the fall of Somerset, I was given more of the inheritance my father had set out for me. Mary's had been secured on her in full soon after his death, but mine had only come in fits and starts. Now with the fall of Somerset, Warwick brought about the full weight of my inheritance on me. I was given estates, money and men into my service. Finally I was emerging from the scandal of Thomas Seymour, into the light of my titles.

My arrival in London; the goodly Protestant Princess, riding with a retinue of all my household and numbering in the hundreds, was a sign to the country of who was to be accepted in this new regime and who was not. The Catholic, the old, the scheming, wrenching power of Somerset was gone. The Protestant, the new, the goodly reign of Edward...and Warwick, was here.

It looked to my advisors as though I was being singled out to replace Mary, with all her contentious politics and religious beliefs, in the line of succession. Perhaps there was a chance that I should be named as Edward's heir; second only to the King in power in the lands of England.

I had emerged from loss and humiliation, and I was reborn to status and glory.

CHAPTER 44
CHRISTMAS, 1549

I rode into London on a bright, cold morning in December, ready to meet with my younger brother and celebrate Christmas with him. I rode at the head of hundreds of men, all garbed in Tudor colours of green and white, wearing the badges of my house and riding with their heads proud and high as we clattered along the roads of London. My long red hair streamed, unadorned and loose around my shoulders, proclaiming me to be a maiden. My gown was simply adorned in green and white and as I passed, the common people cried out to me.

"God bless you Princess Elizabeth!" they yelled and I made sure I waved to every face and met every pair of eyes I could see. I was fresh with youth with my sixteen years of age, beautiful in my joy at being restored to favour, and I waved and shouted back gaily to them.

They loved me for it.

Whenever I heard someone in that crowd comment how like my father I was, I sent them a coin by my servants as a reward. I loved to hear that I reminded them of him. They had loved him more than any other monarch had been loved. To be compared to him, was a great joy to me.

Surrounded by the fresh bright green and white of the Tudor colours, my red hair catching the sun and my pale skin lit in the glow of the winter afternoon, I looked every inch a true Tudor, the embodiment of their royalty.

That Christmas, Warwick and Edward sent forth letters to the Council and to the bishops affirming that the reformation of the English church would move forward with greater zeal that ever before. In order to show that Edward was in full support of this, indeed that it had been his decree rather than that of his ministers, the wording was "*our act and that of the whole realm*". Paulet and Denny sneaked copies of these letters to me through their growing rings of informants at court, so I was well versed in the changes that went ahead on that Christmas Day.

Christmas was quite merry in 1549; my brother was in high spirits after being brought more into his own power, the ladies I brought with me allowed there to be dancing at court, although it was not of an overly-flamboyant style, the new court being given much to seriousness under the rule of my brother. The new man of power, Warwick, was in fine form. Firm in his new positions and favour with the King, he was on fire with wit and laughter.

But I never felt fully at ease with Warwick; although he had done me good by replacing Somerset, a man I disliked as much for his greed as for the murder of his own brother, I was uneasy with his replacement. I knew that I was little more than a means to an end to him, and I preferred to trust friends and servants with my whole being. He welcomed me to court because I was supportive and loyal to my brother, but would he prove a friend if the tide of favour happened to turn once more against me? I knew not, but I suspected much.

Edward, however, was very much taken with his new head of Council. Warwick talked to him like an adult and a King, showing deference for his intelligence and his religious sensibilities. But I could see that Warwick was also an excellent manipulator, and he was working on Edward, working away little by little, so that eventually, the head of the Council, should become the voice, and perhaps the will, of the King.

Trusting in those who set out to charm us usually ends in betrayal, for why else should they need to charm but for reasons of their own?

After that Christmas at court, it was in February of 1550 that I finally came into my full inheritance.

It was vast.

Dozens of manors, houses and stretches of land slipped into my hands detailed on white parchments. Ewelme in Oxfordshire, Ashridge, Hemel Hempstead, Great Missenden, Berkhamstead, Princes Risborough, manors at Huntingdonshire, Collyweston, Uppingham, Preston, Maxey and to my delight, estates in Peterborough that made me the neighbour of my advisor Cecil. It was with ease that I could visit his family home when I would visit my estates there. But this was not the end of my list, oh no! Estates in Newbury, Dorset, Hampshire, Lincolnshire, Enfield, Somerset House followed and finally, Durham Palace in London.

There had been a time, when I was a small child, after my mother was taken to be killed on the orders of my father that my protector, Lady Bryan, had to *beg* for clothes for me from the very author of my mother's fall, Master Thomas Cromwell. I had been so overlooked then that I was not bought clothes to fit the growing body of the child I was.

Now, I was a princess in full possession of vast and substantial estates, money, men and titles.

I had emerged from my childhood in disgrace and wretchedness, a prisoner accused of treason. Now, I was the beloved sister of the King; a rich woman and a powerful woman in my own right. But the grants of land and riches held a nasty little barb in their tail; it was made clear in my grants that these lands and the wealth that came from them were entitled to me only *until* the day on which the Council and the King provided me with a suitable match and husband. When I married, the Council would choose which of those estates may be granted to my husband as my dowry, and which would return to the hands of the King.

On the day I married, I would lose all of the power and property that I had been gifted in my own right as a princess.

On the day I married, I would lose all my own power and influence, placing them into the hands of some unknown man who would have absolute command over me for the rest of my life.

On the day I married... I would have nothing that was truly my own.

CHAPTER 45
1550
LONDON

Early in the new year of 1550, soon after acquiring my inheritance, I made a deal with John Dudley, Earl of Warwick, to exchange houses.

The new rule and his new position were going smoothly and happily for Warwick, as they were for me, but there was something missing in the vast inheritance that I had; one thing I wanted more than anything else, and Warwick was in possession of it.

Hatfield.

Hatfield House was the place I had first lived in when I was a babe. Although my early memories do not contain anything I could say was firm or secure, the house brought back feelings to me; feelings that were not all good, but nonetheless were strong enough that I did not feel it should belong to any but me. I had spent time there as a child with Edward. Mary had looked after me there as a cherished and loved younger sister; I had been held as a captive there. As I said, not all the memories were good, but all were strong.

It was as close a thing as I had, to a real home.

There were reasons practical as well as sentimental for the desire for the house and estate. Hatfield was only twenty miles from London; far enough away to retreat if there was trouble, and yet close enough to be near to the seats of power when needed. It was closer to the capital than Mary's residence and so I had an advantage over her in keeping a close eye on the unfolding politics of the new reign. With the advice in my ear of Cecil, Parry, Denny, Ascham and Paulet, I was becoming aware of the need to have eyes on the centre of power at all times. I was now sixteen, in possession of my own inheritance and money, favoured by the King my brother and rising high in the popularity of the people.

But I also was much attached to the house.

I loved the gardens at Hatfield. Great, flowing, well structured gardens with a huge park for riding and escaping from worldly troubles. In all lives surrounded by the stresses of power games, being able to ride out, *almost* alone was one of life's ultimate rewards for the price of surviving each day.

So, I went to see Warwick at Richmond Palace. He had great and gracious apartments now, as the closest advisor to the King; the King's goodly right-hand, as one might say. The dejected Somerset had by now been released from imprisonment and allowed to rejoin the Council with Warwick's permission. You may think this a strange move for such a man as Warwick, to invite the man he had displaced back to a position of potential power... but however clever he was with politics, he also found a deep satisfaction in watching those he had toppled scrape for his approval. And so was it with Somerset; brought back to the Council so that Warwick could watch him lick at the heels of his boots for favour, all the time knowing that Somerset hated him. For some men, hatred is more important than love. It was so with Warwick, for he had worked his way from the shame and ignominy of his father's fall to become, almost, the most powerful man in England. Such men often revel in the disgrace of others.

Warwick's father had been an excellent servant to my grandfather, Henry VII, but when my own father came to the throne, Warwick's father had found himself without a head, on charges of treason. My father always knew how to appease the common man, and taking the head of one of the old regime that the country had grown tired and disillusioned with had been seen as an excellent and most popular start to a new reign.

Was Warwick's father really a traitor? His crimes had hardly been heinous. But it is the monarch who decides on treachery, and my father had sacrificed the head of *that* Dudley to the altar of popular belief.

This Dudley, Earl of Warwick, had worked his way up from those shameful beginnings to take on his father's repealed titles once more. I had worked my way out from under the scandal of Seymour, out from the scandal of my mother's reputation. Perhaps we had more in common than we thought. But this did not make me trust him, if anything it made me more wary of him.

Warwick seemed amused by my offer, and was happy enough to leave Hatfield in my hands. I swapped it to him for Caistor, a remote estate that I had never seen and cared nothing for, but would pay him rich dividends from its lands.

His brown eyes glinted at me, sparkling with amusement when he looked me over. He was a handsome man; all the Dudleys were. With brown eyes and dark hair, a short beard and a tall and powerful frame, he was just the kind of man able to make my heart quicken. But I had learnt, from the tutelage of Thomas Seymour, how to hide the rush of passion I might feel when I saw a man I desired. No spark of colour flooded to my cheeks when I talked property with the Earl of Warwick.

His sons were often at court, deposited into good offices that gained the family more wealth and titles. I saw Robin in the halls of court when I visited, sometimes with Edward, and that gave me much pleasure. The young Dudley was married now to a pretty little wife. But I was not interested in her... Robin was a pleasure to look on, not yet as sure and confident as his father, he still radiated appeal. So dark, with his body lithe and strong, almost, but still yet not quite a man…. Ah yes, I have to admit to you, even then I watched Robin Dudley with a quiver of excitement in my heart. He was no match for me in status, and was now married too into the bargain. But sometimes we look on things we know we cannot have perhaps with more pleasure than those we are able to get. Their very attraction somewhat enhanced by the very fact they are unattainable.

But I would no more be held in public scorn due to a man. I had learned restraint and control. I had learnt coolness and reserve. So, I looked, but I told my private thoughts to none.

Warwick and I exchanged houses and I took up my main residence at Hatfield. From this canny vantage point I would be able to keep a close eye on the factions and gossip of the court; my advisors and I should be able to take quiet leave of any problems in the capital; and I would be able to work on strengthening my relationship with my brother. With the growing discord between Mary and him over religious matters, with her defiance of his rule and beliefs, with the growing power of Warwick over the King, it was important that I was close at hand to preserve the power I presently held.

CHAPTER 46

HATFIELD HOUSE, 1550

One morning I rose early, as was my habit, with a great sense of expectation and excitement. My ladies dressed me, I washed my hands and face in water infused with herbs, I took a lozenge of mint and lemon-balm to sweeten my breath and rolled it around in my mouth.

When I was ready, I looked into my mirror and saw a young woman there of grave expression. Red hair like fire flowing from her head, dressed in simple colours of fresh white which made the pale nature of her skin and the black snap of her eyes stand out so much better than any complex cloth or gold and jewels could have nurtured.

I was taller, grown more, grown graver and more adult than when *she* had last seen me. Should she recognise her Elizabeth under all this womanly visage? Would she still see the child she held in her arms and spoke comfort to in the hours of her greatest sorrows?

Would she have changed too? Would she still be my greatest friend, the woman who raised and protected me?

Would she still be my Kat?

I went downstairs, but I could little break my fast of the night before. I was too nervous and too excited to eat. Denny and Paulet would not bother me with any further business today, for I had wanted to greet my friend as was her due.

There was no greater business in my head or my heart today, than the business of returning the heart of the house to her place.

It had been almost two years since we had been pulled apart; Kat taken to the Tower with Parry, questioned and abused. Who knew what they had done to my gentle Kat in there to make her talk against me? Two years we had been apart without being allowed to visit or see each other, without being able to write even a few words of comfort to each other. Such was the degree of her disgrace at having allowed Thomas Seymour such liberties with a princess of royal blood.

I had grown in the time we had spent apart, and not only with years. I knew well the levels of danger that her behaviour had encouraged my person into now, and I was unlikely to ever step so far into the jaws of peril willingly again, but to me, she was the woman who had raised me, cared for me, sung to me and above all things, loved me... not because I was a princess, but for my own self. She had made mistakes, as had I, but she was still the most important person in my world.

I was sixteen now, fresh faced and clear of thought. I wanted those around me whom I knew loved me and would protect me.

This was a dangerous world and loyalty counted for a great deal in my eyes. Although Kat had eventually betrayed me to her captors, I did not hold a grudge. I knew somewhere deep within my heart that she would never fail me again. I knew this because she would never have returned to my service if she thought she might be a danger to me. That was the depth of her love.

In the distance, I saw their party from the window. Parry and Jon Ashtley would be there also, riding at her side and no doubt having to remind her of my love for her. Kat was likely to be nervous coming back to my house, fearful that I would love her less. I felt my heart skip in a nervous, yet excited way as I watched the figures of my childhood household ride towards me once more. I was nervous to see her once more, anxious to assure her that my love for her was unchanged. I did not want my Kat to worry anymore.

There are some people with whom the importance of retaining a friendship is dependant upon seeing them every day, feeling their presence and hearing their voice. But true friendships, I believe, come from people who are not able to be always or forever with each other, and although the passage of time may cause them to spread apart for months, or years, when they come back together again, they are able to fall into conversation as though they had only seen each other the day before. In that ease, that acceptance and awareness of minds, therein lays true friendship.

I rushed from the house and into the courtyard as they entered it. As they climbed from their horses and started to bow to me, I ignored them, searching the crowd for the one pair of eyes I had longed to see more than any other.

And there she was. I stopped in my tracks as I saw her. Her gown was severe and black, her face had more lines and her figure was stouter, but her brown warm eyes were everything that had ever meant love to me. I saw her eyes fill with tears as she saw me. Her lips puckered with all the words she had wanted to say, had most likely practised saying, and now, was entirely unable to say.

Without ceremony I took two steps across the courtyard and threw myself crying with joy and pain into the arms of my governess and my best friend.

As the others around us dropped down, bowing to me as their princess and liege lord, I grasped the form of Kat Astley with all the strength in my long-fingered hands and slender arms. She melted into me and we stood, two women in a courtyard, clinging to one another as a drowning sailor clings to a mast in a storm.

There were no words. Those came later and they came in floods.

Silence is the only true sign of such joy that can never be expressed.

When we broke apart weeping, I took Parry, and then John into my arms as well, but returned soon enough to Kat.

I had my family once more.

CHAPTER 47
FEBRUARY, 1603
RICHMOND PALACE

Home.

It is a simple word and yet one filled with thoughts and hopes, with memory and with complexity.

The home we are given to grow up in is not always the home we settle in later in life. For some, the home of childhood is a happy place which will ever be their comfort and safety. Others, not gifted with that same luck may later carve out their own home and hopefully, fill it with the love they were not offered when they were children.

But in whatever form, we all need a home.

I think that we come to understand that home is as much the people that we love as the bricks that shelter our bodies. It is the warmth in the eyes of a friend and the welcome at the end of a day. In many ways we make our home in the hearts of those we love, and doing so, we find our home wherever we find our friends.

When I chose to deal houses with Warwick and won Hatfield House from the deal, I was indeed trying to come home. To a place and a time which were no more innocent than the days that followed, but which *seemed* more innocent because *I* was more innocent, back then. I wanted to have a place where I could remember with ease the events of my childhood, remember the person I was before I started to lose my innocence in the naughty world around me.

But whilst we can scrape a meal from the past, we cannot truly fill our plates without the present and the future. When I took Hatfield back as my own, I filled it with the people who cared for me. With servants who had proven their loyalty, with friends who visited not only because I was the Princess, but because they liked me. Hatfield became the base of my operations to keep careful eye on the throne and the events at court, but it became so much more than that to me. It is impossible and implausible to attribute human emotions to a house made of brick and mortar. But whenever I came back to Hatfield I felt as though the house itself was reaching its arms out to meet me, welcoming its mistress back... home.

We all need a home. It is as deep and basic an instinct to us as needing companionship and affection. It is the steady and unchanging rock against which we place our backs so that we might face the world with a chin held high and eyes that do not waver. It is the root of our strength and the place where we can be ourselves in truth.

Some people find it in their childhood, and some people find it much later. But whether home be a place made of bricks, or the warmth of a friend's heart, we all need one.

Home makes us human, and it makes us strong.

CHAPTER 48

1550, HATFIELD HOUSE

I was surrounded by clever and cautious men.

My household at Hatfield was becoming a little hub for those who were interested in gaining favour at court, via the King's *Sweet Sister Temperance* as he called me, and for those who were interested in the preservation of the Protestant rule.

Mary, by contrast, was bringing together all those who wished to see a return to the authority of Rome. Her house at Hudson was a pilgrimage for those who wanted to continue to worship in the Catholic faith. It was now officially illegal to worship as a Catholic in England. The official religion and accepted practise was Protestant, but Mary stood out in defiance of the laws of her own brother the King, and continued to practise her religion as she always had done; in High Mass; in rosary beads; in Latin sermons; in idols and incense... and in the dangerous and addictive grip of the prospect of martyrdom.

I think Mary had always seen herself as a martyr to the cause of her religion; it would have pleased her mother certainly, to see her daughter stand up or die for the religion into which she was born. The God that gave Mary's grandmother, Queen Isabella of Castile, glory in war, the religious practises that she had clung desperately to through all the years of humiliation and disgrace inflicted on her by our father, these were all things she held dear to her heart.

When she took the oath that proclaimed her a bastard and our father's marriage to her mother invalid, Mary had betrayed her deepest values in order to survive in our father's reign. It had cost her dearly, spiritually, and she was never going to forget that.

Perhaps she hoped her mother would look down on her from the bright light of Heaven, and approve of her actions in defiance of our brother as she was never able to stand strong against the will of our father.

Perhaps she never took the will of our brother seriously as she had done that of our father.

But whatever reason pushed her spirit the most, Mary stood obstinate and proud against our brother's religious fervour. Whenever she was most at risk of being squashed by the machines of politics, she called out for help to her imperial cousin, Charles V of Spain. Where I was alone in the world without any other family but Edward and Mary who had any political importance, Mary had the might of the greatest Catholic Emperor to call on in her hours of need. She held cards that I could only dream of and was quite happy to use them in her defence. As Edward's demands on her conversion to Protestantism came thicker and faster, so Mary threw her powerful Catholic relatives in our brother's face, and held firm in her faith. She could threaten that her cause might be taken up by her powerful cousin. She could threaten invasion of England at the Emperor's hands.

Was invasion ever a real possibility? I think that Charles of Spain saw little value in bringing his army to war with England in order to preserve his distant cousin's religious beliefs, but the threat was always there. Charles may have been a devoted Catholic, but he was also a clever ruler, willing to bide his time and see if Mary should become more or less valuable to him as my brother's reign continued.

But to a small island, the threat of invasion by a foreign power is enough to make men stop and think. To Edward, Mary's insubordination against his power was insupportable, to his Council, it was one of many little bargains they should have to accept when the fist of a foreign power was thrust in the face of England.

It came to a head in the winter of 1550; Christmas is a time for family to gather, and often to argue. It is a strange irony that those we are nearest to in blood, we are often farthest from in beliefs. Mary came to London from Hudson, her train mighty with men dressed in her livery and retainers thronging in their hundreds. My own suite was brought into the capital escorted by over a hundred of the King's guards, a very public sign of favour from the King and Council.

As we settled into the festivities, the atmosphere was fraught. It ended with Edward publicly upbraiding Mary for hearing the Catholic Mass in her chapel at court, and Mary responding that the King of England was not *"yet old enough to make decision on something as deep and old as the practise of religion and the worship of God"*.

Such words to any king are dangerous, such words to a *young* king, even more so. Young people do not take kindly to their age being used to discredit them.

Mary left the court after being publicly scolded by Edward for her disobedience. Especially seeing as her position was such that she was one of the premier nobles of the land, Edward made quite clear how hard he disapproved of her religious rebellion against him. But with the shadow of the Emperor Charles over her shoulder, Mary was steeled in her heart to continue her faith as she would.

In my own faith, I was safe in the realm of my brother's reforming resolve. In public and in the eyes of the Council, I was the *good* sister to the King; I fitted comfortably with their ideals for the formation of the new England. In my heart though, I felt some admiration for Mary. She was determined on keeping true to her beliefs, and although to many it seemed traitorous heresy, I understood well the importance of being always true to one's self.

We entered the New Year of 1551 with Mary leaving court in tears at the rift formed between her young brother and her, and Edward and I stepping forth together, to make merry, to ride, to hunt and to watch entertainments. We both dressed in plain colours, abstaining from ostentatious adornments. We sat and talked often, laughing together when at the baiting or the mummers.

As Mary left court under a cloud of resentment and suspicion, I was brought out to walk at my brother's side, like a consort rather than a sister. It seemed clear to the clever men in my household that a change was on the way, and perhaps it was to be that the old religion would prove the undoing of my elder sister in the line of succession.

There was a great divide forming, not only in the country, over the practise of religion and the worship of God, but in our family too.

CHAPTER 49
1551, THE COURT OF KING EDWARD VI LONDON

I n 1551, Edward was determined to make Mary submit to him as King and Supreme Head of the Church. He summoned her to court and on the 15th of March, she arrived.

Mary rode into London at the head of what looked very much like an *army* of men. She rode into her town residence at St John's as before her rode fifty gentlemen and knights in velvet coats and gold chains, and behind her rode eighty ladies and as many gentlemen again.

Every single one of them carried a rosary in their open hands.

The beads of the rosary were banned as the badge of the ancient superstition of the Catholic faith. It was her most outward and public disobedience against the power of our brother thus far.

Although they wore her badges and colours, it was the symbol of their religion that was most apparent, and that was certainly the thing everyone noticed.

Never before in England had we had such a divide in the worship of God. Never before had we had two royal persons stood on either side of such a great gulf. The King and his direct heir were in public opposition.

Even our father's reign had mitigated the changes to religion with the might of his presence. Never altering the state from being a Catholic one, our father had only replaced the Head of the Church. Now, it felt as though we were on the verge of a war such as had been experienced in the low countries, or Germany, a war based on the fragile differences of the act of worshipping the Lord.

Mary was received at court with all splendour in public... and then was promptly taken upstairs by the Council for a summary scolding in private. She held fast against them, and declared that *"her soul was God's and her faith would not change,"* and they answered her that the King *"constrained not her faith, but willed her as a subject to obey."*

If only Mary had seen enough of the sense in this to simply carry on her worship in private, and not make such a public issue of the matter, then some of the later feuds of our blood may have been unnecessary. But she would not. Our sister had had enough of living in the shadow of the crown.

Mary alerted the Imperial Ambassador of Charles V of Spain, who then stepped in to offer war to the Council should they attempt to impede her right to worship as she wanted. After just one night at court she rode out again from the capital to New Hall in Essex. Later, she would tell me that she thought of fleeing the country at this time, so afraid she was of being forced to submit, to be forced to give up her faith, or be imprisoned in the Tower for treason.

Her choice of place to flee to was most particular, and potentially explosive. East Anglia had been in turmoil since the failed rebellion of 1549 where common men had protested violently on the Protestant faith being forced on them, and the taxes laid on them for war with Scotland. The East of England was not strong for the Protestant crown... not as it was for Mary who represented the old ways, the Catholic ways which the rebels clung to. She was safe there, but had placed herself in a position that was even more likely to make the Council view her with great suspicion. She had placed herself into the centre of Catholic opposition to the Protestant rule.

From Hatfield my advisors and I watched and waited. We talked of the day's events each night and were kept well conversant by informers about the country and court bought by my ample coin. We mused over the power of Warwick, now made Duke of Northumberland, and the growth of the King as a ruler. I was enclosed in a house of clever and cautious men, and for that grace I am ever grateful. They taught me the same lesson as the wary vixen; to wait and to watch, to sniff out the danger ahead, is safest in times of turmoil.

Trouble was coming. It was almost tangible. There was a sense of anticipation in the air.... as though the skies themselves could feel the clashing of the mighty wills of the heirs of Henry VIII and shook beneath their power.

CHAPTER 50
1551 - 1553

I n the years that followed Mary's flight into the East of England, it seemed as though there was an uneasy peace in place amongst the royal family.

Mary and Edward continued to clash on matters religious, but the interference of the Emperor and threat of imperial invasion meant that Edward had to allow Mary to worship as she wished; in private at least. Nowhere else in the country were Catholics allowed such freedom as they were within the bricks of Mary's walls, and it caused them to flock to her. Her retinue grew with those loyal to the old religion, and my brother's Council continued to watch them with a nervous eye. But Mary made no move towards flight from the country, nor outward rebellion against our brother.

Mary never stopped loving Edward; perhaps as his Godmother she saw her role was to educate the young King in the realms of religion. But to Edward of course, this was an insult to his own intelligence and to his right to rule his kingdom as he saw fit.

Mary and I tended to appear at court at different times; either by invitation or because of our responsibilities to our estates. I wanted little to be associated with my sister anyway. However much I respected her stand for her own beliefs, I did not want to be tarnished with the brush of the traitor again. I had learnt my lesson there, and under Edward's governance, as a Protestant heir to the throne, I was safe enough.

Edward and I had grown close in our teenaged years, and I was glad of it. When we met, unlike with Edward and Mary, there was no fraught atmosphere of tension. Edward and I agreed on almost everything and I respected his right to rule as our King, therefore I was always the sister he was more likely to warm to.

But it was not only my young brother who held the whip of power in England and with our growing friendship there came into the minds of his advisors some concern. Power is a jealous master and no one near to the King likes to be replaced by another, no matter what the bonds of blood and kinship may be between them.

In January 1552, after a failed attempt to overthrow the power of Warwick, the unlucky Edward Seymour, Duke of Somerset finally met his end on the same green where his younger brother had met his death. On Tower Hill, between eight and nine of the morning on January 22nd Edward Seymour, once Lord Protector of England, had his head chopped from his body, and departed this life. Warwick may have enjoyed crowing over the dejected man in the Council for a while, but when Somerset tried to assert himself into power once again, Warwick removed him... permanently.

It was after the execution of Somerset that it seemed Warwick became more and more determined to tighten his hands on the reigns of power. At times I was halted from seeing my brother Edward. I would visit the capital only to be told that he was indisposed, and unable to see me. Although Edward had been a healthy enough child, he was not a hale adult, and he did grow sick easily. Even so, I came to suspect that my visitations were hindered less by my brother's inability to hold court to me, but more to allow a separation between the King and the sister he was learning to lean on. The times when I was stopped from seeing my brother became more and more frequent, and they worried me. It seemed to me that Warwick was concerned at the affection Edward had for me.

I wrote to Edward after being stopped from seeing him in the spring of 1553. I wrote to him that I had been on my way to see him, but had been turned back in this progress by the messengers of his Council. I had been twice worried: *"the one for that I doubted your majesty's health, the other because for all my long tarrying I went without that I came for."*

Although I was assured that my brother's health was good enough and his present indisposition was not serious, I continued to worry. I tried to put a cheerful frame on the letter. After all, when one is ill, one hardly needs a berating sister in the ear as well.

When I wrote the letter, I had been informed that Mary *had* been allowed to see Edward four days after I was turned away. Why was I, the favoured sister turned away, where the troublesome one was allowed to see him?

"Perhaps therein, lies the answer," said Denny to me when I mused on this.

"How so?" I asked.

He smiled a little, mirthless smile at me. "Perhaps it is because you *are* favoured that you were not allowed to see the King," he said. "Perhaps there are some who view your relationship with your brother the King as *too* close for the comfort of their positions."

I nodded but did not comment. I could see the sense of his words. Edward, it seemed, was ill oftener than before. Was it real...? Was my brother in danger of his life? Was it but a smokescreen for the machinations of his Councillors or Warwick? I took up my pen and finished my letter to my brother:

"Whatsoever other folks will suspect, I intend not to fear your grace's goodwill, which I know I never deserved to faint, so I trust will stick by me."

I was sure that my brother should never abandon me to the will of his Council, if they were afraid of my influence he would ensure my position and safety all the same.

Once again, I was fooled by love.

Fooled by a notion that because Edward and I shared our father's blood and beliefs, that this would ensure my position as an heir to his throne. Fooled by a notion that the King's friendship with me guaranteed my position in his court and favour.

The Heart is the greatest traitor, and it is always with us, waiting but to trick us once again.

CHAPTER 51
HATFIELD HOUSE, 1553

It deserves its seat at the head of the page, 1553. For this was the year in which all about us was to change in a wealth of confusion and betrayal.

A first, there was nothing but rumours, whispers. Where before the news of the court had come thronging in waves, now it was but a tiny stream of dripping droplets. It seemed as though the court had gone silent. Even our careful messengers paid for by my coin and under the charge of my servants, could prise little from the silent halls and sticky underbelly of the court.

The King was little seen in public. He had suffered and recovered from the dread disease of smallpox in the late winter of the 1552, but now it seemed that symptoms and sickness had returned. And there was something else... something more sinister and craven occurring in the halls of power at the English court.

At Hatfield we watched and waited, as was ever our custom. Kat seemed sure in herself that Edward was dying, and that in the light of Mary's Catholicism, I should be made the heir *apparent* as his rightful Protestant heir and sister. Kat could often make a fine pie from the smallest scraps. But it seemed that there were many others in my household willing to believe this was the truth also.

What did I feel on that matter? It was hard to say.

Through all the years of danger as the bastard daughter of Henry VIII, I had felt as though the crown was far from my fingertips. When I was restored to the succession by our father, I had realized there was a slight and small chance that I could one day become Queen. As Edward's reign began, I submitted to his authority and right to rule; as a young, fit man, we had all thought he would have a long reign over us. As he married, and had children, Mary and I would no longer stand in line to the power of the throne. And so the vague dream of power had faded away within me. It seemed unlikely I should ever become the Queen.

But now Edward was sick, failing; and Mary was a woman, unmarried and Catholic... Not a good replacement in the eyes of the Protestant powers of this realm.

Our cousins and aunts born of the line of the Tudors were far behind us three children of Henry VIII in the right of succession to the throne.

Was there a chance that I could become the first sovereign Queen of England? Was there a chance that Edward would bypass Mary, and put me in his place on the throne if his life was in mortal danger? We agreed enough on religion and politics to make this a possibility. But one thing held me back from the temptation of this idea; even if it was offered to me, I knew I would waver.

The right to rule, the right and order of succession, was a reverend one; a holy estate passed by God unto the heirs of a king's body. Mary was the elder daughter of our father, and whatever differences there may be between us, she had the greater right to hold the crown should our brother be taken into the arms of God.

Mary *was* the rightful heir.

I made this plain to my advisors; I would not take a position over my sister as the legal heir even if it were offered to me.

Perhaps I made it too plain... too public. For the events that were then to unfold were almost made of a fairy story.

I think that both Mary and I became suspicious over the plans at court in May of 1553. Anyone who did not become suspicious should be called a fool.

In quick succession, our cousin Lady Jane Grey, then barely fifteen, was married to Warwick's forth son Guilford, then Catherine Grey, Jane's younger sister, was married to Lord Herbert. Catherine Dudley, Warwick's daughter, was married to Lord Hastings. Margaret Clifford, another Grey family cousin, was betrothed to Warwick's brother. A lot of marriages and alliances, made in a short space of time.

Jane and Catherine Grey and Margaret Clifford were in line to the throne, following Mary and me as descendants of Mary Tudor, our father's youngest sister.

Lord Hastings was of the direct descendant of the Plantagenet kings who ruled before the Tudors.

"Warwick is squaring up both his pawns and his queens," said Denny in a low whisper to me when we heard the news. I nodded but I did not answer. We had a loyal house at Hatfield, but I wanted no talk to take my servants or myself into trouble again.

"He is arranging his chess board," said Cecil quietly.

"Ready for a strike," Parry said, nodding.

Something momentous was going on. Mary knew it as well as I did, I was sure. Exactly what Warwick had in mind, I hardly knew, but making sure his family was entwined securely with all other options to the throne did not bode well for Mary and me as the sometime-bastard daughters of Henry VII as heirs.

Just as it did not bode well for the health of our brother.

We had no news of Edward, no real news. Letters were formal and sent advising us of his good health and plans for future festivities. The lack of his presence in public and the whispers of illness gave lie to these notes scribbled by Councillors.

The truth could only be seen *through* the lies. And it was a hard truth. There could be little other reason for all the subterfuge and the indecently fast marriages… Edward was dying. There was no other explanation for the events that were unfolding with unprecedented speed. My brother was dying, and Warwick and those with him were up to something, something that would not benefit either me or my Catholic sister.

Suspicion was forming in my mind. Somehow and some way, they were going to try and depose us of our positions.

Warwick was going to try and cut us from the line of lawful succession.

We would have to be ready, and I would have to think carefully on any action here undertaken. For the outcome of this one moment in time could decide the path of my life forever, or it could bring about the moment of my death, much sooner.

CHAPTER 52
HATFIELD HOUSE, 1553

Those early summer months in 1553 were a mist of confusion, lies and subterfuge.

I kept to Hatfield and brought our informants ever close to us to hear their news. We heard much, and none of it good. They told us that Mary was being lulled and cozened, not allowed to see her brother, but told only soft lies by clever Councillors and Warwick.

We received whispers that our father's will had been changed by Edward to make the Grey girls, our cousins, the legal heirs of England instead of Mary and me. We heard whispers, too, that many questioned the legality of this "*device,*" as it was called. We got word that the King was desperately ill, despite what the official papers told us; that he coughed black bile and yellow pus; that his body was wasted and he was clinging barely onto life with gnarly and emaciated hands.

In the shade of all these truths, lies and half-truths I resolved to be patient and wait. Who knew which was really the truth and which the fiction? But I suspected much, and none of it good.

In myself and in the quaking centre of my soul, I wished that my brother was not dying. I wished that he, like my father before him, would hold together the rival factions of our land and set forth a rule that brought us peace.

But Edward was made of a different mettle to that of our father. Where our father had ruled with charisma and excitement, Edward was stern and dour. Where our father lit up or cast down the very atmosphere of a palace, Edward was the King relegated to the shadows of everyone's imagination.

I could see why the common people did not love him as they had done our father. The people want a show, and for all the power that one in the public eye may hold, they are little more than a dancing monkey, bent to the whim and will of those who watch them.

Power belongs to a king because the people allow him to hold it. Power belongs to those who have learnt the dance which will make the people warm to them, watch them… even fear them. But Edward was not made of the same spirit as our father had been. He could engender loyalty perhaps, but not love.

Edward, my little brother, was dying. Another of my family was leaving my life. I knew it as well as any other… why else would Warwick be aligning his chess pieces so carefully and with such un-unabashed speed? But I wished it was not so… Edward and I had grown up together, shared our lives as children, listened, learned and laughed together. I loved my pale little brother as I had loved our father, as I had loved Katherine… as I had loved my own mother and all those others I had lost.

Life is about losing people in the end. If you live long enough, you see everyone you loved leave you.

I was mourning for my brother even before I knew he was dead. Remembering his soft voice when we read our Latin together, hearing his grave tone when he found out he was the King, watching him ride at the rings in the mock tourneys he was so fond of, being enfolded in his arms on the day they came to tell us that our father was dead.

His *Sweet Sister Temperance...* I should never have a more inappropriate title gifted to me than that one, and therefore perhaps I remember it the best of all that have been given to me. I might be calm and temperate on the outside, especially when in his presence. But I was anything but temperate and mild inside the prison of my body.

We had no news for a long time.

Then, on the 7th of July the capital was suddenly reinforced by hundreds of guards. On the 8th, the city government was informed of the King's death and on the 10th, they brought my young cousin, the scared and sweet little girl that I remembered from our days in Katherine Parr's household, Lady Jane Grey, to the Tower of London and proclaimed that she was Queen.

Due to Denny's men placed to ride to Hatfield with all speed, we heard the news fast.

I ordered that our remaining men, working as informants, be taken out of the city immediately; there was nothing more they could do to enlighten us. The plan had been made clear, and Warwick had moved his pieces into play. The city was closing down, preparing for the trouble they knew was going to break. It was better that we had our allies away from possible arrest and close to us.

I took my spies back from London and sent them to gather news elsewhere in the country. Warwick and the Council had played their hand now; we had to see what others would do.

Mary had come back to her house at Hunsdon in recent months, but now she fled that house with all her guard as she heard that the Council, headed by Warwick, was sending a detachment of guards to take her into custody. They did not want the Catholic Princess, the rightful heir, to escape just as they pulled off their *coup*.

But they did not catch her. My wily elder sister escaped their clutches.

I could not help but laugh when I imagined my older sister riding out to her estates in East Anglia on the back of a horse running like the wind, with the Council's guards flailing and hopping behind her like the toads they were.

Mary proclaimed herself Queen. Her standard was raised in the hotbed of Catholic unrest and rebellion that was East Anglia. She had chosen well, my sister, her hand surely guided by the will of God as she chose where to start her conquest for the crown. She was the rightful heir and she was not going to be stopped now.

Denny advised that we move. We should either fly to Mary's side, or retreat to an area not so near to London. It was a dangerous time.

"Stop, sir," I said holding up my hand even as he went to tell Parry to issue those commands. "We cannot risk being premature on either side. If we move anywhere then we shall be suspected of something. Should my sister fail to win the day, then my cousin will remain queen. Should my cousin lose, then my sister will be Queen. I would little like to lose my head on either side by choosing to support the other prematurely. Caution costs nothing."

"But the Council will eventually send guards here," he said in exasperation. "They have missed capturing one heir. They will not lose another."

I rose and smiled at him, placing my hand on his arm, "but if we flee my lord, we will have to chose a side, or be accused of treason by both, and that could be disastrous at this early stage." I shook my head and looked at the men about me. I felt strangely calm despite the rushed beating of my heart.

"Do not worry my lord. I have another option, a course of action which was shown to me by a lady who showed most excellent intelligence in the face of mortal danger." As I spoke, I undid the white long-hanging sleeves at the back of my dress, pulled one off and handed it to him as I started to undo the other.

Denny and Parry both stared at me open mouthed as I started to slowly undress before them.

"I am *grievously* ill, my lords," I said calmly. "And should *any* contingent of *any* army arrive here to take possession of me, they will have to do so without my consent. They can lift the whole bed out of my house if they are able, but I will not be seen to go *willingly* with either side. If I commit to either side now, I will place myself in grave danger. But if I commit to neither, I cannot be said to have acted treasonously. Now, bring my ladies to me, for with the death of my brother I am suddenly taken sick unto death."

I paused and eyed them carefully. "And you will make most sure that my *grave* illness is *not* information that stays within these four walls... Do I make myself clear?"

Denny suddenly grinned, from ear to ear like a small delighted dog. Parry was still watching me undress with quite a lot of distraction, but he managed to right himself. "It shall be as you say, your highness," he said.

I smiled at him. "When one studies history, my lord, one learns that there is something most great commanders did that separated them from the others."

"Which is what, my lady?" asked Parry.

I paused and looked out onto the lawns and hedges of my beloved Hatfield. It was a warm and balmy summer's day, and hard to believe that the country was erupting in a riot of civil war over which Queen should reign over it.

I turned back and smiled at him. "The great commanders knew which battles to fight and which to avoid," I said. They bowed to me with respect, smiles all over their faces.

"Now, send Kat and my maids to me. I must be put to bed immediately. None shall be admitted unless they force the door. All news will be brought to me covertly. I will be kept informed of all that is going on, but everyone in this house apart from you *must* believe I am sick unto death. I will not have my servants placed in danger. It is up to *you* gentlemen to make my household believe lies which may save their lives."

I sent them off and went to bed. From my bed I should see what needed to be done next. There was no sense in jumping into one camp or another, not yet.

CHAPTER 53

SUMMER, 1553
HATFIELD HOUSE

During those short weeks of unrest, as England quivered on the edges of civil war, I thought on the figure of my little cousin a lot. Jane Grey, the girl Warwick had proclaimed Queen.

I later heard, that when the title was announced to rest on her head, that monarchs around the globe had be drawn family trees to see where she fitted in. As the daughter of the daughter of my father's sister, you can understand their confusion; especially when there were two direct heirs to the throne alive and well.

Such a farce had been made and they had put her at the head of it! How willing was she, I wondered, to take a throne that was not legally hers over the rights of her cousins, women she had known since she was little?

She and I had spent time together under Katherine. Although I could not say I had a lot of affection for her, mainly due to my own jealousy when Katherine preferred her company to mine, I could not help but feel sympathy for her now. Packaged off like a brood-mare to marry Warwick's fourth son, Guilford Dudley, used as a pawn for the ambitions of Warwick. No doubt the Duke had arranged this marriage not only to enable him to rule through her, but so that his son might in turn become a king and his grandchildren would inherit the throne. Warwick had moved fast to ensure that on the death of Edward, his own power would not only remain intact, but increase.

She was a clever girl, Jane. She must have known that the Dudleys were plotting something. But what options did she have? Her family agreed the match with Guildford, a horribly spoilt young man by all reports, and she could have done little but agree. It was not within her rights, not in reality, to refuse the match approved of by her parents.

Women are bartered and bought in this way in marriage. Her own views would have meant very little to ambitious parents such as the Greys.

And now she was stuck, put in the position of Queen, married to an oaf, or so all around court agreed, and in the grip of the mighty Duke Northumberland, Earl of Warwick, the *queen*-maker as they were laughingly calling him in the villages. None of the common people understood who she was, nor what her claim was to the throne. Warwick might have thought he had neatly sewn up this package but it was not so. He had underestimated the opinion of the people of England. Such a sham… and my little pale and clever cousin was placed right in the heart of it. The greatest traitor to this country was a tiny girl, now but sixteen, more interested in books than in wielding power.

No, it was the Duke himself who was the master of these ill times; Warwick; Northumberland; Dudley; John… anything you called him it all spelt out the same thing.

Traitor.

Thousands of men flocked to Mary's banners; her pennants streaming in the breeze of the summer air, her passionate and devoted speeches brought men seething to her side. A multitude of men, common and noble alike were already behind her, beside her... *with* her, in mind, body and spirit. The daughter of *Great Harry* was in need, they called. The daughter of *Bluff King Hal* was set aside for a woman they had never heard of... *was it to be borne? No!*

Mary was never as well-liked by the people as I. She was too rigid, too dour and too severe. But in those days after the death of our brother, the days when she was forced to fight for her throne; in those days she stood out before her people, her maiden's hair flowing in the wind, as she spoke to them of her *right* to the throne as the daughter of Henry VIII and the statutes he put into place. In those days they loved her, they cheered her, believed in her and they swore to fight and die for her as their true Queen.

In those days, you could see she was truly a descendant of her warrior-like grandmother, Isabella of Castile.

Mary's troops drew together thousands of the common man. It is the common people that give a king the power he holds, and they gave that power to Mary.

They understood little of history, of maps or maths, of philosophy or Latin, but they understood right from wrong. They understood, as I did, the holy right of kingship. Jane was no queen of theirs, and Warwick should never rule over them as he sought to. Protestant and Catholic alike joined together to march with the army of my older sister. Glowing with a beauty that she would never know again as she basked in both the love and outrage of her people, Mary rode at the head of them like a goddess, flanked by the loyal troops of England.

I cheered them silently. The right to rule should not be questioned of a monarch, not when the alternative is so far behind in right of succession. I had refused to counter such a thought, as should anyone who knew right from wrong.

But still, I did not rise from my bed.

I had learnt to be cautious, and whichever side I joined, I was not at this time the most important figurehead, nor the least expendable. It was not in my best interests to enter into this conflict, yet. In my bed, sick, I was committed to neither side, and so could weather this storm without pledging my life to a side. Whichever won, I would still be here to press my own claim, when and if, the time came.

Warwick rode out at the head of the Council's army to face the forces of Queen Mary Tudor. It was a fatal mistake on the part of the false Queen Jane to have sent the one man who held the rebellious *coup* in place into the arms of danger. And it was done by her order.

But knowing Jane, perhaps it was not done by accident at all, but by design. I doubt very much she wanted the role she had been thrust into, and I do not doubt she knew well the dangers she was sending her father-in-law into when she sent him to face the wrath of the people of England.

His forces melted away from him as he marched out to meet Mary. Their hearts were harried by the forces set against them and their loyalty to Warwick was flawed. The troops of the Council escaped Warwick at night and fled even in the daylight hours into the countryside. In London, the Council, now freed from the control of Warwick, started to lose their nerve.

It did not take long for Mary to take London. Her forces were vast, and swelled by the day. The Council bowed to her will and her army and delivered London into her hands with little resistance. Without Warwick to whip them into shape, they floundered and fell.

Warwick was beaten; he fled the ruins of his army outside of London and he *himself* proclaimed Mary Queen, in Cambridge. There were no trumpeters and no drums as he made his proclamation to the astounded crowd, so he threw his own hat in the air as he cried "*God save Queen Mary!*" Those around him just stared at him with amazement. Did he think he could save himself after such open and artful rebellion, simply by naming the rightful Queen as Queen?

Desperation makes men do the most remarkable things... and often, the most stupid of things.

His too-late act of fake loyalty did not help him. He was arrested. The great Duke, the son of a traitor, father to a failed King and father-in-law to a fallen Queen was brought into London tied to the back of a cart. His clothes covered in mud, waste and excrement, his face blackened with filth and fear.

They took him, and every member of his family that they could find, including, to my sorrow, the charming young Robin Dudley. They put them in the Tower. Jane Grey was taken there too.

I heard she went quietly and said to her captors only that Mary was, and had always been, the true Queen of England.

CHAPTER 54

1553

Mary I was proclaimed Queen on the 19th of July, 1553. I made a sudden and complete recovery from the grave illness that had taken hold of me on the death of my brother.

I wrote to the Queen immediately, apparently from my sickbed, to tell her of my grave illness, and subsequent recovery on hearing of her victory. I told her that on the death of our brother I had been so overtaken by illness I feared for my life, and then on hearing of the rebellion against her rightful rule, I had sickened further.

"...As though the treachery and treason that beset this country and your gracious self was a poison to my very blood, so that I could not stand nor walk, nor come to your side as I had wished."

Did Mary believe me? I doubt it.

She had enough understanding of my character and enough of her own suspicions of my wiles to believe that I might have stayed out of the conflict to bide my time.

But I had not joined the other side, so I was no traitor to her.

She wrote back to me, in a letter that glowed with happiness, telling me of her victory, of her people's love, and inviting me to be at her side during the preparations for her coronation. It was only fitting, she wrote, as *I was now her heir,* the next in line to the throne, until such time as she had children of her own. It was right that the people should see us together in unity.

She advised me that we were not to wear mourning for our brother when we met, for although we owed him, as our late King, due deference, this was now a season of joy and not to celebrate that would dishonour the great victory that she had won.

My elder sister had just become the first sovereign Queen of England, borne to the throne on a wave of popular support. Her coronation would make her the first female anointed Head of the English crown and of the English Church.

And I was now the heir to the throne. One step away from becoming Queen.

Through all the troubles of my life, I had endured. Through all the perils of my childhood, I had survived. The Bastard Princess, the shamed daughter of Anne Boleyn, the ignored princess of this realm was now next in power only to the Queen herself.

As I rose from my bed and dressed to prepare myself for the journey to London, I could not help but smile. Over and over, my lips seemed to move on their own, grinning with pleasure and expectation.

Although I was sure this was not the end of my troubles, I was also sure this was not the end of my journey. Mary was thirty-seven years old… old now to marry, old to produce a child. Even as her reign was born, I could feel the embryo of my own rule quickening beneath my heart.

The new Queen of England had little breeding time left to produce an heir to replace me.

I could almost feel the crown quivering above my head.

CHAPTER 55

SUMMER, 1553

O n the 29th of July, 1553, I and my retinue of thousands rode
into London, making for my town house at Somerset House.
We rode through Fleet Street with the roar of the crowds in our
ears.

Dressed in green and white with fabrics donned accorded to
their ranks, but all colours proclaiming the Tudor name, my men
filled the streets before me like a great wave, a cresting, iridescent
sheen over a mighty sea.

Two thousand men and horse rode out before me with spears
and bows and guns, their voices raised in shouts of loyalty to Queen
Mary, and to me.

And in their midst I rode, my red hair loose and streaming
down my back, my horse white and youthful as myself; dressed
in glowing whites and greens, every inch a Tudor, every inch the
daughter of my father.

The crowds cheered us as we rode in and the streets of London
shook with their voices.

After the horror and upheaval of the past months, and especially the past few weeks, the common man was pleased to see an easy and quick return to peace; war does no man who fights any favours. Only those who wait behind the lines of soldiers, protected by their nobility and rank, gain any profit from it. The country had been glad to rise to war for Mary's rights, but they were even more glad to lay down their weapons in quick and easy victory, and return to peace.

Mary had ridden into the seat of power with the whole country at her back, and with her coming, as with any new ideal, the people hoped for a new reign where they would see peace and prosperity.

In the bonfires and bells that crackled and rang out all over the city that night there was the *hope* of the people in the air, the smell of optimism and expectation. People drank together and talked of our father. *Bluff King Hal's daughter was Queen,* they said, and *everything was right with the world again.*

For as long as they had the Tudors, they had their kings.

I think that they even little cared that Mary was a woman… not right then at least. Worries and fears such as those were for the days after the celebrations, when roaring headaches and ale-sickened bellies would give rise to the darker fears and prejudices of their minds. *Then* they would worry that she was a woman, and that a woman had never ruled them before. *Then* they would tell dark stories of the Norman princess Matilda and her failed uprising. *Then* they would tell each other that women had no right to rule over men.

But that was not tonight; tonight was afire with the happiness of prosperity and hope.

All that night in Somerset House I listened to the shouts and the sounds of celebration through the night at my window. I heard the roars against Warwick with pleasure and felt sadness at the shouts against Jane Grey. I heard the slaps on backs and the cheers for Queen Mary and the Lady Elizabeth and I felt warmed in my heart, for although the people did not really know us, they believed in us with all their hearts.

The next morning I rode out to meet my sister, the victorious Queen. I reduced the number of my servants by half, so as to show deference to her...and because I did not want her thinking I had arrived with an army. I did not want to get off on the wrong foot, with my powerful sister.

Mary had been at Beaulieu since her army took the capital, getting ready to enter London in style. It is always good for a new ruler to make a lasting first impression. I met her halfway at Wanstead, just outside London. I was taken to her rooms by some of her servants, and let in to her inner chambers by her ladies. Of course she had seen me arrive; my retinue, although smaller than before, was still enormous.

"Your majesty," I said as I swept to the floor in a curtsey.

"Rise, sister," she said in her gruff voice. The emotion of the moment seemed to have made her voice even deeper than it was normally.

As I rose, I kept my eyes to the floor, wishing to show her all reverence that I could in this most important moment.

She rose from her chair and came towards me, her arms outstretched. I looked up into Mary's worn face. I had not seen her for some time. The years had not done her good service. She looked old before her time; her hair was thin, lines of worry and weariness lined her eyes and almost all her teeth were gone. Those that were left were blackened. She tried to smile now by cupping her lips over the gap where her teeth should have been, it gave her a strange and most sinister bearing, like a snake about to strike.

But her face glowed with happiness and victory. Her cheeks were flushed with success and the hands she held out to me on that day were hot with excitement and pleasure. Her fine eyes glittered as they looked at me and there were small tears in them. She was as sentimental as our father at times. Reuniting with her sister, her closest living relative, in her moment of glory had touched her deeply.

She pulled me to her and embraced her.

"Sister," she said gaily, like a little girl asking me to play. "I am so pleased to see you recovered from your illness, and to be by my side as I enter London as Queen."

I bowed as best I could as she held on to my hands. "I too am grateful to be by your side, your majesty, to see the fruition of your successful campaign to win your rightful throne against the wickedness which had overtaken these lands."

She laughed. "Yes," she said. "I *am* the rightful Queen, and finally I will see the dream of my mother and father come to light as I continue the *legitimate* rule of the Tudor dynasty."

I smiled at her, but was inwardly considering that her idea had never been our father's plan. Had he been happy with a female heir he would never have set aside Mary's mother and married my own, nor set aside *my* mother to marry Edward's. He had not wanted a female ruler.... that was most clear, so this *dream* she spoke of, was not one he would have dreamed.

But this was hardly a place for truth. This was the court and this was the Queen. I was not going to part with the honest thoughts of my head. As close as I was now to the throne, I was also made most vulnerable by that position.

I was about to enter the most dangerous time of my life; about to walk willingly again into danger.

But that morning, I knew this not.

My sister wrapped her arm into mine and we stepped together, out, into the privy gardens.

Under the pale sun of an English summer, with arms linked like the best of friends, talking to each other gently, we two... we Tudors... the last of our father's children, wandered as sisters, basked in the warmth of the clement skies.

Here ends *The Bastard Princess*...Elizabeth's story will continue with *The Heretic Heir* as her journey through the dangerous reign of her sister continues. Only one step from the throne, Elizabeth is about to enter the most dangerous time of her life...

ABOUT THE AUTHOR

I find people talking about themselves in the third person to be entirely unsettling, so, since this section is written by me, I will use my own voice rather than try to make you believe that another person is writing about me to make me sound terribly important.

I am an independent author, publishing my books by myself, with the help of my lovely editor. I write in all the spare time I have. I briefly tried entering into the realm of 'traditional' publishing but, to be honest, found the process so time consuming and convoluted that I quickly decided to go it alone and self-publish.

My passion for history, in particular perhaps the era of the Tudors, began early in life. As a child I lived in Croydon, near London, and my schools were lucky enough to be close to such glorious places as Hampton Court and the Tower of London to mean that field trips often took us to those castles. I think it's hard not to find the Tudors infectious when you hear their stories, especially when surrounded by the bricks and mortar they built their reigns within. There is heroism and scandal, betrayal and belief, politics and passion and a seemingly never-ending cast list of truly fascinating people. So when I sat down to start writing, I could think of no better place to start than somewhere and sometime I loved and was slightly obsessed with.

Expect *many* books from me, but do not necessarily expect them all to be of the Tudor era. I write as many of you read, I suspect; in many genres. My own bookshelves are weighted down with historical volumes and biographies, but they also contain dystopias, sci-fi, horror, humour, children's books, fairy tales, romance and adventure. I can't promise I'll manage to write in *all* the areas I've mentioned there, but I'd love to give it a go. If anything I've published isn't your thing, that's fine, I just hope you like the ones I write which *are* your thing!

The majority of my books *are* historical fiction however, so I hope that if you liked this volume you will give the others in this series (and perhaps not in this series), a look. I want to divert you as readers, to please you with my writing and to have you join me on these adventures.

A book is nothing without a reader.

As to the rest of me; I am in my thirties and live in Cornwall with a rescued dog, a rescued cat and my partner (who wasn't rescued, but may well have rescued me). I studied Literature at University after I fell in love with books as a small child. When I was little I could often be found nestled half-way up the stairs with a pile of books and my head lost in another world between the pages. There is nothing more satisfying to me than finding a new book I adore, to place next to the multitudes I own and love... and nothing more disappointing to me to find a book I am willing to never open again. I do hope that this book was not a disappointment to you; I loved writing it and I hope that showed through the pages.

This is only the first in a large selection of titles coming to you on Amazon. I hope you will try the others.

If you would like to contact me, please do so.

On twitter, I am @TudorTweep and am more than happy to follow back and reply to any and all messages. I may avoid you if you decide to say anything worrying or anything abusive, but I figure that's acceptable.

Via email, I am tudortweep@gmail.com a dedicated email account for my readers to reach me on. I'll try and reply within a few days.

I publish some first drafts and short stories on Wattpad where I can be found at www.wattpad.com/user/GemmaLawrence31. Wattpad was the first place I ever showed my stories, *to anyone*, and in many ways its readers and their response to my works were the influence which pushed me into self-publishing. If you have never been on the site I recommend you try it out. Its free, its fun and its chock-full of real emerging talent. I love Wattpad because its members and their encouragement gave me the boost I needed as a fearful waif to get some confidence in myself and make a go of a life as a real, published writer.

Thank you for taking a risk with an unknown author and reading my book. I do hope now that you've read one you'll want to read more. If you'd like to leave me a review, that would be very much appreciated also!

Gemma Lawrence
Cornwall
2015

THANK YOU

To so many people for helping me make this book possible... to my editor Brooke who entered into this with me and gave me her time, her wonderful guidance and also her encouragement. To my partner Matthew, who will be the first to admit that history is not his thing, and yet is willing to listen to me extol the virtues and vices of the Tudors and every other time period, repeatedly, to him and pushed me to publish even when I feared to. To my family for their ongoing love and support; this includes not only my own blood in my mother and father, sister and brother, but also their families, their partners and all my nieces who I am sure are set to take the world by storm as they grow. To Matthew's family, for their support, and for the extended family I have found myself welcomed to within them. To my friend Petra who took a tour of Tudor palaces and places with me back in 2010 which helped me to prepare for this book and others; her enthusiasm for that strange but amazing holiday brought an early ally to the idea I could actually write a book... And lastly, to the people who wrote all the books I read in order to write this book... all the historical biographers and masters of their craft who brought Elizabeth, and her times, to life in my head.

Thank you to all of you; you'll never know how much you've helped me, but I know what I owe to you.

Gemma
Cornwall
2015

Lightning Source UK Ltd.
Milton Keynes UK
UKHW011826041218
333468UK00028B/1969/P